I thought over my options. They were narrow. "Can you get to Johnny Farmer for me? Can you ask him to take another look at the evidence?"

"You think Farmer would give the least bit of respect to any suggestion from a lowly evidence tech? As if."

He wasn't any more likely to give weight to pleas from a private investigator. Like a lot of police detectives, Farmer's regard for P.I.'s was only a little higher than his opinion of common household vermin, and his opinion of me was maybe just a little lower than that.

"I really need somebody in my corner on this, Toby. I think Annie Holland's innocent."

"Think? Or want to believe?"

I had no answer for that one.

"There's one thing I can do for you, and if you ever tell anyone I did it, you're a dead woman."

I perked up immediately. "What? What can you do?"

"When we get back to the Evidence Department, just sort of neglect to take your purse. You can remember it in half an hour. And you couldn't calculate the size of the favor you're gonna owe me."

### Praise for *Murder Beach:*

"The promising debut of private investigator Caley Burke. A fast-paced adventure with romance and local color, murder and suspense."
—KAREN KIJEWSKI, author of *Copy Kat*

# MORE MYSTERIES FROM THE
# BERKLEY PUBLISHING GROUP . . .

**JENNY McKAY MYSTERIES:** This TV reporter finds out where, when, why . . . *and* whodunit. "A more streetwise version of television's Murphy Brown." —*Booklist*

by Dick Belsky
BROADCAST CLUES                          LIVE FROM NEW YORK
THE MOURNING SHOW

**CAT CALIBAN MYSTERIES:** She was married for thirty-eight years. Raised three kids. Compared to that, tracking down killers is easy . . .

by D.B. Borton
ONE FOR THE MONEY                        TWO POINTS FOR MURDER
THREE IS A CROWD

**KATE JASPER MYSTERIES:** Even in sunny California, there are cold-blooded killers . . . "This series is a treasure!" —Carolyn G. Hart

by Jaqueline Girdner
ADJUSTED TO DEATH                        MURDER MOST MELLOW
THE LAST RESORT                          FAT-FREE AND FATAL
TEA-TOTALLY DEAD

**FREDDIE O'NEAL, P.I., MYSTERIES:** You can bet that this appealing Reno P.I. will get her man . . . "A winner." —Linda Grant

by Catherine Dain
LAY IT ON THE LINE                       SING A SONG OF DEATH
WALK A CROOKED MILE                      LAMENT FOR A DEAD COWBOY
BET AGAINST THE HOUSE

**CALEY BURKE, P.I., MYSTERIES:** This California private investigator has a brand-new license, a gun in her purse, and a knack for solving even the trickiest cases!

by Bridget McKenna
MURDER BEACH                             DEAD AHEAD
CAUGHT DEAD

**CHINA BAYLES MYSTERIES:** She left the big city to run an herb shop in Pecan Springs, Texas. But murder can happen anywhere . . . "A wonderful character!" —*Mostly Murder*

by Susan Wittig Albert
THYME OF DEATH                           WITCHES' BANE

**LIZ WAREHAM MYSTERIES:** In the world of public relations, crime can be a real career-killer . . . "Readers will enjoy feisty Liz!" —*Publishers Weekly*

by Carol Brennan
HEADHUNT                                 FULL COMMISSION

# CAUGHT DEAD

## BRIDGET McKENNA

BERKLEY PRIME CRIME, NEW YORK

CAUGHT DEAD

A Berkley Prime Crime Book / published by arrangement with the author

PRINTING HISTORY
Berkley Prime Crime edition / February 1995

ISBN: 0-425-14493-3

Berkley Prime Crime Books are published by
The Berkley Publishing Group,
200 Madison Avenue, New York, NY 10016.
The name BERKLEY PRIME CRIME and the
BERKLEY PRIME CRIME design are trademarks
belonging to Berkley Publishing Corporation.

PRINTED IN THE UNITED STATES OF AMERICA

10  9  8  7  6  5  4  3  2  1

# CHAPTER 1

U.S. INTERSTATE 5 IS A HIGHWAY GIANT WITH ITS TOES tickling the Mexican border and its head bumping up against British Columbia. Cascade, California, is nestled snugly in its navel, at the far northern end of the great Central Valley from which the folks back east get lettuce in December.

If you're going north on I-5, here's how you'll recognize Cascade: It's the unimpressive middle-sized town just before the place where the land rises into lakes and woods and breathtaking scenery. If you're going south, it's the place where the scenery ends and the mind-numbing highway boredom begins.

As you pass through the middle of town, take a look to the west and you might see the Rio Sacramento Theater and on the second floor, the offices of Baronian Investigations. That's where I work, or did until my boss, Jake Baronian, kicked me out of my office.

"I don't need another week off, Jake—I'm going insane from not working!" I stood in front of Jake's desk, hands on either side of a mountain of papers that concealed every square inch of its antique oak surface—Jake Baronian is a devout believer in the principle that a neat desk is the sign of a sick mind. It was Monday morning at five minutes after nine, and I had been back in town since the previous

Monday, when I had reported in ready to work. That's when Jake had first ordered me to take a week off. Now he was trying to stick me with another one.

"So go see Maggie. She does insane." Jake pushed a card across the desk with "Margaret M. Peck, Ph.D." and "Cascade Counseling Center" printed in a friendly, nonthreatening typeface. His lively black eyes were clouded with concern for my well-being, which his customary quips couldn't disguise. Jake had been my boss and my friend for more than three years now, somehow managing to turn an insecure divorcée into a professional investigator while always being available for advice, conversation, and the occasional Saturday night poker game.

I was getting quite a collection of Maggie Peck's cards— Jake and I had been playing this same scene every day for a week. I put this one in the back pocket of my jeans. "I'll think about it," I told him. It was the same thing I had said every time he brought up the subject of counseling; I was too accustomed to keeping my own secrets to suddenly want to pay someone by the hour to drag them out of me.

"I called her up, Burke," he said finally. "I told her you'd be in tomorrow at nine. Don't make a liar out of me."

I couldn't suppress a sigh of exasperation. "Don't try to be my father, Jake. Just let me come back to work and I'll be fine."

Jake shook his head. "You just told me you haven't had a decent night's sleep in a week."

"I haven't *worked* in a week! All I need is something to keep my mind busy. I know you've got work backed up. You need me here helping you do it. Just let me do my job and I'll sleep like a baby, I promise you."

Or if I don't, I'll keep my mouth shut about it this time, I told myself. The forced inactivity of this leave of absence was giving me entirely too much time to think about the things that were bothering me. There was nothing I wanted more at this moment—not even a solid night's sleep with no nightmares—than to be back at my desk or out on the street investigating something.

"The only promise I want from you is that you'll take care of yourself. You've lost—what—five pounds?"

"I *needed* to lose five pounds."

"Did you need those dark circles under your eyes? Your hands are shaking—you're going to tell me you needed *that*?"

I dropped into a chair, wishing I had a cigarette, though I smoked my last one at least six years ago. My eyes felt like somebody'd sandpapered them, and my stomach was full of sharp rocks. I'd also been drinking at night to get to sleep, but Jake didn't know about that part. He didn't know about the dreams of guns and fire, and neither did anyone else, because keeping my mouth shut is what I do best.

Maybe it's not all that healthy to keep things bottled up inside, but it was what I had done for thirty-two years, and I wasn't comfortable with the idea of doing things differently now. Unfortunately for my entrenched habits, Jake was sticking to his guns about this counseling thing. If I wanted to continue to work for Baronian Investigations, I was going to have to make an effort.

"If I go see Maggie Peck, you'll let me come back to work." It was a question, but I didn't have enough energy to put the inflection on it.

"You go see her tomorrow and every week until you're okay again. It's all covered on your insurance, anyway, and you might find out you like having someone to talk to."

"I've got *you* to talk to."

"There are things you don't tell even me. I think maybe there are things you don't tell *yourself*."

I hated to admit it, but Jake had a point. It wasn't that I had a problem with the idea of people seeking professional help for their problems; I had a problem with seeking help for myself. I was willing to allow that everyone needed an impartial ear to talk into, a friendly shoulder to unload on, as long as "everyone" didn't include me.

The only kinds of therapy I'd ever exposed myself to were work and art. I always took my work home with me, and I carried a sketchbook everywhere I went. Since I got back from my vacation on the south coast I'd been carrying it in a black canvas portfolio—a welcome-back gift from Jake with lots of nifty zippers and pockets—that doubled as a purse, briefcase, and lunch bag. I was enrolled in a summer figure drawing class at the local community college, Tuesdays and Thursdays, and my drawing served as both meditation and emotional outlet. I'd had my share of emotional problems, but dragging my drawing tools out of the bottom of a crate, divorcing my flaky husband, and going to work for Jake Baronian had taken care of them, or so I thought.

As it turned out, going to work as a private investigator had given me a whole new set of problems, too, like getting into dangerous situations way over my head, and just occasionally having to kill someone in order to keep myself alive. That's what was costing me sleep this week—I had killed a man who would certainly have killed me and a friend in cold blood, and who knows how many others who got in his way. The law called it self-defense and so did I, and I had fewer regrets about it than you might suppose, but then there were the nightmares. If I could just get over the goddamned nightmares.

I took the card back out of my pocket. "Okay," I said, holding it up for Jake to see. "You win." I managed a smile. "I'll see Maggie, I'll take the week off, I'll be back here at nine on Monday morning."

"And you'll get some sleep, and get your appetite back."

I didn't comment on how unlikely that seemed at the moment. I just nodded on my way out the door.

I walked out of Jake's office and into a long hallway. Baronian Investigation's offices are long and narrow, the only space above the Rio Sacramento Theater that's not occupied by upstairs auditoriums and storage rooms. There are five offices, all on one side of the hallway, all over-looking Sacramento Street just before it dead-ends into City Center Mall.

At the far end is a file-storage room and general junk-collecting area the public never sees. Next to that is a conference room, then my office, then Jake's. The office closest to the front door and stairway to the street serves as a reception area. From any room, you can hear the audio tracks of four movies playing at once, two of them quite clearly if you don't close your office door.

I walked down the hallway, pausing for just a moment in front of my office, regarding the "Caley Burke" lettered in black and gold on the frosted glass of the door, and even going so far as to turn the doorknob before I decided there wasn't anything in there I was going to need during my latest week off. I'd miss my computer, an IBM-clone 486 with a CD drive, a 14.4 modem, a Super VGA monitor, and a 200 megabyte hard drive that was more than adequate to accommodate all my case files, my favorite word-processing program, and half a dozen games to boot. All work and no play makes Caley go batshit. On the other hand, *no* work wasn't doing me much good, either.

I opened the hallway door and stepped into the reception area, the room with the newest carpet and furniture. Sepia photographic prints of Cascade in the last century were lined up neatly on the walls, showing a bustling small town with high wooden sidewalks and false-fronted stores crowded along unpaved streets. These had been a gift to Jake from me after I got tired of his no-frills decorating style. Like all the rooms, the reception area was well-lit by several floor-to-ceiling sash windows, all open to admit whatever cool air remained this far above the street at a little after nine on a July morning.

Terrie Santini, Jake's new office assistant, was typing out one of Jake's handwritten reports on her desktop computer, her face totally obscured by a mass of curls as she bent over the keys. Terrie was maybe twenty-five, with an unrestrained mop of curly dark-blond hair and generous, lively features. She had a playful sense of humor that had a way of brightening up our dullest days, and was rapidly becoming one of the family after being on the job less than two months. "So, are you back?" she asked, looking up from her keyboard.

I sighed. "Not exactly. I'm taking an involuntary vacation."

"Am I caught in a time warp, or didn't you just have one of those?" She saved her work, then got up and poured two cups of coffee and handed one to me. "Black, right?"

I sat down on the corner of her desk and accepted the coffee. "Right. As to your question, it seems I'm going crazy."

A smile tweaked the corners of Terrie's mouth. "I don't feel like I know you well enough to crack a joke about it, but I want you to know it's killing me."

I smiled back. "Oh, don't think I haven't cracked them all myself. After three years of relatively routine work, I get a couple of tough cases, some people wave some guns around, and I can't seem to take the heat."

"Hey, don't sell yourself short," Terrie said. She added three spoons of sugar and a generous amount of cream to her cup. "I know I'm always saying I want to be a detective, but to tell you the truth, it scares me a little, too. The first time somebody pointed a gun at me, I'd probably faint in my tracks."

"That's what I thought, too, but when you're in a situation like that, something else seems to take over." I paused a moment, trying to find the right words for something difficult to express. "It's like you find out things about yourself you may never have realized or admitted—things you'd probably never have had the chance to know about if someone hadn't threatened your life."

"And then you have to deal with those things, huh?"

"Yeah, that's it," I said. What I didn't say was that one of the things you deal with if you survive the experience is finding out you're capable of killing. "That's about it."

I pointed to the mixture in Terrie's cup, which was less coffee by now than liquid candy. "Do you really drink that crap?"

"Mother's milk," she said, taking a swallow. "Six cups of this contains all the nourishment a human body needs for eight hours. Honest. And it'll make your hair curly, too."

"I believe you about the last part," I said. "I always wanted curly hair."

"Well, I always wanted to be a redhead," said Terrie. "Maybe we should trade."

The thought of Terrie trading in her gorgeous head of curls for my head of coarse, spiky, bright red, and utterly straight hair made me smile. "I think we're stuck with what we've been dealt," I told her. "You should be grateful."

Jake came through the door of the reception area and frowned at me. "I don't want to see your face around here for a week, Burke. Go home and get some rest."

I got up from Terrie's desk. "Oops. Busted. Okay, boss, I'll see you in a week."

"Or any time at all if you need me—you know that."

I did know it. It was a good thing to know.

There was another person, a few hundred miles away, unfortunately, who would also be there if I needed him, or at least if I was willing to tell him I did. The problem was, I hadn't been totally honest with David Hayden about what I was going through.

David and I had been friends in high school fifteen years before, and my recent trip to Morado Beach on California's south coast had given us an opportunity to turn that friendship into something far more sensational and far more complicated. If either of us had been willing to see our time together as no more than a pleasant diversion and say, "Let's do lunch next time you're in town," we could have gone back to our previous lives without all this romantic longing, nagging doubts, and astronomical telephone bills, but that hadn't been the way it had turned out.

Even though he had a busy career as a painter along with the responsibility of looking out for his grandfather, I was sure David would make arrangements and come running if I told him how miserable I was and how much I needed him. I was sure, but somehow I wasn't willing to put it to the test. I couldn't bring myself to spoil our phone calls—the closest contact we'd had for two months—with kvetching about a few bad dreams. At least that's what I told myself.

When David and I talked, which we did a couple of times a week, I put all that nasty, bad, scary stuff so far out of my mind that it almost didn't exist until we'd said goodbye and hung up. We talked about our lives and plans—plans that included weekend visits and perhaps even a longer vacation together sometime later in the year, but which so far did not include any permanent commitments on either of our parts. Those calls and those plans were the only good things I could find in my life lately, and I was stubbornly unwilling to taint them with my day-to-day misery.

"How's life up north?" David would ask, and I'd tell him some story from earlier in the year about pulling an all-night surveillance on an employee suspected of stealing electronics hardware from his employer and reselling it on the street. Coffee and sandwiches in my car and trying to stay awake and wishing I could go to the bathroom, and the buyer never shows and the deal never goes down.

We'd have a good laugh at the absurdity of it all, and I'd sort of forget to mention that Jake wouldn't let me work, that I couldn't make myself drive down and see him because I was too messed up to be any good to anyone else, that I'd awakened the night before with my heart pounding, trying to scream for help as I remembered looking up the barrel of a revolver into the eyes of a man who wanted to kill me.

Having neglected to mention that, there wasn't much point in telling him what had really happened to me on my last trip out of town, the story of which I'd already watered down to a couple of close calls and a bit of adventure in the woods.

He'd called just last night, and I'd been so glad to hear his voice, I'd kept him on the phone far too long, keeping the subject on his life, his family, his career. David was still concerned about what I'd been through in Morado Beach a couple of months before, and it didn't seem right to give him something else to worry about. That's what I told myself.

So I'd painted myself into a tight little corner, and now I had to sit in it. I walked from the office to my apartment feeling more than a little sorry for myself.

# CHAPTER 2

EVERY MORNING AT EIGHT O'CLOCK I GO TO THE CASCADE Hotel Café, located around the corner from my office, for breakfast. It's not a big place or a fancy place. It's not nearly as colorful or as airy or as synthetically cheery as the plethora of more modern coffee shops that have sprung up at the various I-5 off-ramps around town. There's something very appealing, though, about the way the finish on the pine paneling has darkened with age, and the way the light comes in through the windows in the early morning, and let's face it: Any place that hires waitresses over forty can't be all bad.

I'm a regular there, along with a lot of other people who work downtown. Cops and lawyers mingle at the hotel with auto mechanics and pawnbrokers and retired people who live upstairs and haven't really got anywhere else to go. The waitresses know me by name, and know what I invariably order, so I sit down and my coffee appears at my elbow and I can read my newspaper and know breakfast is coming and the world is in order, or at least my little chunk of it. It's a pretty good way to start the day, especially for someone who hates to cook for one.

Although Jake hadn't let me work all last week, I'd been going into the café every morning out of habit since I got back from Cedar Ridge, a charming small town in the northern Sierras where I'd almost gotten myself eaten by pit bulls, shot, and/or burned to death scarcely more than a week before.

It was some comfort, at least, to stick to that much of my usual routine, even though once I left the café I had no idea where to go. I had already seen every movie at the Rio for free, and every other movie in town for money, and television bores me stiff most of the time, except for the news, which just makes me feel helpless. My television had been broken for five months, anyway, and I never seemed to get around to having it fixed.

I felt like one of the hotel pensioners, whom I encountered fairly regularly in my travels these days. I spent a lot of time wandering around aimlessly, and a lot more sitting in my apartment and staring at the wall. I went for walks by the river and took myself out to lunches I couldn't eat, and once, I got so desperate I called up my ex-husband. He had one of his ditzy girlfriends with him at the time, so we didn't say much besides hello and goodbye, not that our conversations are usually all that deep and meaningful.

The thing was, I was bored to death in the daytime and scared to death at night. The walls of the world were beginning to close in, and maybe Jake was right. Maybe I needed someone to talk to. It was Tuesday morning, and I'd be talking to Maggie Peck in less than an hour.

"My mom told me you're a private detective."

I looked up from the front page of the *San Francisco Chronicle* to see a dark-haired boy of about sixteen in kitchen whites and a damp apron standing by my table with a bus tub full of dishes. "That's right," I said. "I work at Baronian Investigations, up above the Rio. Who's your mom?" I added.

"Annie Holland," he said, naming a waitress I'd seen nearly every morning for three years, a big-boned woman with a friendly face whom I'd come to like and look forward to seeing first thing every weekday morning. "I'm

Sam Holland." He set down the tub and held out a hand.

"I'm Caley Burke," I said, taking it.

"I know."

"Is your mom here today?" Usually, Annie was there with coffee and a smile before I had my napkin unfolded. I'd already waved off the attentions of Paula, the woman who worked the other side of the room, but so far there'd been no sign of Annie.

"Uh, she's in back, I guess. She'll be out here in a minute." He stood there looking flustered for a few seconds. "Can I come see you at your office later?"

"Actually, I'm not at my office this week. I'm sort of on vacation right now."

"Oh. Okay." Sam picked up the tub and started to turn away.

"Come to my apartment," I told him, handing him a card with my home address written on the back. "I only live about two blocks from here. It's the apartment above the interior design place."

He took the card between two fingers and smiled at me with undisguised relief. "I'm off at three. I'll be there right after. Oh, and don't say anything to my mom about this, okay?"

"Okay."

Sam walked away. Annie came out of the kitchen a few moments later, dabbing at her eyes, which were red and slightly swollen. Her graying brown hair was drawn back in a neat braid under the requisite uniform cap, but a few wisps of hair strayed down onto her face, which was unlike her usual neat-as-a-pin appearance. I wasn't the only one having a bad day, it seemed. She poured me a cup of coffee and laid out a napkin and flatware. "The usual, Caley?"

"What else? By the way, I just met Sam. He seems like a great kid."

Annie's broad face was suffused by sudden joy. "He's terrific, all right," she replied, smiling proudly as parents do when another adult recognizes the solid gold in their children. Almost as quickly, the joy faded as though she'd remembered something she'd rather not, and was replaced by what seemed to be a kind of sorrowful anxiety. She sighed. "Well, I'll just go get that order in."

As I ate my breakfast I wondered what the deal was with Sam and Annie. When you spend as much time in your own company as I do, you sometimes forget to include other people in your universe. I'd known Annie in a casual way for three years, and this was the first time it had occurred to me to really wonder what her personal problems might be.

Of course, I doubted that Annie had ever concerned herself with my life, either; I was just one of hundreds of customers she saw every week, and I'd never exactly gone out of my way to get to know her personally. I seldom went far out of my way to get to know people. It was a deeply rooted tendency I had been fighting for years to overcome.

I looked at my right wrist, and my heart gave a thump of anxiety. Mickey Mouse posed preciously on my watch face, little gloved hands pointing to nine and eleven, which meant I had five minutes to make my appointment at the Counseling Center. I gave three seconds' thought to blowing off the appointment and facing Jake on Monday; then I threw some money on the table and bolted out the door.

I unlocked the door of the new blue Toyota the insurance company and I had bought just last week, right after I got back to town from Cedar Ridge. I had pulped my old Subaru against the trunk of a eucalyptus tree two months before, and it was *definitely* the other guy's fault. I missed the Subie, but I really loved my new car.

I sat there for fifteen seconds or so deciding what to do next. I'm cool in a sudden crisis, but not at my best against constant stress. Finally I realized I was staring at my car key, and stuck it into the ignition with a sigh. Jake had probably not made this appointment a day too soon.

• • •

The Cascade Counseling Center was located in an old house in a residential neighborhood that had been recently gentrified after falling into disrepute and disrepair decades before. The house itself had been painted in a cheery tint of peach with shades of blue and white and deep orange sparking up the Victorian trimmings. Only a discreet sign hanging on a painted iron hook hinted at what awaited me inside: Jake's counselor, Maggie Peck.

Jake swore by Maggie's concern and insight. He'd had problems of his own over the years, like the alcoholism that had wrecked his law career and his marriage and almost his life before he woke up one morning and realized he couldn't go any further without help. Maggie had seen him through a long and rocky recovery and made him able to face his children again, and his future. He's been sober for nine years now, and he's one of the most well-balanced people I've ever known.

I parked my car on the street and turned off the engine, leaving my hand on the key and waiting to change my mind about all this. I thought of Jake. I've never respected anyone as much as I respect Jake Baronian. If he could face up to his inner demons, I sure as hell wasn't going to chicken out on a harmless chat with a friendly shrink. What could she do—tell me I was crazy? I knew that already.

I got out of the car and walked up the steps.

"So you don't sleep?" Maggie Peck sat at one end of a plump flowered chintz sofa in jeans, a T-shirt, and a cotton blazer, sneakered feet pulled up under her legs. Her face was reserved but not unfriendly under a light brown bob, going gray a bit, that just brushed her shoulders. Her eyes looked kind. "Do you mean 'at all,' or 'some'?"

"Some," I told her, picking up the glass of iced tea she had poured me. We were sitting in front of an open window shaded by tall trees, and the slight breeze coming through was refreshing after the summer heat that was already noticeable at nine in the morning. "I can fall asleep if I have a couple of drinks, but then I usually wake up after an hour or so and can't get back to sleep until it's light."

Maggie nodded. "Liquor interferes with your sleep cycles. Bad dreams?"

"Pretty bad. People trying to kill me, stuff like that."

"Why do you think you're dreaming that people are trying to kill you?"

"Maybe because every now and again someone does."

Maggie raised an eyebrow a fraction of an inch; the first sign of an involuntary reaction I'd seen since I walked in. I felt like I had caught a peek at the woman behind the professional. "Maybe you should tell me about it."

There. The invitation had been spoken. *Tell me about it. Tell Dr. Peck all those things you've been feeling since the night you had to kill your first human being.* Was that what I really wanted to do? The decision was mine alone, but I looked at Maggie Peck for a long moment, hoping for some sign. She smiled at me, and her eyes crinkled a bit at the corners and I saw the concern for others that had drawn Jake to her when he was drowning in liquor and self-hate, like I was drowning in fear and guilt.

"It's not my personal life, it's my job," I said, surprised at the sound of my voice, since I had been certain I wasn't ready to speak yet. "Not that my job is all that dangerous, ordinarily. Usually it's just phone calls and paperwork and watching for people to do something wrong that someone else wants them to do." I settled back into the soft, welcoming chair Maggie had provided for me, and proceeded to get it off my chest.

"You see, I went down to the south coast in May and my old boyfriend proposed to me, and then somebody tried to kill me. Two somebodies, actually, and that doesn't count getting blown against a pier railing when one of them blew up somebody else, or totaling my car when I got run off the road into a eucalyptus tree. Before it was all over, I'd killed someone."

Both of Maggie's eyebrows rose perceptibly. I sighed and went on. "Self-defense. Then I came back up here and I thought I was over it, and I went out of town again, and someone else tried to kill me. Well, a lot of people wanted to, but only one was about to do it, and I killed him, too."

Maggie cocked her head to one side, inviting more detail, which I proceeded to give her. I told her about the investigation I had taken on hoping to clear my old friend Tony Garza of suspicion in the death of not one, but two bitter enemies conveniently murdered within a few days of one another. I told her about Rob Cameron and my attempt to make one last grab at that almost forgotten dream of a home and family.

I recounted the story of one man who wanted to see me drowned in the night-black ocean, and another who stood me up against the wall of a cliffside cave and put a gun to the side of my head. These were not pleasant memories, and neither was the memory of firing bullets into another person and feeling dead weight against you in the darkness and knowing someone was dead because of a conscious act that you had no choice but to take responsibility for.

Maybe I would have gotten over the experience, given enough time, but only a few weeks later, on another out-of-town case, I'd been forced to choose again between my life and another's, on a night that was more full of fear and death than any I've ever experienced. At some point the camel of my serenity had felt the crushing weight of that proverbial straw, and the rest was history.

"I think I can see why you're not sleeping," Maggie commented.

"I've considered not leaving town for the rest of my life," I said.

She nodded. The shadow of a smile played across her lips. "That might cut the risk some. Have you considered changing your line of work?"

"It's not like this, usually. Usually it's background checks and insurance surveillance and industrial undercover and so much boredom you can't think straight. I think I just had a run of bad luck."

"Luck," Maggie said softly, nodding. "Do you believe in luck?"

I thought about it. "I guess not. Not really. People usually get what they're prepared to get from life. But there are exceptions, I guess."

"I imagine there are. But for the most part, I agree with you. People draw certain experiences to themselves because of the way they live. You're putting yourself into dangerous situations. The question is, why?"

That was indeed the question.

# CHAPTER 3

"MY MOTHER WON'T TELL ME WHO MY FATHER IS." SAM Holland sat across from me at the tiny table in the kitchen area of my apartment holding a can of soda and staring at the checkered tablecloth as though it might know the answers he couldn't get anywhere else. "I know she wasn't married to anybody when I was born. She's never been married." He watched me with dark brown eyes surrounded by dark lashes on a slightly narrow face that was going to be nothing short of stunning in a few years. He seemed to be expecting a reaction to the fact of his illegitimacy, but I had none to give him.

"That information is probably on your birth certificate. Have you looked to see if it is?"

"I can't find it. I know my mom's hidden it somewhere, but our place isn't that big, and I've looked everywhere I can think of."

"If it's something she wants to keep secret from you, she may have put it in a safe-deposit box," I ventured.

Sam ran a hand through his straight, dark hair. "If she did, I wouldn't be able to get to it, would I?"

"Not unless she wanted you to." I watched him make a trail in the frost on the can with his thumb, over and over. "There'd be a key somewhere, but if there's something she's keeping from you, I think it'd be pretty well hidden. Have you two talked about this a lot?"

"A few times when I was younger. She never said much then, either, but it didn't really bother me so much back then when she changed the subject. This past year it just got to be real important to me. I started asking her questions, and she wouldn't answer them, and she'd get all upset." His eyes teared up just a bit at the memory. "I don't want to make her feel bad, but it's something I need to know. I don't know how to explain why it matters so much."

"You don't have to," I told him. "It would matter to anybody. So is that why you need a detective?"

"I guess so. I mean, you could try to find out for me, couldn't you? Investigate?"

"That's what I do, all right," I admitted. "But I charge money for it."

"I have some saved. I've been working at the café this summer, saving money to go to veterinary school in a couple of years, and I've got a part-time job at an animal clinic. I've been helping out with the bills at home, but I managed to put a lot of money in the bank. I can afford to pay you."

I'd been planning to cut my usual rate down to nearly nothing for this job, anyway—a sixteen-year-old dishwasher couldn't afford what people usually pay for the services of a private investigator—but now I had a better idea. "I've got a better idea," I told Sam. "You can do the investigating yourself. What state were you born in?"

"California. In Eureka, up near the Oregon border."

"Call the Department of Health in Sacramento and find out how much they charge to search for a copy of your birth certificate. If you don't want your mother to know you're calling, use a pay phone and make sure you're home to get the mail for the next couple of days. You can send them a money order by Express Mail and get the certificate back the same way. It'll only take a couple of days, and you won't be out more than maybe fifteen or twenty bucks for the whole thing."

"Is it really that easy?"

"Piece of cake. Make sure you tell them you want an actual copy of your birth record, and not just a certified abstract. And tell them you have to have it in a hurry, so they'll expedite it. It'll cost you a few dollars more, but it'll save you two weeks. If there's a name on there, you'll have it in your hands practically overnight."

Sam took a pen and notebook out of his backpack and wrote down what I'd told him. "When it comes, maybe I can sit Mom down and make her talk about it." He glanced up, startled. "*If* there's a name?"

"There's always the possibility that she didn't fill in a name."

"You mean like if she didn't know who my father was?"

"Yeah, I guess that's what I mean."

"You don't know my mom like I do," said Sam. "She's not like that."

"Things happen, Sam," I told him. "If you find out there's no name, it doesn't mean your mother was a bad person."

"No, but . . ." He shook his head. "Jesus, it almost figures, now that you mention it, you know? Why would she keep me from meeting my father? Why wouldn't she at least tell me and let me make my own decision about it? She lived around here all her life, so I always figured my father was someone from around here. Somebody she knew. That's what was driving me so nuts—like maybe it was somebody I'd seen or met, you know?"

"Yeah. That'd be tough, all right."

"But if it was—oh, hell, I don't know—if she doesn't know, that might be why she's so afraid to say anything about it to me. Or maybe it was somebody she was ashamed of." He looked very young and frightened as his mind raced through the possibilities.

"Those are the kinds of things you should be prepared to find out. The problem with asking questions is, sometimes we get the answers."

"Would you mind doing something for me, Ms. Burke?"

"That depends. What is it?"

"Ask around. You know, investigate. You could find out if there was anything like that anyone might know about. I'll pay you for your time and everything. I'd like to know what was going on in her life then—what she was going through. It's always been a big mystery to me. Like there was a black hole in her life for about a year, and I can't see into it. Then after the birth certificate comes, maybe even if there's no name on it, if I know more about her, maybe we'll be able to talk about it."

I get paid to snoop. I don't usually like to put that word to it; usually I like to think of it as finding the truth, but when I'm honest with myself I'm forced to admit it comes down to snooping in the end. Sam wanted to pay me to snoop on his mother, in a manner of speaking, though he intended no malice. Was that any worse than snooping on a potential employee for an employer? I decided it wasn't, probably because that was the conclusion that fit the case. Sam needed information, and getting people information they needed was my job. When I was allowed to do it, that is. And this time it wasn't up to Jake. It was my case and my call.

"I'll see what I can do. I'll be as discreet as possible— we don't want to alert your mother to any of this until you get your birth certificate back and decide if you want to talk to her about it."

"Right. I'm going to go make the call right now," he said, getting up and draining the last of his soda. "I've still got time to get a money order in today's mail. Thanks for everything, Ms. Burke."

"Call me Caley, and it was my pleasure," I said. "I'll call you in a couple of days and let you know what I found out. Meanwhile, get back to me if you need any more help with this."

"And you won't say anything to my mother?"

"It's between us. A professional thing."

"Like when you tell things to a priest?"

"Sort of like that. You'll have your answer in a few days, so go home and relax."

Sam snorted. "I wish I could relax. It's my aunt Katherine's birthday, and we have to go to her house for a party. My mom's sister," he added by way of explanation. He shook his head; a barely perceptible expression of disgust.

"Why do I get the feeling you'd rather walk barefoot on hot coals?"

"Probably because I would." Sam contemplated his sneakers, frowning. "My aunt Katherine gives the phrase 'stone bitch' a whole new meaning. She gives these parties so she can show off who she's sleeping around on her husband with this month, and so the rest of the family can sit around and listen to her talk about how important she is and how much of a nothing my mother is."

"She doesn't like your mother?"

He sighed deeply. "I don't think she likes anybody much, but she seems to get some kind of special kick out of baiting Mom. She's been doing the same thing every time I've seen her for as long as I can remember. I wish my mom would just tell her to fuck off." He looked up at me in alarm. "Sorry."

"I understand perfectly," I said, holding the door open for him. Annie Holland had always seemed such a strong and self-sufficient woman. I didn't know anything about her family, but somehow I couldn't see her standing still for her sister's abuse forever. "Maybe tonight will be the night, huh?"

Sam shook his head sadly. "I'm not putting any money on it. Thanks again." We shook hands and he started down the stairs.

I went to my window and watched as Sam walked out onto the street from my stairway and stepped up to a public phone on the corner. There goes a young man taking life by the horns, I thought as I watched him pick up the phone.

I decided I could do no less myself. I slung my bag over my shoulder and let myself out of my apartment. My Tuesday night figure drawing class was still three hours away, but I could use the time to good advantage by sitting in the mall and doing quick sketches of people passing by until it was time to leave. On my way past the phone booth I waved at Sam. "Call me when it comes in," I said.

He smiled and gave me a thumbs-up.

# CHAPTER 4

CASCADE ISN'T REALLY A SMALL TOWN ANYMORE, BUT it's still hard not to know more about people than you really want to. One of the things I knew was that Annie Holland had once been engaged to my art teacher, Robby Fry. That was about seventeen years ago by local gossip, and a bit more than sixteen since Annie had gone out of town and come back with an infant son. Conventional wisdom had it that Robby was not the father, and that was about all I ever knew on the subject, since I've always been disinclined to pursue gossip. Of course, in my present line of work, gossip was a tool. And tools are meant to be used.

As I sketched that night's model over and over, quick sketches aimed at capturing line, mass, and light rather than detail, I kept looking at Robby Fry sitting at his desk buried in the usual paperwork, a boyish shock of gray-streaked brown hair fallen over his forehead, and his gold-rimmed glasses continually slipping down and continually being pushed back up in a gesture as unconscious as it was utterly typical of Robby.

As I watched him, I couldn't help speculating about the past. What had really happened between him and Annie? And if he wasn't Sam's father, who was?

My speculations weren't much more helpful than the

24

town's hearsay, so by the time class was over I had convinced myself that it wouldn't hurt anything to ask him a few questions. I asked him to join me for coffee and pie at a nearby retro-fifties diner after class, something we did about once a month anyway, so I didn't feel totally obvious or totally ashamed of my curiosity. As reluctant as I was to spend Sam's money, he wanted some answers. That, and I desperately needed something to do.

Babe's Diner featured nickel jukeboxes and a never-changing menu of three burgers, six sandwiches, and seven kinds of pie, plus peach in season. It was in season now, and we each ordered a piece. "We'll have that hot, à la mode, and with no guilt on the side," Robby instructed. "And we want the good china this time." Robby had come late to enjoying life, and always seemed to be making up for lost time.

The waitress humphed and retreated down the narrow aisle between the red Naugahyde booths. "And coffee," he added to her back. "And one for my friend. Price is no object."

The waitress turned her head to give him a look, which, since Robby had turned back around to face me, he couldn't see.

"You'd think they'd get used to you in this place," I said. "You practically live here when you're not in class or in your office."

"Well, I think I fulfill a need. I'm that crazy customer they have to humor. It's true their night staff isn't noted for an appreciation of comedy."

The waitress came back a moment later with our coffee, set it down without comment, and walked away again. Robby dug some nickels out of his pocket and punched his selections into the jukebox at our booth. Buddy Holly began to lament over Peggy Sue.

I stared at the steam rising from my cup. "Robby, can I presume on our long acquaintance to ask you some personal stuff?"

"Presume away. I'll probably even answer."

"You used to be engaged to Annie Holland, didn't you?"

"Boy, when you say personal, you really mean it." He laughed, but I could tell it was a subject he wasn't crazy about. "Not officially engaged," he said. "I never actually got around to asking her in so many words, but the relationship was serious. I always assumed we'd be married."

"When did you stop assuming that?"

"Oh, one day, it must be almost seventeen years ago," Robby said, gazing out the window next to our booth, "we had a terrible fight. It was over my mother."

I nodded. I'd heard tales about Robby Fry's mother; an unpleasant, domineering woman who ran her son's life until the day she died. Until that day, Robby had been quiet, almost pathologically shy, and fearful. Since then he'd become a regular free spirit and weekend favorite at the local comedy club.

"Mother hated Annie," Robby continued, "or maybe she just hated the idea of another woman taking me away from her. Whenever I'd start talking about getting married, or spending too much time away from home, she had a way of getting deathly sick." He smiled wryly. "At the time, I guess I thought it was genuine, or I didn't know how to call her bluff, more likely. She'd act like she was dying, and I'd spend less time with Annie for a while, and then Mother would feel better, and I'd go back to seeing more of Annie, and the whole thing would start up again."

"Who broke up with who?"

"It was Annie. I can't blame her for it." He cupped his coffee in both hands and stared into it. "I guess I'd just have gone on like that for the foreseeable future, never having enough backbone to tell my mother to go to hell, and Annie knew that better than I did, and she couldn't see going on that way. She told me we were through.

"She told me not to call, or come by, or write—just to get the hell out of her life." He stopped, took off the glasses, blinked away tears. "I did. Next thing I knew, she'd gone off somewhere up north—Eureka or maybe Trinidad. Then her sister left and went up there to be with her." He looked up at me, the old sorrow surprisingly fresh in his eyes. "She came back six months later with a baby."

"Your baby?"

Robby shook his head. "I wondered. I hoped. If the baby were mine, we could start all over again. We could get married no matter what my mother said. It would have removed the need to make the decision on my own, if you know what I mean."

I did, of course. I was no stranger to letting things happen to me—I'd spent my twenties doing just that, while my life and my marriage fell apart around me. "Did you talk to her about it? Did you ask her if the baby was yours?"

Robby shook his head. "She didn't contact me when she came back into town. I heard about it from another instructor here at the college. I didn't know whether I should call or wait for her to call. Finally I went to see her. She didn't invite me in."

"Did she talk to you at all?"

"She told me the boy wasn't mine."

"Could she have been lying to you? Reacting out of anger? I'm guessing she was hurt pretty badly."

"I thought the same thing at first," Robby said, nodding slowly. "I couldn't believe Annie could have been seeing someone else while we were together. I told her I knew the baby had to be mine. I told her we'd get married no matter what my mother said or did."

"But she said no. And she kept saying no. Every time I went by or called her, she said no. Then I had to believe her. I said we should get married anyway, even if the baby was someone else's, but I think I waited too long to say it. Annie wasn't having any. Finally I quit asking. But I'll tell you one thing for sure: If Sam were my son, she would have told me. Annie wouldn't deprive a father and son of one another, no matter how angry or disappointed she was. I know the boy's not mine."

"Do you have any idea who the father might be?"

"None. Don't think I didn't speculate about it—for years—but I just don't know. There was gossip, of course. People tried to pin it on every guy in town, but Annie didn't care. She just went about making a life for her and Sam." I could see admiration in Robby's eyes, and perhaps something else. It wasn't difficult to think he might still be in love with her, even now.

"Who else did Annie know at the time?"

"Well, she grew up in Cascade, so she knew a lot of people after a fashion, but not very many socially," Robby said. "Neither of us had much social life outside each other."

I didn't remind him that if subsequent events were to be believed, Annie certainly had some sort of social life he didn't know about. The waitress brought our pie, and Robby waited until she was out of earshot before he went on.

"Annie had dropped out of school to support her brother and two sisters when her parents died. After the youngest sister left home, she started thinking about college again. She was working two jobs to save money for tuition at a four-year college, and taking some classes here a couple of nights a week. That's how we met—I'd just started teaching that year."

Annie's former employers might have a clue to who else she knew at the time. I resisted the urge to pull out a notebook and start writing. "Where was she working?" I asked as casually as I could manage.

"This is more than idle curiosity about my youth, isn't it?" Robby asked. "Is this about a case or something?"

"I should have mentioned it earlier. It's sort of a case, but I can't talk about it just yet. I didn't mean to grill you under false pretenses. I don't want you to think I'd take advantage of our friendship."

"Hey, no problem," Robby said. "As long as it doesn't hurt Annie."

"I don't think it will, and it will help someone else a great deal."

"Well, she worked part-time as a clerk at Drake's, and she kept house for old Miss Rose."

"*Old* Miss Rose? I don't suppose she's still with us."

Robby laughed. "You'd be wrong. We only *thought* she was old back then. She's even older now, and still living on Park Street right by the river. That Tudor place with the four-car garage."

I knew the house. Ancient and just a bit run-down, it dominated a huge corner lot with a magnificent river view on a quiet residential street not more than a dozen blocks from my apartment. And Drake's—an expensive clothing store in downtown Cascade—was even closer. I dug into my pie with a growing sense of optimism. I was going to forget about Jake's little leave of absence and talk to a couple of people tomorrow. The more I heard, the more the puzzle of Sam's origins intrigued me, but mostly I wanted to feel like a detective again.

# CHAPTER 5

· · · · · · · · · · · · · · · · ·

MELISSA DRAKE PACED THE FLOOR OF HER SMALL, DARK office, one hand supporting an elbow, the other holding a lit cigarette. She hadn't asked if I minded, so I felt like an idiot asking her not to smother me in secondhand smoke. I kept my peace and wished for oxygen.

I'd put off breakfast temporarily and gotten to Drake's a few minutes after they opened at nine. I'd been shown in here after a brief but frustrating exchange with a receptionist who seemed destined for a stellar career in the security industry. By standing my ground, I was at least able to get her to call and find out if I could be seen without an appointment. Melissa Drake was kept well insulated from casual callers, but she had been only too glad to talk with me when she found out what had brought me here.

"He was sleeping with her, of course—Richard, I mean." It hadn't taken Melissa any time at all to open up once I mentioned the name Annie Holland. She'd lit a cigarette from the butt of the previous one, and started pacing. In fifteen seconds I knew that she and Richard Drake—co-owners of Drake's Clothing Store during the time Annie Holland worked there—were divorced, and Richard was living off his inheritance in Los Angeles with the fifth in a steady succession of ever-younger women.

30

"He always said he was innocent, but I'd caught him at it twice before, and I wasn't falling for his lies a third time. Annie Holland left town on vacation and phoned in her resignation two weeks later. When she came back to town with an illegitimate child, it took me about one minute to divorce Richard's ass and take the house. I'd had it up to here with his bullshit."

"So you think Sam Holland is your ex-husband's son?"

"I know damned well he is," she replied, puffing smoke in twin columns from her nostrils like a medieval dragon.

"If that's true, why do you suppose Richard didn't stick around to help take care of him?" I asked.

"Because he's a moral coward," Melissa Drake replied. "Not to mention a liar and a lecher." She stubbed out the latest cigarette in an onyx ashtray on her desk and reached into her skirt pocket for the pack. "It wasn't the first time he'd gotten a girl pregnant," she said.

I waited without saying anything. She was dying to tell me, anyway.

"There was one other one that I know of," she went on. "I don't know how many he may have been able to keep from me; I was pretty stupid about Richard for a long time. Anyway, he gave this other girl some money to have an abortion and she did. My guess is he made the same offer to Annie, but she turned it down. Or maybe she took the money and went away and had the kid. I never asked."

She paused long enough to light up again, and my stomach did a slow roll. The longer I live, the more I hate cigarette smoke. I honestly don't care if someone else has to breathe it to stay happy; I just want to be in another room when they do.

"I got over being mad at Annie Holland and the others a long time ago," Melissa said wearily. "They were just as taken in by him as I was. I really don't care if I never see or hear from Richard again. He sold me his half of the store at a fraction of what it was worth, you know." She attempted a smile, but only her mouth changed; the rest of her face remained as grim as before. "Now he has his life, and I have mine."

Melissa Drake had her life, but I'd be willing to bet Richard loomed larger in it now than he ever had when they shared a house. She was still keeping track of his girlfriends, and her eyes lit up like little coals when she talked about him. "Thanks for talking with me," I said, standing and offering my hand. "Could I trouble you for Richard's phone number? I'd like to speak to him personally."

Melissa transferred her cigarette to her left hand and scribbled a number on a piece of notepaper, then gave me a businesslike handshake. "My pleasure," she assured me.

It was good to get out on the street again and into the fresh air. It was as good not to be breathing Melissa Drake's bitterness as her secondhand smoke. I wondered if her hatred for her ex-husband would always be the most important thing in her life, but the answer seemed obvious.

I found the nearest pay phone and took the slip of paper Melissa had given me out of my pocket. Whatever her problems might be, I now had Richard Drake's phone number in Los Angeles, and could get one more thing done before I had my morning coffee. I was starting to feel the rush I sometimes get when I've got an intriguing case on my hands and a list of good leads still to follow. Food and caffeine could wait.

The night had been ghastly as usual, the wakefulness nearly as troubling as the dreams because of the questions I now had to torture myself with since my session with Maggie Peck. All night long I'd tossed on my bed and gone over and over them.

Was there some deep underlying reason I'd chosen investigation as a career, or was it as simple as the coincidence of my first meeting with Jake and the fact that I was finished with my marriage, unhappy with my life, and looking for a different line of work? Was I doing a job—one that I did pretty well and always tried to do better—or attempting to fill some hole in my psychological puzzle? I shook my head and put the questions aside as I punched in the numbers for Richard Drake and my telephone credit card.

"Richard Drake," said the voice on the other end of the phone. "Hello."

"Mr. Drake, my name is Caley Burke. I work for Baronian Investigations in Cascade, California."

"Oh, Christ, what's Melissa pulling now?"

"This doesn't have anything to do with your ex-wife, Mr. Drake. I'd like to ask you some questions about Annie Holland."

"If you're asking about Annie Holland, then I *know* Melissa's behind it," Drake replied. "She's nothing short of obsessed with the whole incident."

"*Was* there an incident?"

"Between Melissa and me, yes. Something along the lines of an atomic explosion. Between Annie and me? I barely knew Annie Holland, except as an employee."

"Melissa says you had an affair with her."

"That never happened. Nothing ever happened with Annie and me, but Melissa's paranoia about it ended up wrecking our marriage, as I'm sure she's told you in great detail."

I remained silent for a moment, not knowing whether I should mention that Melissa claimed to have caught him red-handed with two other female employees over the years.

Richard Drake jumped into the gap with both feet. "All right, I messed around a little—what man doesn't? Melissa found out a couple of times, and she wasn't any too happy about it, but that doesn't mean I was automatically guilty the next time she got suspicious, does it?"

"Mrs. Drake thinks you're the father of Annie's son, Sam," I said.

There was a moment of silence from Richard Drake's end of the phone. "If this isn't about some new scheme of Melissa's to wreck my life, why the hell are you saying these things to me?"

"I can't discuss the case with you, but I can tell you that I'm not working for Melissa, and I'm not trying to dig dirt on you. I just want to know if you're Sam Holland's father, or if you know who is."

"Listen, Miss . . ."

"Burke."

"Listen, Miss Burke. I've got no reason to lie about this. I fooled around a lot of times in the years I was married to Melissa—I admit that freely. But it was always a certain type of girl, you know? The pretty ones, not to put too fine a point on it. Annie was a good employee, and she seemed like a pretty nice person, but she wasn't a looker. And there was always a looker around with twelve or fifteen young female employees to choose from, you understand me?"

I understood him better than I wanted to.

"I'm sorry Annie's had a tough life, but that doesn't make me the father of her kid, and I don't know who is."

"Well, thank you, Mr. Drake—you've been very helpful." I always said things like that, but this time I meant it. I would have given a lot to have been able to see his face, but I believed Richard Drake's story. He was not only honest but totally unrepentant about his indiscretions, and I didn't think he was lying about this one. I'd have to look somewhere else for clues to the identity of Sam's father, and there was a place close by where I could look right now.

"Oh, Annie was such a good girl. So many of the young women you can get to come in and help with the house just aren't honest or hard-working at all. Annie was a real gem."

Amelia Rose had seemed delighted by my unannounced visit, and insisted on making a pot of tea for us to chat over. While she was in the kitchen I looked around at the sitting room. The dark woods, heavy red drapes, and high shelves full of leather-bound books seemed to harken back to days when ladies came to tea and young girls had names like Amelia Rose.

I stifled the urge to peek outside and see if I'd really entered a previous century when I'd stepped through

Miss Rose's hand-carved front door. I'd done a lot of research on what Cascade had looked like a hundred years ago, and I could clearly picture the unpaved street that had once run by outside, and the horse-drawn traffic that moved leisurely up and down it. I had almost convinced myself I heard hoofbeats when Miss Rose came back into the room.

She had brought a tray with tea things, and insisted on pouring for us. I declined sugar and cream. Miss Rose was somewhere on the sunny side of ninety, with bright, friendly eyes and a ready smile full of her own teeth. I made a silent request to whoever might be listening to be half this healthy and alert if I made it to her age, which was seeming less likely all the time.

"I knew I couldn't keep her here forever," she went on, handing me a shortbread biscuit on a little linen napkin. "She was made for better things than keeping house for some dried up old thing like me. And then she went away and had that baby. And you know what I never could figure out? Why go away?"

"Excuse me?" I said around a mouthful of biscuit.

"Why go anywhere? Why couldn't she have stayed right here and had it? You know, I always thought maybe she planned to give the baby up for adoption and come back home, then changed her mind. It was only sixteen or seventeen years ago, and we'd already done the sixties, and all that."

Miss Rose reached across the table and patted my hand. "You're too young to remember the way it used to be, but by the seventies things had changed. By that time girls were having babies out of wedlock right and left, and abortions were readily available, too. It just didn't make sense. Still doesn't." She stirred half a teaspoon of sugar into her tea and sipped at it.

I tried my own tea. It was delicious. "My tea never tastes this good," I told Miss Rose. "What's your secret?"

"Loose tea—never bags. This is Oolong."

I made a mental note to throw out all my tea bags. "So you don't have any idea who the father was?"

"Don't think I haven't speculated a time or twenty. I'm an observer of people, you know. I can spot family resemblances better than most, and more than one time I've been certain that it's a wise child that knows his own father, if you take my meaning."

I did.

"Now you take Annie Holland and her siblings, for instance," Miss Rose went on. "Annie's the oldest, then Joey, then Susan, then Katherine. Annie and Joey resemble their mother most strongly, while Susan and Katherine look a lot more like their father, but there are striking resemblances between all of them."

"I think Annie's the only one of them I've ever met," I said. "I've lived here a long time, but I don't really know that many people."

"A loner, eh?"

"I'm trying to quit."

"Well, most people you talk to wouldn't say Joey and Susan resemble one another at all, but they do, if you know what to look for. Or take Annie and Katherine. Annie's a big girl, and Katherine's so petite. That's what most people look at first. And Annie's features aren't quite as pretty as Katherine's. That's the other thing people tend to notice, but the resemblances are there, all right. They're in the shape of the eyes and eyebrows, and in the line of cheek and jaw, mostly. Subtle, but very definite. Their inner differences are much more pronounced than their outer ones.

"The men always seemed to like Katherine," Miss Rose continued. "She's always had a knot of them after her like a pack of stray male dogs. And being married doesn't stop her from taking her pick of them, either."

"Really?"

Miss Rose nodded. "And always the best-looking of them. Katherine could never resist a pretty face."

"Does her husband know about all this?"

"It would be difficult to imagine he doesn't, but people have a nearly infinite capacity for self-delusion, don't you think?"

I did indeed. "Speaking of family resemblances, have you noticed any resemblance between Sam and Robby Fry?"

"That's a little harder to call," Miss Rose admitted. "Robby's features and Annie's are of a similar type—people always said they resembled one another. But if Robby had been Sam's father, Annie would have told him so. She might not have married him, but she wouldn't have kept him from Sam."

"That's what Robby said, too."

"Annie's a good person," said Miss Rose. "She still comes to visit me every now and again; Sam, too, sometimes, but he's young and has lots more interesting things to do. But at any rate, I'm sure Robby Fry had nothing to do with it, and that's the only young man I knew she was seeing."

"Did you know Richard Drake?"

Miss Rose nodded. "I see you've talked to Melissa," she remarked drily. "She divorced Richard over Annie's baby, though why she hadn't dumped him years before I never understood."

I didn't understand it either, especially now that I'd talked to him. "I've never met Richard Drake. Have you seen any resemblance between him and Sam Holland?"

Miss Rose shook her head emphatically. "Absolutely not. Richard had a nose on him you wouldn't believe. A honker, I believe they call it. There's no way he could miss passing on a feature like that in some way. It's too dominant."

I had to agree; Sam's nose bore no resemblance to anything called a honker. None of his features seemed irregular or unattractive at all. He looked a bit like Annie, but there were other influences in the face, too—influences that might come from his father's side, like the slightly lengthened face and the dark eyes that burned with their own inner fire.

"No, Sam doesn't look anything like Richard," Miss Rose continued, "though if you care to know, there are more than a few other young people around here who do."

# CHAPTER 6

AMELIA ROSE'S TEA AND BISCUITS HAD ONLY HEIGHTENED my appetite for my delayed breakfast. I drove from the Rose house by the river to the Cascade Hotel a little faster than was prudent considering the Cascade Police Department was located about halfway between the two. My luck held, and I was through the door and headed for my usual table in about two minutes flat. On the way, I grabbed a *San Francisco Chronicle* from the stack on the counter and put down two quarters. A morning without the *Chron* is a morning without sunshine.

I looked around for Annie Holland, but didn't see her. No sign of Sam, either, but he was most likely stuck back in the kitchen. What I did see were the usual complement of hotel residents—mostly pensioners who ran up a tab all month and paid it off when their government checks came in—and a smattering of business people and professionals meeting one another over the best breakfast in town.

Paula, the other waitress on the morning shift, came up to take my order. "Don't you always have two eggs over medium, bacon, hash browns, and a buttered English muffin?"

"The Heart Attack Special," I agreed. "Where's Annie this morning?"

Paula's mouth opened and closed like a fish out of water. "Oh, my gosh, I guess you must be the last one in town who doesn't know." She turned to the man at the next table, who was reading the sports section of *The Cascade Beacon,* the local paper. "You through with this, hon?" she asked him as she whisked the front section off his table and onto mine. She jabbed a forefinger at the headline.

" 'Wife of Cascade Councilman Murdered in Her Home,' "I read aloud. " 'Cascade civic leader Katherine Garrett killed by unknown intruder.' " The byline was a familiar one: Michael Carlson. I looked up at Paula. "What's this got to do with Annie?"

"Katherine Garrett!" Paula exclaimed, aghast at my ignorance. "That's Annie's youngest sister!"

Holy cow. Never in a zillion years would I have put Annie Holland, coffee-shop waitress, together with Katherine Garrett, Cascade's premiere hostess and social climber.

I remembered what Miss Rose had said about the obvious superficial differences between Annie and her sister Katherine, and the differences of character and personality. I only knew Katherine Garrett by reputation, but it was a considerable one, and didn't disagree with Miss Rose's evaluation of her. While Annie was a warm-hearted, down-to-earth individual, a natural mother figure whose concern for others was famous among her friends and acquaintances, Katherine Garrett was reputed to be of a different character.

Katherine was known, or known of, by nearly everyone in town, and heartily disliked by most or all who knew her. She was relentlessly ambitious—not for herself, but for her husband, Raymond Garrett, a local politician who had served on the City Council and was now a strong contender for the next congressional election. She was probably best known as a tireless destroyer of reputations; a woman who had run through everyone willing to call themselves her friends years since, and had since had to content herself with assassinating the characters of acquaintances and her husband's political rivals.

Sam's Aunt Katherine. The stone bitch. It all fit.

"There must be a list of suspects clear around the block," I commented.

Paula snatched back the paper. "Don't speak ill of the dead," she warned solemnly.

"I'll be good," I promised. "Let me get another look at that. And you could turn in my order, too," I suggested.

Paula humphed and turned away, tossing down the paper. I offered an apologetic smile to the man at the next table. He disappeared behind the sports section, shaking his head. I returned to the front page and the article about Katherine Garrett, nearly without remorse.

Last night, I recalled from my conversation with Sam the day before, had been Katherine Garrett's birthday party. According to the newspaper article, some time after all the guests had departed someone had entered the darkened house and laid into Katherine's skull with a heavy object.

The exact time of death was being withheld, as were the gory details of the crime scene, but it did say the body had been found in the dining room, under the table. It was unlikely, I thought, that you could bludgeon someone under a table with any efficiency. My overactive imagination showed me a little mind movie of the deceased attempting to get away from her attacker after the fact by dragging herself slowly across the carpet—trying to hide where there was no hiding place. It wasn't a pretty picture.

I felt terribly sorry for Annie; from what Sam had said, Katherine and Annie's relationship was pretty unhealthy, and there'd be no time now to heal the damage. Annie would probably remember Katherine's belittling and verbal abuse more vividly than anything else about her, and that seemed an awful shame.

As an only child, I've always been curious about sibling relationships. The ones I've seen run the gamut between sincere respect and affection to the barest toleration for the sake of blood, with a lot of interesting combinations in between. Most work okay, but there are people in the world who really shouldn't be related to one another. These two sisters seemed to fit the latter category.

When I fantasized, as a child, about having a sister or brother, my dream siblings were always perfect, sweet, loving beings of a sort that certainly don't exist on this planet. Maybe I was lucky, after all, not to have been blessed with the real thing. I'd never know.

Annie had apparently gotten stuck with the worst kind, and now this. And how must Sam be taking it, along with his other anxieties? Tomorrow, by my calculations, he'd be expecting his birth certificate by Express Mail. I hoped whatever the news was, it would be news he could handle. I'd hoped to be able to call him later and see if he wanted a rundown on what little information I had. Now, in light of the family tragedy, it seemed best to wait and let him contact me when he was ready.

I was grateful to Sam for coming to me with his problem when he did. I knew Jake cared about my well-being, but I felt hurt that he didn't think I could handle my job, despite my current difficulties. Sam, knowing nothing of my situation, treated me like a detective because he didn't know any better. I'd felt good interviewing people, trying to fit in a few of those elusive puzzle pieces that sometimes come together so satisfyingly.

Then there were those other times. Since last night I had talked to the three people next to her family who could be expected to know the most about Annie Holland's life before she left Cascade so suddenly seventeen years before, and for all I'd been able to turn up, Sam Holland might have been a virgin birth. I couldn't help feeling that Jake would know what to do next, but a lot of good that did me.

I shoved food around on my plate for a few minutes, but my appetite was gone again. I paid the check and walked out onto the street.

Chances were, there'd be a name on the birth certificate when it arrived, and if Sam needed help finding out more about his newly revealed father, I'd be willing to give it. I'd also be happy to tell him what I knew so far about his mother's early life. Nothing unpleasant or unscrupulous had come to light, and I thought he might like to know how highly Robby and Miss Rose thought of Annie. For now, though, I'd done all I could with the information I had. I wasn't in any position to grill Annie's surviving relatives about her past after the events of last night.

I parked my car on the street in front of my apartment and spent the day walking around town and sitting by the river, sketching and thinking. My session with Maggie Peck had opened up a line of thought I didn't particularly welcome. Was I in the wrong line of work? Was there some flaw, some shortcoming in my mental makeup that steered me away from more traditional occupations and into the sometimes risky investigation business? I thought about these things as I captured quick studies of people and objects around me with my pencil.

I'd had a lot of jobs in my life, some half-assed, some less so. None of them had made me feel like getting up in the morning like I had since I went to work for Jake Baronian. Even having my life threatened hadn't changed my mind about it. Even killing another human being hadn't made me want to go back to my previous life. Did that mean there was something basically wrong with me? My drawings began to take on a surreal appearance as I pondered all this. It was an interesting new wrinkle to my style, I decided, looking at the day's sketches. Maybe I ought to go poking around my emotional insides more often.

I got back to my block at a little before six. Julian MacIntyre, my downstairs neighbor who owns Studio J, the interior design studio over which my apartment is located, was pulling the blind down over his front door, when he saw me coming up the sidewalk. "Get in here," he called as he threw open the door to the sound of little bells. "We're having Spaghetti Carbonara, and you're invited." The bells over the door chimed again as he shut it behind us.

Julian, unlike sane people, adores spur-of-the-moment guests. He and his roommate, Carl, frequently thump on their ceiling with a broom and ask me down for dinner and late-night talks, usually when they sense that I'm feeling down. I'd been seeing a lot of them this past week.

"Go pick out some wine," Julian said, pointing at the wine closet in the back of the studio, "but remember it has to breathe for two minutes for each year since the vintage, and I'm thirsty now."

"I'll pick something young," I promised.

"Bring it on back," he said, disappearing through a curtained doorway that led to his apartment. "I'll tell Carl you're here." The sounds of Bach floated in from the kitchen. I smiled to myself. Julian's timing was unusually perfect tonight; this was just what I needed. I mulled over the several dozen bottles of wine lying in the little niches Julian had built for them. Did we want a Cabernet for Carbonara, or a Merlot? Julian was trying to teach me to tell one variety of wine from another, but it was an uphill struggle.

*"Buona sera!"* Carl called from the kitchen as I pushed through the curtain with two bottles of Silver Family Merlot.

"You're not Italian, Carl," I informed him. "Your father's name is Johanssen and your mother is a Rosencranz."

"When I make Carbonara, I'm Italian," Carl assured me. "You should come by when we're having Manchurian Beef."

Brandishing some kind of Swiss Army corkscrew, Julian took the bottles and examined the labels with approval. "Young and sassy," he said, nodding. "Let's get a head start on Carl." We walked into the next room and he switched on the television.

Paul Gregory, the local station's news anchor, posed beside a photograph that was superimposed on the background of the set. It showed Katherine Garrett in happier days, on the arm of Raymond Garrett, both of them smiling at the camera like good politicians. "Let's turn this up a bit," Julian suggested. "Not everyday we have such sensational news in this burg."

"We'll have more on the Katherine Garrett murder case as it develops," Gregory said as the picture of Katherine Garrett faded to be replaced by one representing another local news story. His look of concerned sorrow changed to one of sturdy optimism. Theater was alive and well on local TV.

"Looks like we're too late to learn anything new," Julian said. He muted the TV and uncorked a bottle of Merlot. He pointed to the news anchor, now mouthing silent words next to a picture of a school building. "It looks like Channel 5 is losing its pretty anchorman."

"Paul Gregory? Where's he going?"

"To Washington, if he has his way. He's just announced that he's running for Congress."

"He is? Isn't that the seat Raymond Garrett's running for, too?"

"Well, he's the conservative one. Gregory leans a little farther to the left than Garrett." He handed me a black crystal glass half full of wine.

"Julian, Genghis Khan leans farther left than Garrett. His politics would have been right at home in Dickens's London—workhouses and all that." I suddenly remembered who we were talking about. "I wonder if what happened to his wife is going to have an effect on the election."

"Only if he killed her. Of course that would be the only thing likely to make me vote for him."

"Katherine Garrett was a well-hated woman around here, wasn't she?"

"Possible suspects will have to take numbers to be considered for arrest," Julian agreed.

Carl poked his head through the doorway. "It's ready," he said with a smile of satisfied accomplishment. "Get it while it's hot. And don't forget to bring that wine."

Three hours, six Brandenburg Concerti and four glasses of Merlot later, I said good night and headed up the stairs to my apartment. Belatedly, I realized the light had gone out over my door.

The area at the top of the stairwell was so black that by the time I was halfway up the steps I couldn't tell if my eyes were open or shut. I had a moment of dizziness, and grabbed the banister with one hand until it passed, then continued up the stairs, one at a time.

My heart thumped as I thought I saw a shape in the corner by the door. I stopped on the stairs until I had convinced myself it was a trick of my light-deprived eyes, but now I was decidedly uneasy. I don't go around looking over my shoulder everywhere I go, but it's true there are people out there who will hurt you, and I'd never gotten around to those self-defense classes I was always promising myself.

There was my gun, of course, but if I reached into my bag and took it out, I was admitting I really thought there was somebody up there. On the other hand, why carry around a deadly piece of hardware if you're afraid to use it when you need it? I'd learned that lesson the hard way not long before.

Oh God, this was getting sillier and sillier. Shaking my head at my own foolishness, I took a deep breath and stepped onto the landing. A hand descended onto my shoulder.

# CHAPTER 7

· · · · · · · · · · · · · · · · · ·

BEFORE I COULD TAKE A BREATH TO SCREAM, A VOICE said, "Caley, it's me! It's Sam Holland!"

"Jesus, don't *ever* do that again!" I croaked, sagging against my door. Sam reached up above my head and screwed the light bulb back in. In its dim yellowish light I could see his face, more frightened than mine, with streaks of dried tears staining his cheeks.

I found my keys with shaking hands and tried to open the door to the one large room where I live. "What's wrong, Sam?" I asked. "Is it about your aunt Katherine? I read about it this morning. I'm very sorry."

His mouth quivered, and fresh tears started down the paths left by the last ones. "It's my mom," he sobbed. "They put her in jail!"

The lock turned, finally. My heart was still working overtime on the threat I'd imagined Sam to be, and it was another struggle to get the key back out of the lock. "Come inside," I told him, opening the door. "Tell me everything that happened."

Sam had dodged an officer from Child Protective Services by ducking out a back window of his house after the police had come and arrested Annie Holland for the murder

47

of her sister. He'd brought a few clothes with him, and he held them against his midsection as he paced from one piece of furniture to another while he talked.

"That detective showed up—the one who'd already talked to Mom this morning."

"Do you remember his name?"

Sam thought for a moment. "Farmer. Yeah. What an asshole."

I nodded sympathetically. I was no stranger to the less attractive aspects of Detective Farmer's personality.

"He'd talked to her once at Aunt Katherine's house in the morning," Sam said. "Then he had her go down to the police station and make a statement. He was already treating her like some kind of criminal. He came back in the afternoon and talked to her some more; then he came with some other cops to arrest her around dinner time, and this woman came with him—she was going to take me with her to some kind of . . . I don't know, a home or something."

I had put on some water for tea while Sam paced and talked. Now I took his bundle of clothes and set it on the end of the couch, then led him into the kitchen area and sat him down in one of the two chairs.

"The whole day has just been so fucked, you know?"

"Yeah," I replied, taking a pitcher of milk out of the refrigerator. "I think I do."

"I mean, first what happened to Aunt Katherine, then all that shit at the police station. I spent a lot of the day just trying to take care of Mom, you know, make her feel better. Sometimes she'd seem to be okay for a few minutes and then she'd look at me and start crying again. I felt like I was making her cry somehow, and I didn't know what I could do about it."

"It wasn't your fault. Your mom was lucky she had you there when she needed you. So what happened when Farmer came back to the house the last time?"

"He told her she was under arrest for suspicion of murder. He told her all about her rights and all that, but he seemed so goddamned happy about it. I wanted to break his fucking neck. Then they took her away, and this woman said she was taking me somewhere in her car."

He shivered despite the warmth of the air coming in through the open balcony doors. I walked over and closed them, then rummaged through the closet for a crocheted afghan my mother had sent me last Christmas. The poor kid had been through a lot the past couple of days and I wondered how he was holding up as well as he was. I handed him the afghan and he managed a smile of gratitude as he put it over his shoulders.

The teakettle screeched, and I turned off the burner under it. "So how did you get away from this woman from the juvenile authorities?" I asked him, pouring hot water over a tea bag and putting the mug down on the table in front of him. I sat down opposite him with my own cup.

"I told her I needed something out of my room, and I'd be right back. I grabbed some clothes and went out the window."

"You know, you're lucky they didn't have some uniforms stationed in the yard. They do that, sometimes."

"There was one, I think, but they were already taking Mom out the front door, and he was heading around the corner to the front of the house when I hit the ground. I took off before they could figure out I wasn't coming back out of my room."

With his change of clothing bundled under his arm, Sam had hidden out under a bridge in a nearby park until dark, then run to my front door. When he got no answer to his knock, he disabled the light over the door and waited for me.

"Mom couldn't have killed Aunt Katherine." Sam had repeated that same sentiment several times since I'd let him into my apartment. His hands shook too badly to hold the cup of tea I'd made him; the hot liquid slopped onto his hand and onto the table, but he didn't seem to notice.

I took the cup away from him and dried his hand with a paper towel. "Sam, I want you to tell me everything that happened Tuesday at your aunt Katherine's house. You went to her birthday party, right?"

"Yeah. I tried to talk Mom out of going, as usual, and she told me we had to go. Well, she didn't say I had to go, exactly, but Aunt Katherine had asked her to bring me. I knew what that meant. Once when I didn't go to one of Aunt Katherine's parties I found out later that she had a total fit about it—at Mom, of course. So I always went after that. Sometimes I didn't stay too long, but she couldn't say I didn't show up."

"And what happened when you got there?"

"The usual happy family bullshit at first. You know, the whole happy birthday routine."

"And then?"

Sam sighed deeply. "And then Aunt Katherine started in, the way she always does." He paused. "Did. Little digs about Mom, how she looked, her clothes, her hair. Hadn't she gained a little weight? Wasn't that the same dress she wore to the New Year's party? She'd be so much prettier if she'd wear some makeup. Shit like that."

"How did your mother react to that?"

"Same as always, pretty much. Mom always tries to see the best in people. She always tries to pretend what Aunt Katherine says isn't really insulting, and she smiles, but I know her, and I can see how hurt she is." He looked across the table at me, eyes blazing with anger. "I can't tell you how much it pisses me off to have her treat my mom that way."

"You don't have to tell me. I think I can guess." Sam's devotion to his mother had never been clearer to me than when I saw that look in his eyes.

"I used to tell Mom that if she didn't tell Aunt Katherine to fuck off, I would. Any time I said anything like that, she'd get all upset again. She'd beg me not to say anything to Aunt Katherine, just to let it pass. She said that was just her way, and she didn't mean anything by it. But she did. She *liked* doing it. I could tell. She was getting some kind of weird kick out of it." The dark eyes were less angry now, and more puzzled. "She wanted to make Mom feel bad—like small. Like she wasn't anything or anybody, you know?"

"Yeah," I said, sorry that honesty forced me to agree with him, "I know. There are a lot of people like that in the world, Sam, and you're going to run into a lot more of them in your life."

"Okay, I guess I can understand that, but her own sister? Why would anyone want her own sister to feel like that— and then be so goddamned happy about it?"

I didn't even attempt an answer to that one, but it didn't seem Sam was expecting one.

"So you got mad," I prompted him.

"Yeah. I told Aunt Katherine to stop talking that way to my mother, and I told Mom to stand up for once in her life and give Aunt Katherine what she deserved."

I flinched visibly. Someone had done just that only a few hours later.

Sam read my mind. "My mom didn't kill her, Ms. Burke."

"It's Caley, remember? And I'm not saying she did. But please understand, Sam—there has to be some evidence that points to her, and pretty strongly, or the police wouldn't have arrested her. They have to be very careful about who they charge with a crime."

"Then why did they arrest my mother?" Sam's voice broke completely, and he put his head down on the table and sobbed like a small child. I got up and found a box of tissues and brought it over to him. I'm never sure how to comfort people when they're deeply unhappy, or whether they want me to. I usually end up fluttering my hands around, afraid to touch someone who won't welcome it.

I put two tissues in Sam's hand and put my own hand over his. "It's going to be all right," I told him, and tried to sound like I meant it. In my personal experience, things frequently—though not always—work out for the best, but the way in which they work out isn't always the way we'd have planned it.

He looked up at me. "I told Mom I'd find someone who could help her. You can help, can't you?"

No need to mention I wasn't having much luck helping myself these days. "I'll try. What she really needs right now is an attorney. Does she have one that you know of?"

"No. I'm pretty sure she doesn't."

I thought of a more immediate problem. "Sam, is there anyone you can stay with until this gets straightened out?"

He looked at me through a haze of tears, then finally seemed to be processing the question. "Nowhere they won't find me," he said. "Can't I stay here with you?"

I opened my mouth to speak, uncertain of what was going to come out. Of course my automatic response should have been to say, "No, of course you can't stay here—you're a minor, and the police want you in a foster home for your own protection, and I don't want to be dragged into this whole mess and maybe arrested for hiding you."

That's not what I told him, though, because before I could say any of this I looked at the frightened boy sitting at my kitchen table, and I knew I couldn't turn him in or turn him away. "You can sleep on the couch," I said. "I've got an extra blanket and pillow in the closet. You should probably call the café and the vet hospital in the morning to let them know you won't be in for a few days."

"Will you be able to find out something that soon?"

"I don't know, Sam," I admitted. "I hope so, anyway. At the very least, by next week I should know if there's nothing more I can do. Maybe you can use the time to sort things out for yourself, and I'll try to do the worrying for both of us. Meanwhile, I'll go see your mother in the morning and let her know you're all right."

# CHAPTER 8

. . . . . . . . . . . . . . . . . . . .

THE CASCADE CITY JAIL IS NEWER THAN SOME, AND SMELLS
better than most, but hanging out there is way down on my
list of fun things to do around town. To get from the reception
desk to the visitors' center I had to subject myself to a certain
amount of minor indignity and the touch of claustrophobia
that I always get in a place where I know they can lock the
doors behind me. It may be experiences like this that keep
me such a law-abiding citizen—who knows?

I waited on one side of a reinforced double plate-glass
partition for Annie to be brought in. A few minutes later
she appeared in a doorway across the room, dressed in a
faded blue denim tunic and shapeless trousers to match.
She was accompanied by a poker-faced female officer with
grandmotherly white hair under a dark blue uniform cap.
Annie looked confused when she saw me. She had probably
been expecting someone else.

"First off, Sam's safe," I told her as soon as the officer
had retreated to her folding chair by the door and Annie had
picked up the telephone receiver on her side of the partition.
"That's all I want to say over this thing, but don't worry
about him another minute." Sam was still a bit dazed by
the events of the day before, but I'd left him in hopeful
spirits and instructed him not to answer the phone. My

answering machine would take care of my messages, and I really didn't want to advertise the fact that he was there.

Annie's face was puffy with crying, her eyes swollen. She seemed foggy and disoriented, the way I might be if someone had come into my house, handcuffed me, and brought me to this dismal place. "Caley? What are you doing here?"

"Did you hear what I just said?"

"Yes. Sam's okay. Thank you. But I still don't understand. . . ." She shook her head slowly.

"It's a little hard to explain. I'm going to talk to some people and see if I can find out anything. . . ." How to put this? I was going to see how hopeless her situation was? I was going to try and find out how much evidence they had against Annie for the murder of her sister? "I'm going to try and help you any way I can. Do you have a lawyer?"

She shook her head, eyes filling with tears. Right now she probably felt like she didn't have anyone at all. It was a feeling I'd had a time or two myself, and though I had never considered Annie a friend, it hurt me to think what she must be going through. She had probably spent the night in a tiny holding cell with no real cot, only a bench built into the wall, and a naked overhead light bulb that never went out.

The holding cell experience had a way of softening one up before interrogation, which was the whole purpose, but the police wouldn't interrogate Annie without an attorney present, and if she didn't get one herself they'd appoint a public defender to represent her. I found it a little surprising that Susan or Joey hadn't arranged something for her by now.

"Has anyone in your family offered to get you an attorney?"

She shook her head. "I haven't seen Joey yet," she said, "and Susan doesn't have any money. She's trying to hold on to her house after her divorce, and she's completely broke. She suggested I have the court appoint one."

I thought about this for all of two seconds before deciding I'd rather see her case handled by someone I trusted, and worry about the money later. "Do you know Mike Gold?" I asked.

Annie nodded. "He comes in the cafe most mornings."

Mike Gold practiced at Jake's old law firm, Saperstein, Kendall, and Moss. He and Jake had been friends for twenty years or more, and Baronian Investigations did a lot of case work for him. Most of all, he was a terrific human being. He didn't specialize in criminal work anymore, but I knew if I asked, he'd come and talk to Annie about taking the case.

"He's good. Would you like me to call him?"

"Would you?" Annie's voice cracked completely. "They said I needed an attorney, but I've never needed one before, and I wasn't sure who to call or how, or . . ."

"I'll take care of it. I don't want you to worry. Have they moved you to a regular cell yet?"

"Just a little while ago. Caley, it's so awful in here!" Annie looked around at the walls of the ugly green room like a trapped rabbit. "I'm so frightened. I don't know what to do. Somebody killed my sister and I'm just so afraid for myself, and I know that's wrong, but I can't help it!" Her shoulders shook with sobs. The officer at the door raised her head from her magazine and narrowed her eyes, but didn't get up.

"There'd be something wrong if you *weren't* afraid at a time like this," I assured her. "I'm going to do everything I can. I'll get Mike in here today to talk with you and explain what's going on. He'll talk to the police and get more information on your case than either you or I can drag out of them. If they find out I'm poking around in an active case, they'll make sure I don't get any cooperation they don't absolutely have to give me. Meanwhile, I'll see what I can find out on my own."

"You're . . . investigating for me?" Annie's eyes got wider, then filled up with tears. Her lip started to tremble. "I can't afford any of this."

"These things have a way of working themselves out," I assured her. Now it was time to get down to the hard stuff. "Annie, can you tell me what happened? At Katherine's? I know you and Sam went to her birthday party. Why don't you start there?"

"Katherine and I had an argument."

I sighed. This was not particularly good news. "An argument? A bad one? When did that happen?"

"Not at first. First, we were just all there . . ."

"Who all was there?"

"Katherine—" Her voice broke on her sister's name. She swallowed hard and went on. "Raymond. Susan and Joey. Raymond's business partner and his wife."

"Names?" I opened my portfolio and rummaged around in the pockets for one of my little spiral notebooks and a pencil.

"His partner's name is Chip DeLora. I think that's short for Charles. His wife's name is Liz. Lila was there, too—that's Katherine's housekeeper, Lila Jensen. She lives at the house. Sam was there for a while, but he got mad and left before dinner."

"He was mad at Katherine?"

"At Katherine, yes. And at me for not standing up to her. Katherine had a way of saying things that hurt. Mostly to me, I guess. Sam was always telling me to write her off. He's very protective of me, you know."

"I know."

"So when she started in sniping at me, Sam got mad and left the house."

"Then what happened?"

"After dinner Katherine and I got into an argument."

"Is that unusual?"

"I don't recall ever really arguing with her before—not like this. Arguing with Katherine has always been useless, anyway. We all just sort of got into the habit of giving her what she wanted and getting it over with. But I shouted at her. This time, I mean."

"Did anyone else hear the argument?"

"Chip and Liz had just left. I don't know where Lila was. Raymond was in his office down the hall. Joey and Susan were in the family room, so I don't think they heard everything, but they heard it when . . . they heard me. They came running in then. Katherine never raised her voice."

"But you did?"

Annie nodded. "I was so angry. I just lost control. I screamed."

"What did you say to her?"

"I said I'd kill her. Yes, I did say that. . . ." Her eyes wandered to the far wall. "Susan and Joey heard me say it. Oh, the looks on their faces. I don't think they'd ever heard me lose my temper before, not at Katherine. But I didn't mean I was going to . . . you know . . . hurt her or do anything to her. What I was saying was that before I'd let her—" She stopped suddenly and looked at me. "I didn't kill my sister—you've got to believe me, Caley!"

I decided to leave for now the issue of what the argument was about. Annie obviously wasn't willing to talk about it just yet, and we could always get back to it later when she was feeling stronger. "Why are the police so certain you killed her? They must have some kind of evidence, even if it's wrong. What happened after the argument?"

Annie stared up at the ceiling. "Joey and Susan came in from the family room, and they were looking at us, and I realized what I'd said. I knew I should apologize, but I couldn't. I knew I should explain why I said those things, but I couldn't say anything. I ran out of the house and got into my car. That's when I realized I'd left my purse with my keys in it on a chair in the living room. I couldn't go back in. There was a spare key in the ashtray, and I used that to start the car."

She went home, but the spare house key that was usually under the pot of geraniums wasn't there, and Sam wasn't home. She went to a coffee shop and sat for a while, but it was getting late and she had to be at work the next day. She went back by the house, but no key and no Sam. She hated the idea, but her only choice was to go back to Katherine's and get her purse.

"What time was it by then?"

"A little after midnight, I guess. I'm usually in bed right after ten, because I have to be at the coffee shop by six-thirty."

Annie had gone back to Katherine's and up to the front door. The house was dark, and she stood there for a few moments, afraid to knock for fear it would be Katherine who answered. On impulse, she tried the door; it was unlocked.

She went inside. She was afraid to turn on a light for fear of rousing someone, so she felt her way across the living room toward the dining room. She remembered having left her purse on a chair near the dining room doorway, and hoped Lila hadn't moved it when she cleaned up after the party.

There was some moonlight coming through the living room window, but the dense row of green plants on the windowsill cast a shadow over the floor and made it hard to see where she was stepping. She went slowly, feeling her way carefully.

"I was just about to the dining room doorway when the cat jumped out from behind a chair and scared me half to death."

"Katherine had a cat?" I couldn't keep the incredulity out of my voice. My recent crash course in Katherine Garrett, combined with the stories I'd heard while she was alive, had produced an image of a woman who would have no affection to spare for pets.

"She's Raymond's cat, actually. Peony. A Siamese. Katherine hates her. Hated her." Annie swallowed hard.

"Anyway, Peony's usually so calm, but she was acting like something had frightened her. She came leaping out from behind one of the chairs, and she was howling. It scared the heck out of me. I jumped back and bumped into something. I turned around, and it was Katherine's new vase—the one Raymond had bought for her birthday. I had bumped into the stand and it was about to tip over. It was some kind of special vase—the type of pottery and the designer—I can't remember what she said about it, but it cost hundreds of dollars and it was falling. All I could think of was what Katherine would say."

"Did it break?"

"I grabbed it." She clenched her hands reflexively at the memory. "It almost fell through my hands, but I held on and kept it from hitting the floor. Of course, once I had it in my hands, I could see how heavy it was—how thick. I think I could have thrown it against the wall and it would have bounced right off." She looked into her empty palms as though she could still see the vase resting there. "They told me someone killed Katherine with a heavy vase. Was it that one, do you think?"

"I don't know. What happened then?"

"I put the vase back, picked up my purse, and went out the same way I came in. When I got home Sam was there. He'd been called in to assist with an emergency surgery at the animal hospital. He's a part-time tech there, and someone always has to be on call after hours to assist if a vet gets called in. That night it was him. He'd put the key in his pocket when he came in from Katherine's, and he forgot to put it back where I could find it."

"Did you tell him about your fight with Katherine?"

She shook her head. "I was still too upset, too embarrassed. I knew he'd want to know I'd finally stood up to her, but I was too worried about the consequences. Katherine would make me pay in a thousand little ways for doing that. I decided I'd tell him in the morning, but then Susan called me while I was getting ready for work."

"Your other sister?"

"Yes. Raymond had called her right after he found the . . . after he found Katherine. She got there right after the police. She and Joey. That's my brother. Then they called me."

"Did you go to Katherine's house then?"

"I don't remember driving there. I just remember getting in my car. Then it seemed like I was just there, at the house. They wouldn't let me see Katherine before they took her away."

"Did the police talk to you there?"

"Yes, and then a few hours later they came to my house and talked to me again. Then they came back a third time and arrested me. That time they said I could have a lawyer before I said anything to them, but I couldn't think why I'd need one. I didn't kill Katherine. I could never have hurt my sister."

"I'm going to get Mike Gold in here to talk to you right away. Is there anything I can bring you? Anything you need?"

Annie named a few items the city didn't provide for prisoners, and I made a list. "I'll drop these off later for you," I told her. "Keep your head up. Sam believes in you."

Annie smiled for the first time since she'd come into the room. "He's like that," she said.

"Well, I think you've probably given him good reason to be."

The white-haired officer came over and stood behind Annie. "Time to go back, Holland," she said, not unkindly. "Your visitor can see you again tomorrow."

Annie gave me a little wave as she stepped through the doorway and was led down a brightly lit hallway. The door closed slowly behind her.

I let out a breath, conscious of how much effort I'd been putting into my show of optimism. When you've been arrested for murder, there isn't all that much to be optimistic about. I'd be glad to think I'd been able to make her feel a little more hopeful, but at the same time I also hoped I hadn't given her any false expectations.

# CHAPTER 9

A PHONE CALL LATER MIKE GOLD HAD PUT THE REST OF his morning on hold and was on his way to the jail. I was on my way to the Technical Services Department in the building next door to see Toby Takahashi, the evidence technician I had lunch with now and again.

I was never sure what shift Toby was working from week to week, and neither was she—evidence techs were the ugly stepchildren of the Cascade Police Department—overworked, underpaid, and largely without respect. The department had about half as many as they needed, and the ones they had were always getting switched from shift to shift and called in for extra shifts on little or no notice. Toby could be found here—or not—any hour of any day. That day, I got lucky.

"She's shut up in there developing crime scene pictures," one of the other techs informed me, pointing at the door to the cluttered room that served as a crime lab, locker room, and coffee break hangout. "Just knock."

"Whaddya want?" was the answer to my light tap on the door.

"Oh, I don't know—for you to break down and buy lunch for once?"

"Hey, Caley! Hang on. I'll be out of here in two shakes."

61

There was the sound of a slamming locker, and a young woman emerged, stripping off a pair of disposable surgical gloves.

Toby is two hairs over five feet tall, with a round face and black almond-shaped eyes between a small, straight nose and a shock of heavy black hair that today was pulled back from her face in a thick ponytail. "I shoulda been out of this dump hours ago, but we're still processing shit from the Garrett homicide. What a fucking mess. Marky, tell Ash I'm history. Tell her I've racked up some mondo overtime, too. Tell her Caley's taking me to the Grill for lunch."

I sighed. I usually picked up the check, but the cost of an occasional lunch at the Grill was more than worth Toby's company and the education I was slowly gaining about evidence.

"So were you the on-scene tech at the Garrett house yesterday?" Toby and I were sitting at a table in the River City Grill sharing a platter of batter-fried mushrooms and ranch dressing while we waited for the rest of our order. My appetite had picked up since I'd sidelined my forced vacation, and I was fighting for my share of the mushrooms. Toby probably weighs ninety pounds with her boots on, but she eats like a jungle predator.

"Yep, that was me," she confirmed around a mouthful of mushroom. "I'd worked my shift and the last half of Beverly's, 'cause she had to go home to take care of a sick kid. About six a.m. we get a call on the radio—a homicide, called in by the vic's husband. I'm making side bets with myself the husband did it, 'cause that's how this kind of thing usually turns out, but you never know until you see it, shoot it, bag it, and tag it, you know?"

"Not as well as you, but go on."

"Well, when I get there, Farmer John's already talking to the husband in the family room . . ."

"Johnny Farmer?" Of course, I knew that from talking to Sam, but the name never failed to make me cringe. Farmer and I went way back.

"Yeah, it was our very own Detective Sergeant John J. Farmer with his shiny shield, which is several degrees brighter than he is, by the way. So the body's in the dining room, and the patrol guys have set up a perimeter, and I go to work. Six rolls of thirty-six, and you wouldn't believe how many rooms there are in that place, and how much shit that woman had around the house to collect fingerprints."

Toby speared a mushroom and drowned it in dressing before popping it into her mouth. "We were there five and a half hours, or I was. Farmer John left after he talked to the vic's family for an hour and a half, and I got to spend the rest of the morning and a chunk of the afternoon doing the scene. Shit, I'm still doing it, but once Farmer heard some Q and A about this hairy argument between Katherine Garrett and her oldest sister, he knew right where he was going with this. He was pretty proud of himself when he made an arrest that afternoon, but I didn't see him developing the prints on the murder weapon."

"Wasn't that a little hasty? Why did it have to be yesterday?"

"Farmer John was hot to move on it, 'cause the last time he pussyfooted around with a homicide suspect who was expected to sit tight, the guy blew town and nobody's seen him since. You know how it is around a cop shop—nobody's ever let him forget it." She closed in on the last mushroom with a fork, and I decided it was the better part of valor to let her have it.

"So what makes everyone so certain her sister did the deed?"

Toby raised an eyebrow. "Are you doing something on this case?"

"Yes. Answer the question?"

Toby cocked her head and frowned at me for a few seconds. Finally, she shrugged. "Oh, why not? Fingerprints. A real nice set of them—left and right hands, fingers and palms—on a heavy pottery vase, just about where you'd have to grab it to bash someone's skull in. Farmer had comparison prints done on the whole family, since they could have touched anything, and it wasn't very likely any of them had a record. And whaddya know, the only set of prints on that vase were Annie Holland's."

"Not Katherine's? Or Raymond's? He bought it for her."

"Apparently the housekeeper had been in to clean up after the party, and something had been splashed on the vase. She wiped it down with a sponge and dried it with a towel. A perfect clean field for a careless perpetrator."

"So careless she didn't wipe off the prints?"

Toby dismissed this argument with a wave of her hand. "Happens every day. Most people aren't offed by strangers; they're killed by people they know—people they've really pissed off in a major way.

"Think about it for a minute. Someone gets you mad enough to kill them, and there's actually something on hand to do the job with. But after you do it, you're scared shitless. All you want to do is get the hell out of there—get as far away as you can. You don't stop and wipe down everything you might have touched."

"What if I told you I don't think she did it?"

"Tell it to Farmer and the D.A.'s office. They wouldn't have made an arrest if they didn't think they could take it to trial."

"What if I told you there's another explanation for how Annie got her prints on the vase?"

"I'd tell you I hope it's a good one. I just shoot the scene, find the prints, and bag the evidence. It's up to the detectives what they decide to make of it."

I thought over my options. They were narrow. "Can you get to Johnny Farmer for me? Can you ask him to take another look at the evidence?"

"You think Farmer would give the least bit of respect to any suggestion from a lowly evidence tech? As if."

I was in complete sympathy. He wasn't any more likely to give weight to pleas from a private investigator. Like a lot of police detectives, Farmer's regard for P.I.'s was only a little higher than his opinion of common household vermin, and his opinion of me was maybe just a little lower than that. The knowledge that I was poking around in this case wasn't likely to make him receptive to my arguments, either.

Our lunch arrived and Toby lit into hers like a starving woman. I watched her tackle a half-pound burger in fascination for a minute or so before I remembered my own sandwich. We ate our lunch, keeping to safe topics like the weather and Police Department gossip, but eventually I had no choice but to try again.

"I really need somebody in my corner on this, Toby. I think Annie Holland's innocent."

"Think? Or want to believe?"

I had no answer for that one.

Toby set down what was left of her burger. "There's one thing I can do for you, and if you ever tell anyone I did it, you're a dead woman."

I perked up immediately. "What? What can you do?"

"When we get back to the Evidence Department, just sort of neglect to take your purse. You can remember it in half an hour. And you couldn't calculate the size of the favor you're gonna owe me."

After retrieving my keys, I conveniently forgot my portfolio near the door to the Tech Services lab. I decided to use the half hour Toby had specified to go back to my place and check up on Sam. He'd been sleeping when I left the apartment that morning. Apparently it had taken him a while to get to sleep, which was understandable. I'd had my best sleep in weeks, which was kind of difficult to explain given my recent problems and all the restless soul-searching of the previous night, but I didn't want to question it too hard. I felt better than I had since I got back to town, and I was determined to enjoy it.

Sam was reading when I got back. He looked up anxiously from the sofa when I stepped inside. "Did you see Mom?"

"Yes, and she's fine. Well, as fine as you can be when you're where she is. She's got a lawyer, and I'm going to drop off some things she needs a little later today."

"Will she have to stay there? In jail?"

"They'll probably hold a hearing tomorrow or the next day to decide whether they've got enough evidence to hold her over for trial, but frankly, Sam, I don't think they'd have made the arrest if they didn't think they had enough evidence to go to trial with."

I caught sight of his face. "That doesn't mean she'll be convicted," I assured him quickly. "But it does mean she might have to stay in jail longer. They don't have to set bail right away." Or at all, I thought, but didn't pass that bit of information along to Sam. "We should know something by tomorrow, like exactly what the charges are."

The message light on the phone was blinking. "Caley, it's David. I called your office and Terrie said you were out of the office all week and I should try reaching you at home. So I'm trying, but no luck." He laughed softly, a sound that made my heart go funny. "I miss you. Call me when you get this. Bye."

I stood with my finger resting lightly on the play button. I sometimes replay David's messages, especially when I'm feeling down, but I wasn't going to do it in front of Sam. I also wasn't going to call him back from here. Sam and I would both be made uncomfortable by the fact that there was no place for him to go in a one-room apartment to get away from my private conversation. I figured I could always use a pay phone while I was out later. I let the tape rewind while I opened the pair of French doors that looked out onto my tiny balcony, and sat down in my one comfortable chair. A breeze came in, not particularly cool, but welcome. I knew I couldn't sit for long—something was waiting for me back at the Tech Services Department and I was dying to know what it was.

"So what do you think will happen?" Sam said. "When they charge her, I mean."

"The worst-case scenario is that they'll charge her with first-degree murder," I told him. "They know she had a terrible argument with Katherine, and that she had plenty of time between then and the time Katherine was actually killed to go away and contemplate it. Premeditation is the deciding factor."

"Is that what you think will happen?"

"Yeah, Sam, that's what I think. I wish I could say something different, but I think you'd want me to be honest."

Sam sighed deeply. "I keep hoping I'll wake up," he said. "Isn't there anything we can do to help her?"

I gave him a smile of encouragement. "We're doing it." I got up and walked into the corner of the apartment that serves as a kitchen. "Have you eaten yet?"

He shook his head. "I just didn't feel like it."

"Your mom would be righteously pissed if I let you starve to death." I opened the refrigerator and surveyed the contents with dismay. "On the other hand, she'd be even more upset if you perished from food poisoning. You like pizza? There are about three dozen pizza parlors in this town, and they all deliver."

"What I really need is my mail."

"Your mail?"

"I sent the money order to Sacramento two days ago by Express Mail. The lady on the phone said she'd express it back yesterday. Only I don't really feel like I can go anywhere right now—not with those people looking for me." He reached into his pocket and removed a brass key on a key ring. "Could you go by and check our mailbox? It's box forty-eight eleven in the downtown post office." His hands shook a little as he handed me the key.

"You've got a lot at stake in what's on that birth certificate, don't you?"

The dark eyes stared me down. "Do you know who your father is?"

"As nearly as anyone else, I guess."

He smiled at that. "Well, most people at least have someone to pin it on. I never had. It always made me feel like I should be looking at every guy my mom's age I saw on the street, you know?"

I nodded.

"Excuse me, sir," he said to an imaginary man. "Are you my father? No? How about *you,* then?" He turned to me. "Get it? No matter how much my mother took care of me, or loved me, or gave up things for me, and I know she gave up a lot . . . I still wanted to know who the other half of me was."

"Then I hope you find out today," I told him. I put the key in the pocket of my jeans, and took out some cash. "Call out for pizza while I'm gone. I'll be back with your mail in an hour or so, I hope."

"I have money in the bank," Sam said. "I don't want to sponge off you or anything."

"We'll settle up later," I assured him.

My portfolio was waiting on a desk just inside the front door of the evidence department, but Toby was out on a burglary scene. "I must have left this here after lunch," I said to the tech who was bent over a crime scene sketch at the next desk.

"Yeah, Toby said you'd be back for it when you figured out where you'd left it," the tech said, not looking up from her drawing. "Took you a while, huh?"

"I've never been bright," I admitted on my way out the door.

I put the bag on the passenger seat and resisted the urge to look inside until I was three blocks from the police department parking lot. Then I pulled over into an empty parking space and let the engine idle while I unzipped the bag.

Inside, along with a battered sketchpad, some pencils, a Tim Powers paperback, and a Walther PP .32 caliber semiautomatic pistol, was a manila envelope at least four inches thick. I peeked inside at a bundle of color photographs secured with heavy rubber bands. I wasn't sure I would welcome the sight of sudden death in living color, but I understood the reason—every detail counts.

The picture on top was of an expensive-looking ranch-style home in the pale light of early morning, but this was not about real estate; I'd seen prints like these before, sitting around the department with Toby and the rest of the evidence crew. These photographs were a chronicle of the Katherine Garrett homicide scene and the resulting medico-legal autopsy.

I couldn't take the pictures home and let Sam see them, and the Cascade Hotel Café was right out. I had to find some neutral ground to get a look at these. This was everything the police had on Annie Holland, and it was also all the evidence available to prove that someone else had killed Katherine Garrett. I put the envelope back in my bag, checked my mirrors, and pulled off in the direction of Riverview Park and my favorite picnic table by the water.

# CHAPTER 10

IT WAS SOMETHING LIKE WATCHING A MOVIE, FRAME BY frame. First the establishing shots: the exterior of the house from every possible angle—each exterior wall and corner depicted, each window and door examined for signs of forced entry. Any bare earth or soft ground observed for signs of shoe prints, with low angle light to pick out depressions that might be missed from directly overhead.

Next were photos of the yard, the rambling decks and red brick patios, the cement walk lined with neat green shrubs, the street outside. A shot of every car that was parked within a block of the house, followed by a close-up of its license plate. A formality? Katherine had been dead at least six hours when her body was discovered, and the chances that the perp's car would be parked outside were slim at best. But no, one of these people might have seen or heard something that could be material to the case. The crime-scene camera missed nothing, because any tiny detail could make or break a case.

As I turned over the prints, one after another, the park, the river, the midday summer heat faded from existence. I was there at the Garrett house, looking through the camera lens, waiting to see what Raymond Garrett had seen when he walked into his dining room that morning at six o'clock.

The camera moves inside the front door into the marble-floored entryway. Shots of the walls on either side of the wide hallway, lined with antique half-tables and mirrors, a cluster of Japanese wood-block prints, doubtlessly genuine, an ikebana arrangement in a blue and white porcelain vase next to the antique hall tree where a man's and a woman's raincoat hang side by side.

Into the family room—up to the high, vaulted ceilings with sunlight pouring through tall, narrow windows—down to the massive fieldstone fireplace. Once around the room to take in the expensive furniture, the Aubusson carpet laid over the polished oak floor, the niches set with more beautiful vases of all kinds. Nothing seems out of place; if I'd just thrown a birthday party, the place would have looked like a war zone, but then I don't have a live-in housekeeper.

A bright, modern kitchen is next, flawlessly appointed with every imaginable convenience and big, showy jars of multicolored pasta, beans, rice, and what-have-you. Knives are neatly arrayed in hardwood racks, and stainless steel pots with bright copper bottoms hang next to heavy cast-iron pans from ceiling hooks over an immense butcher-block table. Arrayed around the walls and under countertops are enough cupboards and cabinets to hold everything in my apartment twice over.

Next door to the kitchen is a small but attractive suite of rooms, modestly furnished and neatly made up. This must be where Lila Jensen lives.

Now the camera travels down the back hallway on the other side of the family room, toward the bedrooms. A wall of family photos. Close-ups of the photos: Annie, Susan, Joey, and Katherine as children, I assume. Forever young, forever trapped in gilded wooden frames, they look at one another and at me, never guessing this lies somewhere in their future.

The camera looks left, into a small bedroom—probably a guest room. Dark, rustic antiques are accented by white drapes and bedspread, white cotton rugs, a dozen little *white throw pillows. Painted wooden boxes are stacked on the dressers and chests. The bed has been slept in since it was made, but there's nothing out of the ordinary here—so far, I might be looking at a photo spread for a decorating magazine.*

*The next room is a library, looking even more untouched than the rest of the house. Leather furniture and duck prints are the motif here, with a porcelain retriever on the mantelpiece forever on point at a porcelain pheasant rising from porcelain grass. No signs of life, or even dust, as though the whole room had been wrapped in plastic until the photographer arrived. Light filters in through sheer white curtains—the heavy green drapes have been pulled back and tied to brass fixtures in the shape of quail.*

*There are a few other incidental rooms and a couple of bathrooms, all decorator-perfect, all with the feeling that no one has walked in since the decorator left. The camera records each one as carefully as though it were crowded with important evidence, because anything at this stage might be crucial.*

*Here is an office with a huge, leather-topped desk holding a computer, printer, telephone, external modem, and fax machine. Finally, some clutter! File folders scattered on a desk; crumpled papers that have missed the mahogany veneer wastebasket and hit the Oriental carpet. A few yellow pencils punctuate the dark expanse of desktop. There are no pictures in this room, no decorative objects of any kind. It is utterly devoid of character or personality.*

*The master bedroom shows indications of occupancy. The bedcovers on the king-size bed are rumpled on one side and pretty much untouched on the other. A pair of men's trousers and a shirt lie on an upholstered bench at the foot of the bed. There is a nightstand on each side of the bed, and in the next shots, the drawers have been opened to reveal their contents.*

*On the rumpled side, the drawer contains a paperback book by a popular author of glitzy fiction, some pens and*

*notepads, miscellaneous clutter, a money clip with a sheaf
of currency, and a silver pocket flask. On top of the nightstand is an amber pill bottle and a glass of water. A second
glass holds a small amount of golden liquid that might be
whiskey.*

*On the side of the bed that hasn't been slept in, we see
an expensive-looking fountain pen, some notepaper and
envelopes, several cosmetic items, and a worn book with
the word "Missal" engraved in gold on the cover.*

*The camera pulls back and pans to an immense
nineteenth-century wardrobe carved with scenes of men
and dogs and leaping stags. More shots detail the contents: men's suits and jackets, drawers of shirts, socks,
and underwear. No sign of women's clothing, but later
prints show a walk-in closet the size of a small bedroom, lined with cedar and custom-fitted with racks and
drawers and shelves crowded with clothes and shoes, all
Katherine's.*

*The end of the closet is taken up by a full-length, three-
way mirror of the sort that every impeccably turned-out
woman should probably own to assure herself not a hair
is out of place before she ventures out into the world.
The often accidental way I face the world can possibly
be blamed on the fact that I own no such aid to perfection.
Or maybe not.*

*The adjoining bathroom is covered in a few shots of
cream marble and deep red carpet and nothing at all out
of the ordinary. Pull back out to the hallway looking back
down toward the entry hall, and beyond, the doorway to
the formal living room.*

*The living room furniture looks freshly polished and
dusted in the morning light from the long picture window.
Tall plants, probably real, though it's hard to tell in a
photograph, fill the window. Upholstery in subdued tints
of blue and green sets off the dark fruitwood to perfection. A
shot of each wall and each corner establishes the relationship of each part of the whole. Close-up on the pearl-gray*

*carpet and follow it toward the doorway that leads to the dining room.*

*There's something on this side of the doorway . . . some dirt on the carpet? A closer shot. Dark brownish speckles, just a few tiny ones—then, as the camera moves closer to the dining room, the speckles give way to oblate drops on carpet, walls, and furniture.*

*The camera constructs the dining room as it has all the other rooms, covering all angles, all features, one by one. As it moves down and across the room, the brown spatters begin to intrude on the furniture, the drapes, the expensive accessories, becoming larger and more dense as the photos progress down the length of the room.*

*Here's a shot of the top of the dining room table with a bright reflection from a nearby window on its mirror-polished surface marred by what I can now recognize as dull, dried blood—not spatters or spots, but streaks and smears and splashes of blood.*

*Tilt down under the table: a pair of legs, feet in nylons, one high-heeled shoe nearby. Tilt further down: a woman's body lies crumpled. Blood is everywhere. Pan across to the head, crushed, broken; the face unrecognizably battered, a pool of dark blood beneath it on the pale carpet. Here and there on the carpet are smears that might be footprints, but no details are evident.*

*Katherine Garrett's arms are flung over her head, out-stretched, reaching. For what? From one angle, the arms, covered in blood, are all you can see sticking out from under the table. Close-ups of her hands show a diamond-studded wedding band on the left and an emerald and diamond cocktail ring on the right.*

*The next few shots detail a white ceramic vase smeared with blood and hair, found next to the body. The vase is photographed where it was found; then every inch of its surface is turned to the camera and photographed. The bottom is blackened with dried blood, and one side of the vase is completely covered in blood gone from red to deep iron-brown, with only traces of the white glaze showing through.*

I sat for a moment and listened to the persistent rushing sound of the river, staring at the face-down photographs and seeing Katherine Garrett's ruined face. It was going to get worse before it got better, I knew. When Toby was through photographing the crime scene and the body *in situ,* Katherine Garrett would have been transported to the county morgue, and the next series of photographs would detail her autopsy.

After a few moments, I returned to the photos with a sigh. When I was finished I went back through them one by one, taking notes as I went. I wanted to talk with Toby again, and have her explain some things to me. I had to find a phone and let Sam know I'd be late getting back with his mail.

# CHAPTER 11

"THE THING ABOUT BLOOD IS, IT CAN SPRAY IN ALL DI-rections from the point of impact." Toby Takahashi took a healthy bite of her steak sandwich—medium rare. I was toying with a small salad, the photos having murdered any appetite I might have had that soon after lunch.

She riffled through the stack of prints and pulled out the first photograph that showed any traces of blood on Katherine Garrett's pale gray carpet. "Like this. This is a fairly even pattern caused by a high-speed impact. You can see how small the droplets are. This," she said, pointing to a series of rust-red arcs on the wall, "is a severed artery. It's more like a fountain of blood with the pump running down as the victim bleeds out. Every one of those arcs is a heartbeat."

I nodded, glad I had decided against the tomato soup.

We were in a back booth in an off-ramp coffee shop in the little town south of Cascade where Toby lives. Toby was wearing her usual civilian uniform of black jeans and a T-shirt silk-screened with grinning skulls and the name of a heavy metal band. I felt positively overdressed in a cotton shirt with buttons, jeans, and a lightweight blazer.

Toby had gotten off duty at three and had not hesitated to accept my offer of more free food in exchange for her first-hand knowledge of crime scenes. First, though, I'd called Sam to let him know I'd be gone a while longer and I hadn't forgotten about checking his mail.

I'd filled Toby in on Annie's story about why she was in Katherine's house at that hour, and about her grabbing the vase to keep it from falling. Now we were going over some of the crime scene photos and Toby was filling me in, at my request, on the dynamics of flying blood.

"That shot's maybe six feet or less from where the blows were struck," Toby explained, pointing at a close-up of a small area of carpet with a few dozen visible brown speckles. "The smallest droplets fly that far in a sort of spray, like an aerosol. The bigger drops hit closer in."

"Like these?" I pointed to some elongated spatters on the upholstery of a side chair that was sitting against the wall a few feet from the table.

"Yeah, and you can see how their shape shows the impact. They flatten out like that when they hit something. Gravity pulls the drop downward." She uncovered another photo from the pile on the table between us and moved it closer for comparison. "These even bigger ones are from closer yet. The heavier drops fall closer to the source." The source being Katherine Garrett's head.

"So the bigger the splatters, the closer they are to the source of bleeding."

"That's how it works."

"That's what I thought. Now look at this." I went through the prints and pulled out the pictures of the white glazed pottery vase smeared with blackish-red. "The murder weapon, right?"

Toby nodded. "Without a doubt. It's got Katherine's hair and blood all over it. And Annie Holland's fingerprints, too, I'm sorry to add."

"Yeah, yeah, I know all that. But look at what else it's got." I pulled out the series of close-ups of the vase, taken after it had been removed from the spot where it was found, and photographed from all sides, and laid them out in front of her. On the side away from the part of the vase that had supposedly been used to bludgeon its owner to death, and clearly visible when you knew what you were looking for, were red-brown spots that could only be still more dried blood. "How far away would the point of impact need to be to produce spatters like these?"

Toby looked up from the picture. "Maybe five feet or so," she said, putting down her sandwich and picking up the photo. "So how did they get on there?"

I handed her another picture. This one showed the dining room from the doorway, and a tall Oriental-style wooden stand about the right size to hold an object like the white vase, standing near the doorway on the living room side. It was empty.

"What if the vase were on this stand? Would the spatter patterns fit then?"

She compared the pictures of the stand and the vase, laying a few more out on the table to establish distance and position. "It's not impossible. If we knew exactly where it was sitting and how it was turned, I could tell for sure. But I can tell you one thing right now—it couldn't have gotten those spatters on it while the perp was bashing in Katherine's head—it just doesn't work that way."

"So how *does* it work?"

Toby had another mouthful of steak sandwich by this time, so she settled for a shrug and shook her head as if to say she didn't have a clue.

"I'll tell you what my guess is," I told her. "I think whoever killed Katherine did the job with the white vase because they knew Annie had touched it. I think they may have hit her with something else first, enough times to render her unconscious and quiet by the time Annie got there, so she didn't know her sister was lying on the floor under the table only a few feet away when she picked up her purse and left.

"Now that I think about it, it's even possible that Katherine might even have been dead already when she was hit with the vase, and the perp went back and struck her with it a few times to establish it as a murder weapon. Is there any way to tell that?"

Toby nodded. "Blows only bruise if there's blood circulating. If you hit a dead person, the results look different. Of course, if you bludgeon somebody to death, then hit them a couple more times in the same place for good measure after they're dead, the results could be pretty confusing."

"But theoretically, you could tell the difference in an autopsy."

"Allow me to point out that they've already done an autopsy," Toby said. "The body's been released to the family already."

"Could the police get it back for further investigation?"

"Uh-huh. If they wanted to. But Farmer John's got his case all sewn up. He's got a suspect who threatened to kill the victim, then left her prints all over the murder weapon. If somebody else did use the vase on Katherine," Toby pointed out, "they didn't disturb Annie's prints or leave any of their own.

"Besides, the medical examiner said the skull fractures were compatible with an object the size and shape and weight of that vase, and there wasn't anything missing, or anything else in the house that could have been used to do the job. Trust me—we looked."

"Then explain those blood splatters that say it was sitting five or six feet away while Katherine was spraying blood all over her dining room."

"I can't. But *you* can't explain why there are nobody else's prints on the vase, and the vase has been elected the official murder weapon. You can't argue with the M.E." A frown creased Toby's forehead for a moment, then was gone.

"Okay, what are you thinking? Spill it."

"Just that Kagan, the regular medical examiner, didn't do the post on Katherine. He's been out of town on vacation. Just got back today."

"And?"

"His assistant picked up the job. Winette. He's . . . well, you didn't hear this from me, but he's not the most careful guy I ever worked with. They say he got through med school by the hairs on his ass, and he's been doing a little tap dance ever since. Now *him* you could argue with. The chances that Kagan would have missed something important are square between slim and none, but Lon Winette is a whole other story."

I pushed a piece of lettuce around my plate halfheartedly, and finally decided to spare its life. "Okay," I said, putting down my fork. "Tell me why Farmer moved so fast to get Annie behind bars. If she didn't run right away, what made him think she wasn't going to be around to be arrested later?"

"First, you've got to remember that everything Farmer John does is a reaction to something else. He's like one of those Superballs, always bouncing off something and going in the other direction, only unlike a Superball, you can always tell which way he's going to bounce. If he gets his fingers burned by being too cautious one day, he's going to jump the gun the next. If that backfires on him, he bounces right back to careful and calculating."

"The amazing bungee detective."

"You got it. And like I mentioned before, he'd just been burned by caution, and his manhood was wilting some on account of it. You have no idea the level cop-shop humor can sink to."

Toby was right. I didn't, and didn't want to, particularly. But there were a lot of things about the Garrett case I did want to know, and I was sitting across from the one person who could, and possibly would, tell me. "So can you fill me in on some minor details?" I asked.

Toby smirked. "Are you willing to owe me your firstborn?"

"I don't think there's going to be one. Settle for a few pints of A-Negative?"

"If they're accompanied by an equal number of steak dinners."

"You want lobster tails with those?"

"I wouldn't turn 'em down. What do you want to know?"

"How does a man not only not know his wife is being beaten to death a few rooms away, but doesn't even think it's strange when he wakes up in the morning and she's not there?"

"Well, according to Raymond Garrett you couldn't hear much from the master bedroom—that room and his private office are the two farthest away from the dining room. Besides that, he said he took something to help him sleep that night. He has a prescription—the bottle was by the bed, so that's probably the truth. There was a glass, too, with some liquor in the bottom yet. If he took the pills with alcohol, he was *really* out of it.

"I also heard him tell Farmer that it wasn't uncommon for Mrs. Garrett to sleep in a different room. So when he woke up and she wasn't there, he figured she was asleep somewhere else. Around six he got up and went into the front of the house, and the rest is history."

I wrote the gist of this down in a notebook. "Okay. Why would the front door be open that late at night? Annie didn't have a key to Katherine's house—she just tried the door and it was unlocked."

"Farmer John was pretty sure it was the maid, but he couldn't get her to cop to it. Look here." She went through the prints until she found the ones of Lila Jensen's rooms. "What's wrong with this picture?"

I looked at the pictures of the neat but unexciting rooms off the Garretts' kitchen. "I give up."

"No outside entrance. The only way for Lila to get outside was to go through the house to one of the outside doors."

"I get it. The only way for someone to get *in* to Lila's room was *also* through the house."

"Right. But she swears she locked it before she went to bed, and Katherine Garrett was already in bed."

"In one of the spare rooms," I guessed. "The one with the unmade bed."

"Yep. But Katherine got up for something. Maybe when she heard someone come in."

"Yeah, but who?"

"Well, I don't have to tell you the official version."

I sighed. "I guess not. And I don't have to tell you I'm proceeding on a different set of assumptions."

"Yeah, well, good luck. The D.A.'s going for murder one, you know."

"I figured as much. Is there any way you could show him these pictures and get Farmer to reopen the investigation?"

Toby let out a short laugh. "Let me tell you what happened the last time a tech tried to tell Farmer John about her interpretation of crime-scene evidence. First, he told her, 'You just shoot the fucking pictures, sweetie, and I'll handle the investigation.' No harm done there, except for being an asshole, but then he requests her personally on every investigation he's got on every day she's working, and treats her like shit the whole time she's working the scene.

"Ten days later, she's laid off. Laid off! We're at least two bodies short to get this job done every day anyway. They can't find a cause to fire her, so she's laid off! I don't personally think that was a coincidence. I think Farmer called in a favor and had her axed."

"Okay, I give up. I don't know where to go from here."

"Has Annie got a lawyer?"

"Yes. Mike Gold."

"Have him talk to Kagan about a new autopsy. But don't take all day about it—the body's been released to a funeral home, and they're planning to cremate her tomorrow morning."

She picked up a menu from the table. "You up for dessert?"

# CHAPTER 12

MIKE GOLD LOOKED HAPPY TO SEE ME, BUT THEN MIKE looks happy about nearly everything until you get him really pissed. He has a round, cheerful face with round, gold-rimmed glasses that make his big brown eyes even bigger. The sight of Mike Gold always makes me smile involuntarily no matter how awful I might be feeling, and I wasn't feeling all that hot just now. Tiresome lawyer jokes aside, Mike's a fine attorney and a fine human being. If Jews had saints, I'd nominate Mike for the position.

I'd no sooner arrived and exchanged my usual greetings with Lorna, Mike's assistant, than Mike spotted me through his office door and came out into the front office.

"Caley! Come in, sit down, have some coffee." Mike beckoned me into his private office.

"I guess we'll just have to exchange those brownie recipes and household hints another time, Lorna. Sorry."

"Damn." Lorna snapped her fingers in a pantomime of disappointment. "I was sure you were going to tell me a foolproof way to get puppy stains out of my white carpet."

Mike looked back and forth between Lorna and me. "Have you two been talking sex and politics again without me?"

Lorna smiled innocently, which is only a little easier for her than a cat with feathers in its mouth. "We're just a couple of poor, dumb womenfolk, boss."

"Yeah. I knew that." Mike gestured and I proceeded ahead of him into his office, a quiet and welcoming place of deep carpeting and huge leather armchairs taking up half the floor space. An oak desk occupied the other side of the room, with papers scattered here and there, and a computer monitor and keyboard dominating the top surface. Mike poured us coffee and opened a tin of Danish butter cookies.

I accepted a mug of coffee and a chair, sinking into the soft leather with an audible sigh. "No thanks on the cookies, but I'll gladly take a rain check."

"Hard day?" Mike asked as he sat down in the chair opposite me and helped himself to a fluted paper of little cookies.

"Hard week. How did your talk with Annie Holland go?"

"Well, she's a little shell-shocked by all this, which is easy enough to understand. She's adamant about being innocent."

"Do you believe her?"

Mike nodded thoughtfully as he nibbled on a cookie. "Yes, I do. You could say that's my job, but the reality is, not everyone you defend in a criminal action is going to be innocent. I've been fooled, but I can usually tell, one way or another."

"I usually think of it as my job not to believe anyone's innocent," I told him, "but I think she is, too. Of course I've been fooled, too, and of course I don't have any proof."

"Proof is the problem, all right," Mike agreed, "but we've got to try. I've talked to Farmer, and I know the physical evidence at the crime scene is pretty overwhelmingly against her. . . ."

"Maybe not all of it," I interrupted, opening my bag and pulling out Toby's extra set of crime scene prints, with the picture of the blood-spattered white vase on top of the stack. I handed the prints over to Mike.

"Where did you get these?" he asked, clearly amazed by my possession of them.

"If I tell you, my source will kill me." And probably eat me, I added to myself. "Let's just say someone did me a huge favor. Look at those top few pictures and tell me what you see."

Mike shuffled through the pictures of the vase, then set down his cookies and went through them again more slowly. "I guess I see the murder weapon. And a hell of a lot of blood."

"There's even more in the carpet, but right now it's the vase I'm concerned with. I'm not sure it's the murder weapon at all."

Mike raised his eyes from the pictures and looked at me over the rims of his glasses.

"If it is, I'm not sure it's the only one," I concluded.

Mike continued to stare. "You're going to clarify that statement, right?"

"Right."

I explained as best I could what the two different patterns of blood splatters meant according to the forensic wisdom of Toby Takahashi, who remained nameless for the purposes of the present discussion, and how it tied in with Annie's story of accidentally handling the vase. I told him about the autopsy that might prove to be less than thorough if the police could be convinced to reclaim Katherine Garrett's body before it was too late.

"If you can get to Gerry Kagan and tell him you don't trust Winette's opinion and you want him to take a look, you might be able to get a second autopsy, but whatever you do, you can't ever admit you've seen these."

Mike tossed down the prints and shook his head, smiling. "Annie told me you're helping her. It sounds like that was a slight understatement."

"I'm doing what I can."

His eyes sparkled with humor. "Does that include hiding a juvenile from Child Protective Services?"

I feigned shock. "Mr. Gold! Do I look like a criminal to you?"

He laughed quietly as he sipped his coffee. "You look like a good friend. If I'm ever in trouble, I hope I've got you and Jake on my side."

I winced. "Baronian Investigations isn't in on this one, Mike. I'm on my own. And you can't tell Jake I'm doing this."

Mike regarded me calmly over the rim of his coffee cup for several seconds. "Okay," he said finally. "If you say so. Why all the secrecy?"

"I'm on vacation."

He cocked his head and grinned. "I'll just sit here and wait for you to explain."

I did explain—everything I could think of that might make Mike understand what I was up against and why my involvement with Sam and Annie Holland had to be kept from Jake. This week, as far as Jake was concerned, I was supposed to be resting and healing. As far as Maggie Peck was concerned, I would be reviewing my life and deciding whether I had chosen a line of work incompatible with long life and day-to-day happiness, and if so, why.

As far as I was concerned, I had a job to do. Several jobs. Annie needed the things I'd promised to drop off at the jail, and Sam's post office box key was still in my pocket. I could imagine his emotional state as he waited for that piece of mail from the Department of Health.

That was where this had all started—where my life had taken a 90-degree turn back into what passed, for me, for normalcy. If Sam hadn't sought me out in the coffee shop Tuesday morning and involved me in his life, I would have read of Katherine Garrett's death and Annie's subsequent arrest and felt sad, perhaps, in a distant sort of way, but not necessarily involved. How much happens around us every day, I wondered, that tears other people's lives apart, and we're just not involved?

As soon as we had gone over Toby's prints and separated out the ones most important to Annie's defense, and as soon as Mike could send Lorna out to take a set of color copies from the photos for his personal use, I excused myself and hurried to the mall.

I'd promised to do some shopping for Annie, and I figured receiving a care package from the outside world would cheer her up a bit. I was hurrying toward the big super drugstore at one end of the mall, eyes on my shopping list, when I ran full-tilt into the other Michael in my life.

"Whoa, Ms. Burke!" he exclaimed, stepping back and steadying me against a fall. "I've got friends on the force, and I could get you cited for reckless walking."

"Hi, Michael," I said, forcing a smile. The one he gave me in return looked more genuine.

I'd been married to Michael Carlson once, what seemed like a million years ago, but was really only a little more than three. The marriage had lasted ten years encompassing two unsuccessful pregnancies, and hadn't been particularly healthy or beneficial to either of us. I'd retreated into depression and a heavy sleep habit; he'd followed his usual habit of turning his back on anything that made him think too hard, like me and my problems.

Eventually, I'd dissolved the marriage and started a new career. He'd continued moving up in his existing one as a writer for the *Cascade Beacon*. Once he and I had both been sure he was destined for bigger and better things, but somehow they never seemed to materialize.

"Got time for a cup of coffee?" he asked, indicating the nearby yogurt shop.

I hesitated, thinking about all the other things I still had to do today.

"I'm sorry we couldn't talk when you called the other day. You sounded so down. I'm glad I ran into you, or should I say I'm glad you ran into me?" He grinned, a smile full of the unself-conscious charm that had hooked me so hard so many years ago. "It's time I caught up with what's happening to you these days."

I started to say there was nothing in particular happening to me these days. I started to say I was just fine, thank you, and maybe I'd call up and chat some time soon. What I did say was, "I've been falling apart at the seams. Let's get some coffee and I'll tell you all about it."

By the time I divorced Michael, just before I went to work for Jake, we had long been out of the habit of talking about anything important. By that time, we usually each contrived to be out when the other was in, and kept our contact as brief and impersonal as possible. It took us more than a year of living in the same not very large town after our divorce to establish a different kind of relationship, one that allowed us to have an occasional lunch or dinner together and tell one another our problems.

Michael's problems usually involved women—the ones he dated got younger and dumber all the time—but since I'd been repulsed by the singles scene early in my new life, my problems seldom had anything to do with men. Following one disastrous relationship soon after our divorce, I'd kept myself too busy until very recently just figuring out how to get good at my new profession and be at home in my own skin. Now suddenly I had a whole new class of problems.

"So you're seeing a shrink now?" Michael asked with his usual tact after we'd been talking for a few minutes in a back booth at the Yogurt Palace.

"I think she might be able to help me get over the rough spots," I replied guardedly.

"Oh, hey, I didn't mean anything by it. And yeah, maybe it'll help you with the bad dreams and stuff. But honestly, Caley, it's that job of yours that's making you crazy. Shit, you have to shoot people sometimes!"

The diners in the next booth turned around and stared.

"That almost never happens," I told him, giving our neighbors a smile of reassurance. "You know how routine my job is most of the time."

"Well, it isn't most of the time that put those scars on your face, is it?"

My fingers went automatically to a small, fading scar on my right cheekbone. There was another one, only a little larger, almost hidden by my left eyebrow. They could hardly be called disfiguring, but I still wasn't used to them or to the memories they evoked, sometimes when I wasn't expecting it.

"No, I guess not. But sometimes if you want to make a difference, you have to take risks. Do you remember what I was like when I was so depressed?"

"Vividly. You slept fourteen hours a day and stared at the walls the rest of the time you weren't at work."

"I haven't had a day like that since I went to work for Jake." Or since the day I moved out of our house, which come to think of it was the same day, I thought, but I didn't see the need to say it. "This job has been good for me. Better than good. It's given me a whole new life."

Michael smiled. "I have to admit you're a different person than the woman I was married to. Sometimes I wonder what it would be like if we were married now. I think it would be a lot different."

"You're right," I agreed. "It would be totally different. Back then when you'd make me so angry I wanted to kill you, I'd turn my anger inward and get depressed. Nowadays I carry a gun."

He scored an invisible point for my side in the air between us. "Better just to be friends," he said. "You don't usually kill your friends, right?"

"Not usually," I said with a smile. "So I saw your story on the Katherine Garrett homicide. How did you get to be the guy on the scene?"

"Those friends on the force I was talking about. They're not all in the Traffic Division. Somebody called me and thought I might like to cover it for the *Beacon*. Boy, would I! I wrote another piece about Annie Holland's arrest, and I'll be following the trial, too. Not everyday we have such spectacular happenings in our little town."

"Thankfully. I know I could have done without this one."

Michael looked at me quizzically. "Did you know Katherine Garrett?"

"Only by reputation. But I know Annie Holland. In fact, I'm doing some investigation for her."

He frowned. "You said Jake wouldn't let you come back to work."

"Jake doesn't know I'm doing it."

"I see. So did you want to take advantage of our association to pump me for information?"

"Have you got any?"

He pulled himself up and looked important. "Well, I've seen the crime scene."

"So have I."

"You never!"

"You're right," I admitted with careful honesty. "I haven't, actually. So fill me in."

# CHAPTER 13

MICHAEL'S INFORMATION TOLD ME NOTHING NEW, BUT IT made him happy to share it with me, and I was still way ahead in the favor department. I made sure he kept his voice down while describing the bloody crime scene and Katherine's body, but the people in the next booth left anyway. Maybe they were just finished with their yogurt.

When he'd told me all he knew we made the usual well-meant promises to meet again soon under more pleasant circumstances—lunch, dinner, drinks—whatever. Sometimes it was months between meetings or even phone conversations, especially after he met some brand new brainless young woman who couldn't resist his million-dollar charm. I enjoyed Michael's company when I saw him, without missing him in the slightest when I didn't, and whatever else happened I'd always see him again when he broke up with his current bimbo and needed a friendly shoulder.

Nobody should get married at nineteen, when the strongest criteria most girls have for picking a mate seems to be sex appeal and a willingness to ask the big question. When I met Michael Carlson I had just moved out on my own, and was ready for something terrific to happen to me. Boy, did I have a lot to learn. Many things were going to happen, few of them terrific, and none of them, in hindsight, that I was in the least ready for.

My parents had done their two years in Cascade—the longest amount of time they could bear to stay in one place—and were itching to find greener pastures, somewhere in Arizona this time, though I've never associated Arizona with either pastures or the color green. Whatever it was they were after, it looked to be in Arizona, at least for a year or two.

I'd done my last year of high school in Cascade, gotten a job to postpone decisions about college, and when the urge to relocate hit Mom and Dad again I refused to move away. I'd spent my whole life moving away from one place, one school, one set of acquaintances—but seldom friends—to another, and I was sick of it. I rented my own, inexpensive apartment the day I waved goodbye to them heading south on I-5.

So there I was—young, independent, and poor—feeling only a little insecure and a whole lot grown-up at eighteen and a bit, with a full-time job at a bookstore, and a basement hole-in-the-wall I shared with half of Cascade's cockroach population. When a handsome young newspaper reporter started paying me outrageous amounts of attention, I was all prepared for a great romance.

In order to have that romance turn out anything like my fantasies, I had to reinvent Michael as "the man of my dreams." His self-centeredness I magically transformed into self-assurance, his thoughtlessness into high spirits. I believed him to be an unrecognized genius rather than a man who was always engineering his own failures. I resolutely refused to notice that he was loving only when it suited him, and that his trademark boyish charm was always reserved for the benefit of someone else.

When he asked me to marry him, I leaped at the chance to play the American dream fantasy out to its stunning conclusion, but ten years later I just felt stunned. It took me that long to admit how dreadfully unhappy I was, how dreadful each day of my life had become. The day I woke up was the day I walked.

For his part, Michael had also expected certain things of our marriage that he failed to receive. Like a lot of young women of my generation, too old to have feminists for mothers and caught in the middle of a struggle they didn't understand enough to believe in, I led the man of my life to expect he was getting exactly what he bargained for: a girl ready for molding into his perfect woman.

In fact, I was not at all responsive to Michael's attempts to re-create me, but instead of standing up for myself and becoming an adult, I chose to go along with his manipulation as much as possible on the outside, while stubbornly resisting it on the inside. This did not, as one might imagine, make for a healthy relationship.

Things only got worse when I got pregnant and couldn't deliver a living baby. By the time I'd done that twice, I was practically eager to withdraw into the gray existence of depression. Better that than to stand up and face my problems.

Four years of that, and Michael was ready to write me off, and who could blame him, really? He stopped coming home except to change dirty laundry for clean and make obligatory husband noises. In a total of ten and a half years we went from disaster to debacle to divorce without ever seeming to have the power to reverse our course. It was less like an event in which we participated than a tragic movie we were forced to watch.

It would all be terribly sad to contemplate if it weren't for the fact that the day I divorced Michael was the day I took my life in my own hands and started facing life as an adult. It was also the day I met Jake Baronian. A good day all around, I'd have to say.

Now I found myself back at the drugstore, and not bumping into anyone this time. I fished in my pocket for my list. It felt good to think I could bring a little comfort into Annie's life with a few dollars' worth of minor conveniences. It would feel even better to bring her good news about the rest of her life. Well, one task at a time.

When I'd filled Annie's list and added a few extra items I thought she might enjoy, I dropped the package off at the jail along with what I hoped was an encouraging note saying I'd be by in the morning to see her again.

I used a nearby phone booth to call Annie's sister Susan Brock and their brother Joey, using a list of telephone numbers and addresses Annie had provided that morning. They had apparently been the only ones to overhear the argument between Katherine and Annie, or at least the loudest parts of it, and I was curious about their reaction to it, and to Annie's arrest.

Susan Brock, personnel director at a local chemical products company, was not at her office. I reached her at home, and she seemed pleasant enough, agreeing to see me tomorrow any time after noon. She would be taking the day off to attend Katherine's cremation in the morning, and would be home in the afternoon.

Joey wasn't at work either. He supervised the sales department for a company that manufactured heavy farm equipment in the industrial section of town west of the freeway. The woman who answered his phone said he'd been at home since last week on a leave of absence. She didn't tell me his wife had just left and taken the kids, but that's what had happened to Joey the week before, according to Annie. She felt terribly sorry for him; Joey had never been very good at taking care of himself. He wasn't at home when I called there, but I left a message on the answering machine saying I needed to talk to him about Annie's case.

I called Raymond Garrett, too, while I was wasting quarters. At his office a young woman fielded my call and informed me that he was not expected in the rest of the week, as there'd been a death in the family. I feigned polite surprise and said I'd call back at a better time. I dialed his home number, hoping to make contact anyhow. No one answered, so I left a message on his machine explaining the urgency of my need to talk with him, and leaving *my* home number. Tag. You're it.

Too late to take the message back, it occurred to me that it might have been more interesting to drop in unannounced. Toby was right—most of these cases turned out to be husbands killing their wives and hanging it on a mysterious intruder. Even if that weren't the case here, Raymond Garrett might be more likely to reveal his true feelings toward his late wife if he didn't have time to rehearse for my questions.

I love hindsight—it's so brilliantly obvious.

The fact that I was holding a phone receiver in my hand reminded me that I owed David an answer to his message. I toyed with the idea of calling later, but after staring at the receiver until it squawked angrily at me, I dialed his number and the digits for my phone card. I hadn't even realized I was hoping for a safe encounter with his answering machine until I heard him answer the phone.

"Hello." My heart did its usual thing at the sound of his voice.

"Hi. It's Caley."

"It's good to hear your voice," David said. "I've been sort of expecting you to call."

"Well, I meant to, but life sort of happened while I was making other plans. I'm sorry."

"Don't be. It's not like we have a schedule to keep or anything. I just wanted to talk to you. . . ."

"And it was my turn to call, and I totally spaced it. I'm sorry. Again." I slumped against the back of the booth. I hated thinking I was so thoughtless. My recent problems were one thing, but David Hayden was more important than all of it, and I didn't want him to think otherwise for even a second.

"Terrie said you wouldn't be back at work until Monday. Are you okay?"

I felt the full impact of the pattern of dishonesty I'd established with David. If I'd clued him in to my emotional state from the beginning instead of trying to pretend everything was just peachy in my life, I'd have the perfect opportunity now to take advantage of the emotional support he could offer. "It's relative," I said with a sigh. "I'm not sick or anything, but I'm taking the week off."

The tone of David's voice changed, grew serious. "Caley, is something wrong? Would you like me to drive up there? Or maybe you'd rather come down here. We could spend a few days together."

That sounded like the best idea I'd heard in years. "I wish we could, but I'm on a case."

"How can you be on a case while you're taking the week off?"

"Well, let's say I'm not supposed to be on a case, but I am. I know that doesn't seem to make any sense, but it does. Really."

"And you don't want to tell me about it, do you?" There was no mistaking the hurt in his voice.

"I do. I just can't do it right now." Silence. "I've been having some problems." There. I'd finally said it, though I'd certainly left out the details.

"What kind of problems, and how can I help?"

"You can help by letting me talk about it, but I can't do that now. I'm in a phone booth on a public street and I'm about to burst into tears, and I really hate doing that in front of people."

"When will you be home? I'll call you. We can talk all day, if you need to."

"I can't talk at home, either. I've got someone staying there."

"Not some irresistibly sexy man, I hope."

"He will be some day, but right now he's a frightened kid who needs a friend. Please understand, David, I'm working this out—these problems I've been having—and this case has been really therapeutic."

"I don't think I know enough to understand. Is it all right if I just accept, for now?"

That was when I realized how much I loved him. I stood there for a moment and let it hit me, but I didn't say the words. I'd save that for later. "That would be terrific," was what I did say. "I'll call you again in a few days."

"You'd better. I'll just wait here by the phone, if that's okay."

"No. Go paint something."

"Tony says hi." Tony Garza was David's grandfather and an old friend of mine.

"Hi, Tony. Bye, David. I'll call you."

My next stop was the downtown post office. Annie and Sam's box was stuffed with mail, not having been emptied for the last few days. It was mostly junk, I noted as I shuffled through it on my way out of the post office; mail-order catalogs and sweepstakes come-ons and once-in-a-lifetime offers, much like the vast majority of my own mail. So it wasn't just *me* who was responsible for the wholesale death of forests. That was a relief.

I dug through a dozen useless items before I saw it. There, between a phone bill and a sale leaflet from a chain supermarket, was an official-looking envelope from the California Department of Health in Sacramento. It made me nervous just looking at it, and I had nothing at stake here, really. I clutched the stack of letters to my chest and walked through the big glass doors, leaving the artificial coolness of the building behind in a gust of late-afternoon heat.

As I stepped outside onto the wide stone steps of the Cascade Post Office, I noticed an ugly blue sedan in need of a paint job which was pulled up in the No Parking zone, efficiently obstructing both curbside postal boxes. A man in brown slacks, cheap oxfords, and a tan double-knit sport coat leaned against the front fender like a fashion model for the polyester industry. He wore a smile of smarmy self-satisfaction, and didn't seem even slightly worried about copping an illegal parking ticket.

# CHAPTER 14

I LET OUT AN INVOLUNTARY SIGH. DETECTIVE SERGEANT Johnny Farmer didn't even have a place on my list of people I like to run into, and this meeting smacked of a certain amount of deliberation on his part. I gave him a nod and a smile that I hoped looked more sincere than it felt and walked past him. I heard his footsteps behind me as I reached the curb beside my car, and caught a whiff of his repulsive cologne.

"Been a long time, Burke," a sarcastic voice said as I reached for the door handle.

This time I suppressed the sigh. "We don't exactly travel in the same circles, Johnny."

"We have been today, though."

I let go the door handle and turned to face him. The smile was gone, replaced by something resembling annoyance. "This is the first time I've seen *you*," I told him.

"Maybe I'm a better detective than you are," he remarked, and the self-satisfied smile was back.

"Or maybe you're just shiftier."

The smile faded again. I wondered how many times I could just turn it off and on like a light switch. The plain truth was Johnny Farmer just didn't like me much, and I returned the feeling twofold.

I know most of the detectives on the Cascade force, and my relations with them are largely amiable. It's been a long time since I've fooled myself about the level of intelligence necessary to achieve the rank of Detective, but nonetheless many *are* intelligent, and a few are genuine good guys despite being in a profession known to sour the milk of human kindness. Many are committed to wading into the fight between good and evil for the sake of people they'll never meet, because it's the job. It's what they do. Johnny Farmer had never struck me as one of these.

"What do you want, Johnny? I've got places to go."

"What are you doing fucking around in the Garrett homicide?"

"What makes you think I am?" I put as much innocence as I could muster into this one.

"I have my ways," he said, settling back and getting comfortable again. Now he was leaning against *my* car, and I felt more than a little crowded. He examined his fingernails with a sort of forced casualness, a gesture he probably saw on TV once. "When you visit someone in jail, it's a matter of public record. I just looked on the sign-in sheet."

"Okay, I visited a friend in jail. Did that become illegal while I wasn't paying attention?" I tried a jocular tone, but it wasn't working. I knew that Farmer knew how much he irritated me, and the fact that I couldn't put a congenial face on it irritated me even more.

"You also spent some time at the Tech Services office this morning. I hope you weren't trying to get information on an active homicide investigation. I think you know about how well that would go over with the Department. And then there's Takahashi's job to consider."

Gosh, that sounded a lot like a threat. I decided to take it seriously. I didn't want to get Toby in trouble with Farmer, especially considering his track record with evidence techs. I quickly stifled my first impulse, which was to suggest some anatomically difficult sexual activity or other, and forced myself to take a different tack.

I had to make this convincing. I did my best to look busted, hanging my head slightly and manufacturing an expression of disgusted disappointment. "Okay, I'm on the case. And yes, I tried to get something out of Toby, and she told me to go to hell. She said it wasn't worth getting fired over." I didn't experience the least spasm of guilt for my lie, but I did feel more than a glimmer of satisfaction when he seemed to go for it.

"That was smart." Farmer nodded his satisfaction with Toby's apparent level of intelligence. "Now *I'm* telling you the same thing."

I glared at him.

He glared back. "You're a duly licensed investigator with the State of California. I know, 'cause I checked you out the first time I ran into you."

"Get to the point, Farmer; this may come as a surprise, but you're not telling me anything I don't already know."

"The point is, my authority doesn't include telling you what cases to take or how to investigate them as long as you don't step over the line. But I can tell you this—" He punctuated the rest of his speech with a forefinger pointed too close for good manners to the center of my chest. "Stay the fuck out of my way on this, or I'll make getting police cooperation in this town seem like taking a walk in hell."

I turned away, opened my passenger side door as casually as possible and deposited Sam and Annie's mail facedown on the seat. "Thanks for the advice, Johnny," I said, walking around to the street side of the car and opening the driver's door. "I'll be a good girl, and I'll stay out of your way if that's possible. But I won't stop trying to keep Annie Holland from being indicted for murder."

Farmer followed me and leaned against the fender on that side. "That's your job," he acknowledged, but before I could mistake this remark for a sign of professional courtesy, he added, "You get to take the family's money and make believe you're actually doing something for them.

But nothing you do is going to keep Annie Holland from doing hard time for caving in her sister's skull. And that's if she's lucky."

"Are you tired, Johnny?" I asked him as I sat down and inserted the key in the starter.

"Not especially."

"Then stand the hell *up*," I said, and gunned the motor to life.

Farmer moved away from the car. "Just don't forget what I told you," he said, and did the thing with the finger again.

"I never forget good advice," I assured him as I checked my side mirror. He was still standing in the street as I pulled away and drove down the side street toward my apartment. This time I remembered to drive very slowly and carefully, seeing as how Johnny had pulled out behind me and was looking less than happy in my rearview mirror. When I turned onto my street he kept going straight.

My first encounter with Johnny Farmer had gotten our relationship, if you could call it that, off to the worst possible start. A couple of years back I'd been following a guy suspected of embezzling from a local corporation. His bosses wanted the matter handled without police intervention and had hired Jake, who'd passed some of the legwork along to me. The Cascade police, meanwhile, were on his tail for what he was *doing* with the stolen money, namely buying large quantities of illegal drugs with the intention of turning a neat profit on the resale.

I was pretty inexperienced in those days, and I didn't have a clue that anybody but me was following this clown. Farmer didn't know who I was, either, so one night as I was closing in on my target and about seventy thousand dollars of our client's money, I ended up getting arrested right along with him and his dealer. That's how I found out what the inside of a holding cell is like.

Fortunately, I didn't have long to make a study of it. Jake and Mike Gold had me out of there in two hours flat, and the next time I saw Johnny Farmer was at my arraignment the next morning, when he had to tell the judge that the charges had been dropped. He wasn't a bit happy about it, and his mood, where I was concerned, hadn't improved materially since then.

Since Johnny was only one sour grape in the whole bunch, I hadn't let his attitude get me down until now. We saw one another around town, but that had been about the extent of it. His beat was homicide and robbery these days, and the cases I handled didn't tend to put me afoul of him. Now it seemed likely that our paths would cross again before this case was resolved, and I couldn't say I was looking forward to it with any degree of enthusiasm.

A digital sign on top of a bank building reminded me of the day, date, and temperature in Fahrenheit and Celsius. I decided I liked the Celsius figure better—it was only two digits. Summers in Cascade usually include at least two weeks of blistering heat in the middle of ten weeks of simmering misery.

A few seconds later I uttered an expletive still considered unladylike in some circles. "It's Thursday!" I added to that. "I've got class tonight, and I don't even know if Robby knows what's happened to Annie! What's *wrong* with me?" I chewed myself out some more as I scanned the vicinity for a pay phone. I'd been driving past the mall again, and was almost on top of it, so I turned in and found a parking spot. This was not a call I wanted to make in front of Sam.

As it turned out, Robby already knew.

"Don't feel bad, Caley," Robby tried to reassure me. "You couldn't have gotten the news to me any quicker than the dean's wife. She must have been watching the jail with binoculars."

"Well, I'm still sorry. If you had to hear it, it should have been from a friend. And as if that weren't bad enough, I don't see any way I can make it to class tonight."

"Hot date?"

"Unexpected house guest. So, have you given any thought to visiting Annie?"

"I'd like to. I know she needs all the friends she can get right now, but it's been seventeen years since Annie thought of me as a friend, or since I gave her any reason to. I don't think I'd be welcome." His voice held a terrible melancholy I was helpless to comfort.

"I understand," I told him. "She's doing okay, but you can imagine what a shock all this is to her."

"Yeah. I can. Keep me posted on how she's doing, will you?"

"I'd be glad to. And I hope I'll be back in class on Tuesday, but at this point I can't be sure."

"Oh, don't worry about it," he said. "I probably won't flunk you."

Sam was sitting on the edge of one of my two kitchen chairs. He looked up when I walked in, and I could see how hard the wait had been on him.

"Sorry it took me so long to get back, but things kept coming up. We're making important progress on your mom's case."

"What kind of progress?"

"I think we might be able to get a second autopsy."

"What will that prove?"

"It might lend some weight to the idea that someone else actually killed your aunt Katherine."

"I *know* somebody else did." He put down the book he'd been reading and began pacing again, arms folded and head slightly lowered.

"Well, the police don't know it yet, but they might start to get a glimmer if the medical examiner takes another look at the body. There has to be someone else. I really believe that. Someone who wanted your aunt Katherine dead and didn't mind if your mother took the fall."

"I don't know who'd want Mom to go down for it, but there must be a hundred people who wanted to kill Aunt

Katherine at one time or another. There were a few times I wanted to, myself." He sat down again on the edge of the chair, hands clenched into fists between his knees.

"Yeah, I guess I can understand that," I said. I sincerely hoped he *hadn't* killed her, since he was a client, since he was hiding from the juvenile authorities in my apartment, and since I'd grown to like him. "Well, I've got your letter here," I said, proffering the stack of mail with the fateful envelope on top. "You want to open it?"

Sam took the mail, but handed the envelope back to me. "Could *you*? I mean would you *please* open it and tell me what it says?" He got up from the chair and walked across the kitchen area—all of four steps—with his arms crossed in front of his chest as though to ward off a blow to the midsection. "It's driving me totally apeshit. I want to know and I don't want to know."

"It's not too late to tear it up," I said.

"No. I want to know. I need to. Open it. I mean, please."

I wedged a finger under one corner of the flap and ripped open the top of the envelope. Inside was a form with words filling in blanks from top to bottom: name, place of birth, day, date, time.

I skipped to the blank marked "Father's Name." The name printed there was certainly not one that had come up in any of my previous discussions on the subject. I had to think for a moment to put a face to the name—Paul Allen Gregory. Paul Gregory. The guy on the news.

I was so surprised I almost didn't see what was printed in the blank marked "Mother's Name."

The name in that blank was Katherine Holland.

# CHAPTER 15

. . . . . . . . . . . . . . . . . . .

MY HEART STOPPED UTTERLY, THEN THUMPED INTO ACTION again, painfully. Katherine Holland, later to become Katherine Garrett. Not Annie Holland, whom everyone in town believed had borne Sam out of wedlock and kept his father's identity secret, but her younger sister who had presumably gone out of town to help Annie in her time of need.

But it was Katherine who had needed someone, and Annie who had answered the call. And it was Annie who had raised Katherine's son as her own for the past sixteen years.

"Sit down," I told Sam.

He sat.

"This is more than you bargained for," I said. "You'd better prepare yourself for a shock."

"I've been doing that for two days. If I'm not ready now, I never will be." His young face showed a lot of personal courage, but, underneath that, he was scared to death.

I turned the piece of paper over in my hands. "You want me to read it to you?" I hoped he didn't, even as I offered.

"No, I guess I ought to read it myself. I guess you'd

better just give it to me." He held out a hand that shook just a little.

I handed it over and watched his face as he read the information printed so dispassionately on the form. His face seemed to crumple as he took in the words and realized their meaning. He read it again from the top, but the meaning hadn't changed.

I spoke into the silence that seemed unbearably loud in the little room. "Sam, I'm sorry. I had no idea when I said you ought to send for this . . ."

"Jesus!" he exclaimed softly. He let his arms fall to his lap; the birth certificate fluttered to the floor. "Now I know why my mom didn't want me to see this. She didn't *ever* want me to know this."

"She wanted to protect you, Sam. I hope you understand that."

"And that's why she had to put up with Aunt Katherine. All those years she just took whatever Aunt Katherine dished out, and I couldn't figure out why. All those years Aunt Katherine was really my mother. They never wanted me to know. Neither one of them wanted me to know."

"Would you rather have known the truth?"

"I don't know." He pushed at the birth certificate with the toe of one shoe. His eyes were full of hurt and confusion, and his voice was full of unshed tears. "I guess I don't know much, do I? I don't even know who this Paul Gregory guy is."

"He works for a local television station. He's a newscaster. You may have seen him on the evening news." I remembered what Julian had told me Tuesday night. "He's running for Congress against your uncle Raymond. That's about all I know."

Sam just nodded, still dazed.

I pulled up the other chair and sat down opposite him. "You're going to need some time to think about this. Would you like me to go away and leave you alone? I could go out for a while."

He put out a hand as if to stop me physically from leaving. "No. Not right now, anyway. God, I need to talk to my mom. I mean . . ."

"She's still your mother, Sam—the only mother you've ever had. It takes a lot more than giving birth to make someone a mother."

He nodded. "I know. I know. This is just all such shit." Tears welled up in his eyes and he blinked them away. "My mother's dead—my real mother, I mean, and I never loved her. I never even *liked* her." He took a deep, ragged breath and scrubbed tears away with the back of one hand. "My mom's in jail and everyone thinks she killed her sister. My father's some guy on television, and I've never met him."

He sighed deeply, then leaned over and picked up the paper. "I wanted to know. I wasn't going to be happy until I knew, but I never thought it'd be something like this. I didn't want to know *this*."

It was past one before either of us got to sleep, if you could call it that. Every time a car went by on the street outside I'd wake to a feeling of helplessness, and I'd hear Sam tossing on the couch and wonder if his life could ever get back on track after this. Nothing like this had ever happened to me, and I didn't know how to make it right for him.

It was a long goddamned night, and there wasn't a chance I was going to be at my best tomorrow; I don't do lack of sleep at all well. When the alarm started to chirp at seven, I slapped it off and buried it under my mattress. Things only got worse when Mike Gold called at eight-thirty. From a position facedown on my pillow I put out my left hand blindly, caught the phone on the first ring, and muttered something unintelligible into the mouthpiece.

"I've got bad news and bad news," Mike began. What a way to start the day.

"Okay," I said, turning onto my back and wedging the phone between my head and the extra pillow without allowing my eyes to open. "Give me the bad news first."

"Annie had her arraignment this morning, with Judge Anderson. The charge is murder one."

I sighed. "That's bad, but not any worse than we expected."

"The judge refused to set bail."

"That's bad."

"I asked for a separate bail hearing, but he wouldn't give me a court date until the middle of next month. It looks like Annie's going to have to stay in jail for a few weeks."

I shook my head. "Okay. Give me the *bad* news."

"Kagan isn't going to give us a second autopsy."

That opened my eyes. "Oh, shit." I said it quietly, since it looked as though Sam was finally getting some sleep.

"You echo my own sentiments, Ms. Burke," said Mike. "This is what we call, in legal terms, being fucked. At five minutes after ten o'clock, Katherine Garrett will be a small container of ashes."

"You couldn't move Kagan on the autopsy thing at all?"

"Not an inch. I caught him at his office and talked to him for half an hour yesterday after you left, but he's standing behind Lon Winette."

"*Why,* for God's sake?" I asked in a whisper. "My connection in the department says the guy's a medical disaster!"

"I don't think Kagan would disagree with you, necessarily, but he's got his own reasons for sticking by his homeboy—he recommended Winette for the job."

"I'd love to hear the story behind that. I guess our luck can only improve from this point, huh?"

"That seems logical," Mike admitted. "Nowhere to go from the basement but up, they say."

"Unless you happen to believe in hell," I pointed out, just to cheer things up a bit.

"Well, I don't."

"Me neither. So it's going to get better, right?"

"Right. What's on your agenda today?"

I sat up and squinted at the light coming in around the

edges of the window shades. "I'm going by to see Annie again, and I've got an appointment to talk with Susan Brock."

"That's the surviving sister, right?"

"Yeah. She heard the argument between Annie and Katherine. I want to get her take on it, and on the relationship between them, and on who the hell else might have done it. I want to get a look at Raymond Garrett, too, but I haven't been able to reach him yet."

"How about the brother, Joey Holland? Doesn't he live in town, too?"

"Yeah. I couldn't reach him, either. I left a message. I've left a trail of recorded messages about a block long. Someone's got to answer one sooner or later."

"I hope so. Sam okay?"

I looked over at Sam, who was curled up in a tight ball on the couch. "Not really."

"Hey, I'm really sorry I had to spoil your morning, Caley."

"That's okay, Mike. Next time it'll be *good* news."

"From your mouth to God's ear. Or at least Judge Anderson's."


I slipped out of bed and grabbed some clothes to put on in the bathroom. Having someone else in the apartment was a little awkward, but I was willing to put up with that for a while if it helped Sam and Annie. I'd had very little else *but* privacy since my divorce more than three years earlier, and it probably wasn't going to kill me outright to give a little of it up.

I took a quick shower, ran my fingers through my hair, considered makeup, decided against it, threw on some presentable clothes, checked the results, shrugged, and was out the door in less than fifteen minutes total, after leaving a note for Sam saying I'd check back with him later and bring home some real food. I might not be ready for this day, but I could fake it.

I rolled down the window of my car after pulling away from the curb. The last of the morning's cool air blew in, and I smiled in spite of myself at the sensation of it against my face and my hair. One of the many things that sometimes amaze me is how small joys can intrude on the lousiest days.

After finding a parking place, checking my things-to-do list, and waiting for Mickey to raise his little three-fingered minute hand straight up to announce that it was nine o'clock, I walked to a pay phone across from the jail. I tried Raymond Garrett's office once more, but with no more luck than the first time. The young woman on the other end recognized my name and gave me just a bit of attitude about calling back when she'd already *said* he'd be out the rest of the week. I didn't bother to apologize.

I didn't reach Garrett at home, either, but added a few feet of tape to my message total. Leaving a voice message can feel almost as much like a real accomplishment as actually talking to someone when you're trying to build a barrier of tiny achievements against an avalanche of disappointments.


Annie Holland looked even more dazed today than the day before. There are people who can take an experience like jail in stride, but most of us after two days behind bars would have pretty much the same jacklighted look I saw on Annie's face that morning. The reality of being imprisoned is so much more desperate than any imagining.

I've had my own token jail experience, of course, and it taught me a lot about what I don't want to do again, and I've seen that look in the eyes of ordinary people who have found themselves in circumstances like these. When the whole force of law and society has turned against a person, it's like being caught in the gears of an immense, cruel machine.

I really hated to add another calamity to Annie's life after she'd been formally charged that morning with her

sister's murder—the same sister who'd be cremated less
than an hour from now—but there was no way I could
avoid telling her about what had happened last night. She
was already sitting down, so I took a deep breath and leapt
in. "Sam has seen his birth certificate."

# CHAPTER 16

ANNIE STARED, UNBLINKING, FOR A FULL THREE SECONDS, holding the telephone receiver against her ear. Finally the words sank in. "But he couldn't have. It's locked away at the bank."

"He sent for a copy from Sacramento."

She seemed to wilt in her chair. "I guess I knew he'd find out someday, no matter how hard I tried. I just couldn't tell him myself." Her eyes seemed to beg for my understanding. "I promised Katherine I'd never tell anyone."

"That wasn't a very realistic promise."

Annie leaned forward on her elbows in a posture of sorrow, cradling the phone against her head. "There wasn't anything realistic about the whole arrangement," she said. "About Sam and Katherine and me. It didn't have anything to do with realism or being practical or sensible. If I'd been sensible, I suppose I would have let Katherine go through with her plan. All I could think of was how much I didn't want to let Sam go to live with strangers, and how I could get Katherine to change her mind about the adoption."

"Why don't you tell me about it?" I offered. "I know you had a fight with Robby Fry and left town. I guess later everyone thought you left because you were pregnant. What happened?"

"Robby and I were very serious," Annie began. "I've never loved anyone as much as I loved him, and at the time I thought he felt the same way." Her heartache at losing that love was obvious, even after seventeen years. It reminded me of Robby's sadness when we'd discussed this same thing only a few days ago.

"I'm sure he did," I said. "As a matter of fact, he told me he did."

"Maybe. I don't know anymore. But his mother hated me."

"From what I hear, she hated everybody except maybe Robby."

Annie nodded. "I think she thought she loved him, but love isn't supposed to smother. Robby didn't know any better—she had him bamboozled. She did everything she could to keep us apart, and I did everything I could to keep us together."

"And Robby was caught in the middle."

"Yes. I guess it was pretty awful for him, but all I could see back then was that if something or someone didn't stop her, Robby and I were doomed. I expected Robby to stop her. I expected him to stand up to her, and he just wasn't grown-up enough. One day I figured out that he wasn't ever going to be."

"When was the last time you talked to him?"

She thought back. "Sam would have been about seven or eight months old when Robby finally stopped coming around and trying to get me to marry him."

"He's grown up a lot since then," I told her. "After his mother died, he seemed to sort of . . . bloom. And he realizes now how wrong he was to let her run his life. I think you might be surprised at Robby if you talked to him now."

Annie shook her head. "It's been too long. He has a whole different life now."

"Don't be too certain," I said. "So you gave up on Robby and went out of town."

"I couldn't stand my life the way it was. I couldn't stand Robby's caving in to his mother. I couldn't stand my job at Drake's. I'd helped Susan and Joey go to college in Sacramento, and after that I couldn't afford to go myself.

"It was April, and the weather was so nice. I decided I wanted to spend some time near the ocean. Katherine was eighteen by then—she could take care of herself for a week or two, and she wasn't home that much, anyway. I took some vacation time and went up to Trinidad on the north coast and got a room in a motel. Susan knew where I was, but I asked her not to tell anyone. Then Katherine called."

Katherine was eighteen and pregnant. She said the father was Paul Gregory, then a news reporter for the local television station. He was married, and he was not interested in a divorce.

"I'd thought Katherine's life was taking a turn for the better," Annie said. "A boy she was going out with, Don Harris, was involved in a young people's service club at St. Martin's. They visited people in convalescent hospitals and volunteered to cheer up sick kids. It was a good thing for her. She stopped dating Don after a while, but she stayed active in the club and kept going to church. I thought maybe, finally, she'd found a direction for her life."

I remembered the old missal in Katherine's nightstand drawer. She seemed to have hung on to it for sentimental reasons, though the newspaper story mentioned her attending a Presbyterian church with Raymond—she probably figured that for a politically safe denomination.

Katherine's life had taken a completely different direction than Annie had anticipated from her days as a volunteer with St. Martin's. She'd gotten involved with Paul Gregory, who had refused to leave his wife and marry her. Finally, he had come through with a sizable chunk of cash and given it to Katherine on the condition that she leave town and get an abortion. But Katherine didn't want an abortion.

"That was what I couldn't understand," Annie said. "I know I would have considered it if I'd been in her situation, and Katherine had never wanted children. She wouldn't tell me why, but she wanted to have the baby and arrange for an adoption through a lawyer. She needed help."

Annie had given her the help she needed. She quit both her jobs and dropped her own life to be there for her sister. Paul Gregory's cash and Annie's savings paid for an apartment in Eureka, where Sam was born that fall. A couple was waiting to adopt him, but when Annie saw him through the nursery window it was love at first sight.

"I told Katherine I'd do anything she wanted—help her any way I could if she'd call off the adoption and keep him. But she wouldn't even go see him, or let the nurse bring him in to her. She just wanted to give him to the Stanleys—that was the name of the couple the attorney had found—and go back home and forget the whole thing had ever happened. It was breaking my heart to think of never seeing him again."

Katherine hadn't planned on naming her baby, but Annie wanted him to have a name, and when Katherine told Annie to choose one for him, she named him Sam after their grandfather. She thought if the baby had a name it might be easier for Katherine to form an attachment to him, but that didn't happen. She wouldn't even let the nurses bring him into the room. Seventy-two hours after Sam was born she'd be allowed to sign the official papers releasing him to the adoptive parents, and that was what she was determined to do.

All her life, Annie had given in to Katherine, just as their parents had done until the day they died, and Annie never saw a way to change things after they were gone. From the time that Katherine was born, she'd demanded her own way and gotten it; it was easier to give her what she wanted than to suffer through her moods and tantrums. This time, however, Annie wouldn't give up. She begged and pleaded, reasoned and promised. But Katherine wanted no part of raising a baby.

"I said, 'Then give him to me. Let me raise him.' I swore it was the only thing I'd ever ask of her, but I couldn't live with the thought of strangers taking Sam away when I knew I could give him a good life and all the love he'd ever need."

"And she agreed?"

"She agreed to think about it, finally. The Stanleys were coming the next day to take Sam home from the hospital, right after Katherine signed the papers. She said she'd let me know the next morning what she'd decided. I asked her to come to the nursery window and look at him just once—you can't imagine how beautiful he was—but she wouldn't.

"The next morning I went back to the hospital, and Katherine told me she'd decided to call off the adoption and let me keep Sam. There were two conditions—at first. Later, there were new conditions whenever it suited Katherine. But right then the conditions were that I keep him in my bedroom in the apartment until I went back to Cascade. She didn't want to see him."

"What was the other condition?"

"I had to tell everyone he was mine. And I couldn't ever tell him, or anyone, who his father was."

So Annie had come back to Cascade with Sam a couple of weeks after he was born, and let people think what they wanted to think. She never offered explanations or excuses to anyone, and she gave up any future she had with Robby Fry. It was a hard way to go, but she went with her head high and her courage intact. She also went without a legal adoption arrangement between herself and Katherine.

"Katherine said we'd work something out later, but she didn't come back to town for another two and a half years, and then she said it would have to be after she had married Raymond, and after that there was always some reason we couldn't do it right then. She was always going to tell Raymond about Sam and get the legal papers drawn up, but it never happened. After a while I quit asking. It was obvious she didn't want to make the adoption legal."

"Because she wanted more of a hold over you?"

Annie shrugged. "Of course. That was Katherine's way. It took me years to realize it, to admit it, but she held Sam over my head from the day she came back to town. There was always some new threat to take him away if she didn't get something she wanted from me."

"And something that happened at the birthday party the other night was the last straw, wasn't it?"

Annie nodded. "Sam and I had a fight about Katherine that morning—when I told him we had to go to her party. Oh, not a real fight, but we fussed at each other, you know. He didn't want to go to Katherine's. He didn't want me to go, either."

I found myself wishing fervently Sam had been able to succeed in convincing Annie to stay home just this once.

"One time—it was several years ago—Sam refused to go to one of Katherine's family get-togethers and I told him he could stay away if it meant that much to him. Well, I showed up without him and she got me alone in the kitchen at the party and threatened to call him right then and tell him she was his mother, and make him come and live with her and Raymond.

"I got down on my knees and begged her not to do it. If anyone had come in and seen me, I don't know how I would have lived with the embarrassment, but right then it didn't matter. I couldn't let her take my boy away from me. I promised her I'd make sure he didn't miss any of her parties from then on."

"And now he didn't want to go to this one either?"

"He hated Katherine. And sometimes I think he hated me for always letting her have her way." She looked away from me, ashamed.

"I know he hated the way she treated you."

She seemed to think about that for a moment, and a look of quiet pain crossed her face. "Katherine talked to me the way she did because she could. She was always testing people to see what she could and couldn't do to them. And if she could do something, she did."

And that about summed up my opinion of the deceased, corroborated by the testimony of some of her victims. If I could reach beyond death to speak to Katherine Garrett and ask her two questions, they would be, first: Who killed you? and second: What gave you the right to arrange others' lives as though they were furniture in your personal living room? That question was its own answer, I guess. There are people to whom other people don't exist except as props for their own lives. They call them sociopaths.

# CHAPTER 17

SAM WAS GOING STIR CRAZY. MY COLLECTION OF SCIENCE fiction magazines and paperbacks wasn't proving sufficient to keep the walls of my tiny apartment from closing in on him. When I came home after seeing Annie, bearing two bags of much-needed groceries, he was pacing the room like a caged lion. "How's Mom?" he asked as he took one of the bags and walked it to the kitchen counter.

"She's doing pretty well, but it hasn't been easy on her. She was arraigned this morning."

"What does that mean, exactly?" he asked, unable to hide the anxiety in his eyes.

"Just that she's been formally charged with murder in the first degree." I started taking things out of the bags and putting them into cupboards. "That's pretty much what we figured would happen, you know." I handed Sam several items for the refrigerator.

"Yeah. I know. I guess I was just hoping . . . Will she be able to come home now?"

"Not just yet. There'll be another hearing about bail, but that won't be until next month."

Sam turned away and opened the refrigerator door. "I don't know if I can stand hiding out for that long." He put the vegetables in a bin and set the milk on a shelf.

"You still have an aunt and uncle in town," I ventured. "The juvenile authorities would probably allow you to stay with one of them. I think Mike Gold could arrange that without your having to spend any time in custody, if that's what you're worried about."

He closed the refrigerator door. "You're probably getting tired of having me around, huh?"

"No! No, I'm not." And I really wasn't, I realized after I had said it. "I'll admit I'm pretty used to living alone, but that's not necessarily a good thing. I just thought you'd be happier if you could go outside, go back to work, sleep in a real bed, you know."

"I wish I knew what was the right thing to do. Aunt Susan's always treated me kind of strange, and Uncle Joey's a dweeb. I've never been close to either of them, but I guess I *should* probably go and stay with one of them."

I could tell he wasn't looking forward to the prospect. "Not unless it's what you want to do," I said. "There's no sense being any unhappier than you have to be. Why don't you just plan on staying here until something better comes along? Tuna salad sandwiches okay?"

"Yeah. And thanks. I'm going nuts staying inside, but I guess it's a better kind of nuts than I'd be going otherwise. At least I've got plenty of good reading material."

I rummaged in a kitchen drawer for a can opener for the tuna. "You know, I've got an idea. If you can't go out by yourself, at least we can do something together. Nobody will be looking for you with an adult, and we could keep our eyes out for cops. We could go over to the mall tonight and get you some clothes. Hey, with any luck at all we'll have your mom out of jail before the bail hearing and before you completely flip your lid."

"Do you really think so?"

"I hope so. That's the best I can do right now. Meantime, look in the fridge and see if you can find me some mayonnaise."

"Do you think that sometimes people deserve to die?" Sam asked me while we assembled the ingredients for the tuna salad.

"Whew! That's a tough one. People do horrible things sometimes, and there are people we probably don't want on the street, but dead is forever. I just don't know."

"Let me put it this way, then. Do you think there's such a thing as a person who doesn't deserve to live? A person who's just bad all the way through, and whatever bad thing happens to them is okay?"

I put down the chopping knife and looked at him. "We're talking about Katherine Garrett, right?"

"I guess so. I hated her guts. I never told Mom that in so many words, but I did. There were times I wanted her dead, or thought I did. But somebody really killed her, and it had to have been . . . really awful for her. Painful, I mean, and frightening." He stopped spreading mayonnaise on bread and looked at me with tear-filled eyes. "She must have been so afraid, and there was no one to help her."

"Yeah," I agreed. "It must have been pretty awful." I had been pretty certain I was about to die a time or two, and it wasn't a feeling I wanted to experience again.

Sam wiped at his eyes with a shirt sleeve. "I don't feel any different about her. I can't find anything about her to like no matter how much I think about it, and finding out she was my real mother doesn't make me like her any better. But I just can't help thinking nobody deserves to have something like that happen to them."

I had to agree with Sam on principle, but someone Katherine knew certainly felt she deserved to die in a particularly nasty manner. There was no sign of forced entry, and the perpetrator hadn't even tried to make it look like a burglary, which seemed to me like a logical way of attempting to cover up something like that.

It was definitely someone she knew, the way I figured it. A stranger might find cause to pick up a vase and bash your skull in, but only someone who knows you will destroy your face in the process. Whoever had ended Katherine Garrett's life had known her very well indeed.

I kept coming back to that damned vase. One set of fingerprints, two types of blood splatters, mutually exclusive. I had looked at the photos over and over without being able to make much sense of it, other than to come to the logical conclusion that the vase had to have been in one place at some point during the attack on Katherine and in another place before the attacker was finished with her. If Annie didn't kill Katherine with the vase, why weren't there any fingerprints on it other than hers?

I wished I had a way of getting my hands on the vase itself—I had what seemed an irrational notion that I could figure something out if I could only hold it in my hands— but it was now the premier piece of evidence against Annie Holland, and the chances I could get close enough to touch it were too small to calculate.

I went back to eating my lunch, accompanied by unappetizing mental images of splattering blood. A series of loud thumps from downstairs reminded me that I knew someone who might be able to tell me something more about the fatal vase. I finished my sandwich and made a couple of reading recommendations for Sam, who volunteered to do the lunch dishes. Then I grabbed the manila envelope containing the crime scene prints out of my portfolio and went downstairs.

I opened the door of Studio J to the tune of bells. Julian, who was showing samples to a customer, gave me a smile and a wave. I waved back and continued to the freight room off the office, where, as expected, I found Carl knee-deep in multicolored foam pellets, unpacking crates. "Hey, buddy, you think you could manage to do that a little quieter?"

"Well some of us have to work for a living," Carl replied, "unlike certain individuals who can sit in a car all day and bill their clients an hourly rate for surveillance."

"Surveillance. Ugh. I'd rather unpack a crate of statuary any day. But I came here for your expert opinion, actually."

"Oh?" Carl straightened up and kicked his way toward me through a small mountain of packing material. "Which of my many areas of expertise would you care to plumb this afternoon?"

"Pottery and ceramics and that sort of thing." I hitched myself up onto a packing table and rummaged through the prints until I found what I wanted—a few shots of the fatal birthday vase taken in good light with a minimum of blood displayed. I handed them to Carl. "Tell me something about this."

He went through the pictures and turned them toward the window with a thoughtful expression on his face. "I take it the spots are extraneous?"

"Totally."

Carl raised an eyebrow, but kept his thoughts to himself. "In that case it seems to be stoneware with a mutton-fat glaze."

"Mutton fat?"

"Well, there are no real sheep involved. It's called that because of the texture of the glaze." He put the prints down on his desk, turned to a shelf full of oversized books, and pulled down a large volume, riffling through the pages rapidly.

"Here's another example of it," he said, holding the book out to me, open to a picture of a dish with a glaze similar to the one on Katherine's vase. "It's not really super glossy, like a lot of glazed surfaces, but it has a sort of soft, diffused light to it. Almost oily. It looks a lot like fat that's been melted down and cooled off again, doesn't it?"

"I guess it does," I admitted. "I haven't spent a lot of time contemplating melted fat."

"It's a Chinese glaze. And the potter was heavily influenced by the Asian Peasant school. I mean it has that rough, utilitarian sort of air about it, but it just misses being real peasant pottery by trying a bit too hard to hit the mark, if you know what I mean."

"Yes. I think so, anyway. You mean this person may be an artist, but a real Asian peasant could do it better."

"Exactly. I'm guessing it's a Souvelle. Jacqueline Souvelle. She has quite a rep right now for this kind of self-conscious simplicity, and some of her more recent pieces have this kind of glaze. Her name on the bottom would pretty nearly triple the price. Is there a name on the bottom?"

I remembered the print that detailed the vase's bottom section. Anything that might have been written or inscribed on it would have been impossible to read for the thick, dark blood. "I really don't know," I said.

"This vase could set you back almost a thousand dollars," Carl remarked. "I wish I could say the owner had bought it here, and a few more besides, but we've never had a Souvelle in the place."

"What would the inside look like?" I asked him. "There's a shot of it, but all I can see is dark." I handed him the picture of the vase's interior, a brown murkiness with no apparent detail.

"It would be unglazed, probably," he said. "Stoneware turns vitreous at firing temperatures, so there's no need to glaze the inside, and that wouldn't be consistent with the style, anyway. It would be very heavy. And it would be rough."

"Rough?"

"Yes, on the inside. The stoneware clay has ground up bits of fired stoneware mixed in, so it's very abrasive."

"Well, thanks, Carl. Any ideas where it might have been purchased?"

"There are maybe two dozen galleries in California that might carry something like this. Can't you ask the person who bought it?"

I thought about my numerous phone calls to Raymond Garrett's home and office, and the total lack of response to any of them. "Yes," I agreed. "If I can ever get him to answer my calls, I can."

# CHAPTER 18

RAYMOND GARRETT'S BUSINESS, GARRETT FINANCIAL Services, Inc., was located not far from the offices of Baronian Investigations. For that matter, it wasn't far from the jail or Julian's studio and my apartment, either. In downtown Cascade, nothing's too far from anything else.

GFS, Inc. took up the second floor of a two-story Spanish-style building, one of the few of that style in town. It was shaded by two large oak trees that had escaped being cut down when the building was constructed back in some decade before trees were considered an unnatural feature in a business district.

Next door was a tiny burger joint—White Mountain Burgers—that despite the recent salutary trend to healthier foods, was still one of the most popular lunch spots for blocks around. When I got a whiff of the tantalizing burger and fries aromas coming from inside, I almost regretted the fact that I practically never eat beef anymore, and never anything that's been ground beyond recognition. Old habits die hard.

I parked the car and fed a quarter to the meter before heading up the shaded stairs to the upper level. I didn't expect Raymond Garrett to be in his office, but on the off chance that he was, I wanted to be ignored in person for once, instead of by proxy. I approached a large antique desk, and a young woman in a silk suit and an expensive haircut leaned around from behind a computer monitor and gave me a practiced smile.

"I'm here to see Raymond Garrett," I said, handing her my card.

She read it without any visible change of expression. "Mr. Garrett isn't in," she said, in precisely the same tones I'd heard on the phone twice before. "I can leave him a message if you like."

"I *would* like, but I've already left two messages that haven't been returned." I softened my words with a pleasant expression. "I understand this is a difficult time for Mr. Garrett, but I really do need to speak to him personally, if only for a few minutes." I scanned the windows of the offices I could see from the reception area for the familiar silver mane and patrician profile that had been cropping up on political posters and brochures around town. If Raymond Garrett was in, he wasn't visible from here.

"I wish I could be more help . . ." The young woman stood up, frowning slightly at the direction of my gaze. I was dismissed, it seemed, which, seeing as how I wasn't going to see Garrett anyhow, was just peachy with me.

"That's all right," I said brightly. "I'll keep trying." And the next place I planned to try would be the Garrett house, but I'd be damned if Garrett's young blond Cerberus was going to know it. "I'll call back Monday."

A slender, dark-haired man in his early thirties with a finely sculpted face and eyes like Valentino looked in from the other front office. "Sherry, is this something I can help with?"

"Oh, no, Mr. DeLora—" Sherry began, but she never got to finish.

"My name is Caley Burke, Mr. DeLora. Can I have a few minutes of your time?"

"Sure thing." He flashed a smile, which was as dazzling as the rest of him. "Come on back." He disappeared around the doorway.

Sherry couldn't hide her annoyance as I walked past her desk and into Chip DeLora's office, and I couldn't hide my expression of triumph. To be honest, I don't think I tried very hard.

"Please have a seat, Ms. Burke," he said, indicating a burgundy leather visitor's chair. "Can I get you something to drink?"

I always make it a rule to accept hospitality from people I'm interviewing if my purpose is to make them feel more at ease. People who've been raised to be hospitable, and that includes most of us, I think, feel somewhat uncomfortable if a guest refuses offers of food or drink. Conversely, being able to offer something to a person who's entered your territory makes you feel all the more in control of it. A cup of coffee or a glass of iced tea makes good social cement.

The good news is I get to drink a lot of free tea and coffee and lemonade; the bad news is I spend a lot of time looking for a bathroom. This time I accepted a can of soda from a handy office refrigerator. There'd always be a bathroom around if I needed one.

Chip DeLora poured my soda into a frosted glass from a little freezer compartment, and poured one for himself, too, then settled himself into the high-back executive chair behind his desk. The liquid brown eyes were framed by long, straight lashes of the kind most women find extremely difficult to resist. He smiled pleasantly, perfecting the picture. "Now what is it you needed to see Mr. Garrett about, Ms. Burke?"

I handed a Baronian Investigations card with my name on it across the black marble desktop. "I'm investigating the death of Katherine Garrett, Mr. DeLora."

Chip DeLora looked at the card, then at me. "Call me Chip. And I'll admit I don't know much about how these things work, but I've already spoken to the police, and isn't that what *they're* doing?"

"Yes, they are, but their investigation is proceeding in a different direction. At this point they're going on the assumption that Katherine was killed by her sister, Annie Holland."

Chip set his soda can down on the polished surface of his desk three times, making three intersecting rings of condensation. His lashes made gorgeous shadows on his cheeks. After a moment he looked up at me. "And what direction is *your* investigation taking?"

"All of the other directions. I don't want to see Annie go to trial for murder."

"So you want to ask me some questions, is that it? My wife and I left the house several hours before the murder took place, if that's what you want to know."

"Yes, I already know that," I replied with a reassuring smile. Of course I didn't know that he hadn't come back later and walked in through the unlocked front door, but that was neither here nor there for the moment. "The questions I want to ask are of a more general nature."

He nodded. "Go ahead, then."

"A lot of people I've talked to have suggested that Katherine wasn't well-liked."

He waited a moment in silence before he responded. "Is that a question?"

I shrugged. "I thought you might have something to add. Or you might have a different opinion."

Chip sighed. "No. Not entirely, at any rate. Women tended to dislike Katherine intensely. Men had a . . . different reaction."

What a surprise. And with just a bit more imagination I could make a guess as to Katherine's reaction to Chip's spectacular good looks. "Is that so?" I asked casually. "Was your wife one of the women who disliked her?"

At the mention of his wife, a wounded look came and went on Chip's face. "No more than a lot of other women," he said. "She didn't care much for the obligatory socializing we had to do with Katherine and Raymond, but she accepted it with pretty good grace. Liz knows whatever is best for my career is best for us, and my association with Raymond Garrett has been very good for my career."

"Has it been good for your marriage?"

Chip's eyes blazed anger at me for half a second before he recovered from my unanticipated question. "What does that have to do with your investigation?" he asked, back in control and being marginally polite.

"Probably nothing, and I apologize for upsetting you."

"You didn't upset me," he said evenly.

I wasn't buying that for a second. My best guess was that Chip's association with Raymond, and especially with Katherine, had been *very* bad for his marriage.

"Katherine was very active in Raymond's political affairs," I went on matter-of-factly. "She seems to have been very ambitious for him. Do you think it's possible she might have made some enemies of her own along the campaign trail?"

Chip nodded thoughtfully. "I suppose it's possible. Katherine was known for setting her sights on something and never resting until she got it. I think she probably didn't pay a lot of attention to who might be mowed down along the way."

His voice had grown quieter, and his words sounded less prepared. I was willing to bet this much of what Chip DeLora was telling me was the absolute truth. I wanted to prolong this unconscious honesty as long as I could. "And if it was something she wasn't supposed to have?"

"Then she wanted it all the more, and went after it all the harder. I think the only things Katherine ever really wanted were the things someone told her she couldn't have."

"And did that include other women's husbands?"

Chip seemed to snap back to his guarded professional self. "I really didn't know that much about her personal life. I was speaking in the public sense."

"Of course. Now I'd like to ask a few questions about what went on at the Garrett house while you were at Katherine's birthday party, and then I'll let you get back to running your business." I took a spiral notebook out of my portfolio and clicked a pen to the ready, smiling pleasantly to let Chip know we were still buddies. I had my own theories about how well he knew Katherine Garrett, and the price he may have paid for it, and if he wouldn't come clean with me, maybe Liz DeLora would.

The address in the phone book beside DeLora, Charles and Elizabeth, was on the other side of town in one of the newer and more expensive developments. I took the one freeway that crosses Cascade from east to west, rolling up my car window against the pounding mid-July heat and cranking up my nifty new non-CFC air-conditioning system. I felt the cool air drying my sweaty hair and wondered—not for the first time—why I had wilted every summer of all those years before I broke down and got it.

I drove across town from west to east, watching downtown turn to typically uninspiring suburbs, then modest houses on lots of an acre or more, many with gardens and livestock pens nearby. After six or seven miles I could see neighborhoods made up of pricey two-story houses and lush lawns on lots large enough to convince the residents they were getting away from it all. I took an off-ramp that would lead me to the DeLora residence and some questions I wasn't looking forward to asking.

As a kid I was shy. As an adult I can be nothing short of standoffish. I guess it's a sort of defense mechanism, but I don't make friends easily, and I don't care to be surrounded by acquaintances. It's fortunate that I enjoy my own company, because I spend a lot of time alone. For this reason, perhaps, I value my right of privacy more than most people I know. If I feel something is no one's business but my own, I'm not at all shy about clamming up, and I understand perfectly when someone refuses to answer my questions, or turns my attention in another, more comfortable direction.

So what am I doing in a business where it's my job to uncover the very things people don't want me to know? I asked again as I pulled up to the DeLora residence, where a slender woman in shorts and a wide-brimmed hat was digging in the yard with a hand trowel. Liz DeLora's sense of privacy was about to take a beating for the sake of my case and my clients. As I got out of the car and approached her, I reminded myself that in spite of any unpleasantness I might be about to face, this might, with any luck, do more good than harm.

# CHAPTER 19

LIZ DELORA WAS BUSY ACCEPTING HER OWN HOSPITAL-
ity at an alarming rate. We had taken seats on high oak
stools at a tiled pass-through counter between the kitchen
and family room of the DeLora's spacious, sunny home,
and had scarcely begun talking when she uncapped a bottle of Scotch that was sitting on the counter and poured
some into a crystal highball glass. It was good Scotch,
too, but I was sticking to mineral water and lime just
the same.

I looked around at the expensive and ever-so-slightly
tacky decor, heavy on the pastel pink upholstery, *faux*
brocade throw pillows, and genuine wood-grain plastic wall
embellishments, and tried to think of something compli-
mentary to say. "You've certainly done a lot with the
place," I said, which seemed truthful enough.

"Yes, I'm always adding something new," she said, but
her smile of satisfaction faded rapidly. She tossed down the
Scotch and poured another. "You said you wanted to talk
to me about Katherine Garrett."

I wondered briefly if she always pronounced the words
"Katherine Garrett" as though she meant to say "tarantula,"
but decided against asking. "I'm talking to a lot of people

who knew Mrs. Garrett when she was alive—sort of trying to figure out her relationships to some of the people around her."

"And you're with the police or something?"

"More like 'something.' I'm a private investigator." I passed her a card. "I believe you and Mr. DeLora were among the guests at her birthday party the night she was killed. Did you attend parties at the Garretts' often?"

"Every goddamned Christmas and every goddamned New Year's Eve, and every goddamned one of her birthdays ever since Chip went to work for Raymond Garrett," Liz spat. "There was no getting away from Katherine's goddamned parties."

I like it when people are honest. It makes my job so much easier. "What was it about Katherine's parties you didn't like?"

Liz's hand tightened around her glass. Her eyes were getting a little bleary behind a curtain of false eyelashes, and her carefully arranged hair was beginning to come down around her face. "It'd take less time to say what I *did* like."

"Which was?" I hoped I could keep this streak of frankness alive and well until Liz had confirmed what I already suspected about Katherine and Chip.

"Which was nothing. Not Katherine prancing around like a queen on her home territory, not flaunting herself to some man she had her eye on that week, not her condescending attitude toward me, not . . ." She faltered, knocking back the second drink like a veteran.

"Not displaying your husband like a trophy?"

Liz seemed to prepare herself for a sharp denial, then crumpled, cradling her head in her arms on the counter. "She just had to have him! You know what I mean? She had to prove she could take him right out from under my nose. She had to have any man who belonged to somebody else! And she didn't even have enough class to be subtle about it!"

Katherine Garrett had been reduced to ashes just a few hours before, and it was pretty obvious that Liz DeLora preferred her that way. So far, Annie seemed to be the only person in town who was genuinely sorry that Katherine was dead, and the prevailing wisdom was that she had killed her. If she did, I wondered how she could have beat all these other people to it. "What did Raymond think of all this?" I asked.

"He knew. How could he *not* know? All those long looks and possessive gestures. She'd manage to sit beside Chip and put her hand on his leg just for a moment while they were talking, just long enough to let everyone know she owned him. God, I was humiliated!" She started crying all over again.

I waited a minute to let her get it out. There was a box of tissues on the other side of the counter. I moved them next to her and she tried a smile of thanks as she grabbed a handful.

"She didn't care what I was going through, of course," Liz went on when she had regained some of her composure. "Katherine never cared about anyone but herself. Sex was her way of controlling men and destroying their wives, one of Katherine's favorite little games. Before Chip, there were a dozen others."

"And after Chip?"

"This all happened just this year," she said. "I suspected for a long time, but Chip always denied everything. I think he resisted her at first." She laughed harshly. "I *have* to think that, I guess. He was afraid she'd get to Raymond— that she'd cost him his job, but he broke it off last month, finally. It was her or me—I made that clear."

"You're pretty sure Raymond knew what was going on the whole time?"

"Positive. Raymond's not especially bright, but he's not stupid, either. He stays out of Katherine's affairs, but he knows about them, all right."

"And when did *you* know?"

Liz poured a third Scotch. "One night I called the office to find out if he'd be home for dinner. He said he had some work to catch up on and not to wait up for him. I drove into town and waited outside the office. I followed him when he left, and he drove straight to her house." Liz DeLora looked at me with a look that remembered the pain of that moment. "Raymond was out of town all that week. And all that week Chip worked late."

This was not an experience I'd ever lived through personally. If Michael was cheating on me—and I'd made it a point never to ask him—he kept the knowledge from me and I, in turn, didn't pursue it. But I felt a stab of sympathy for Liz DeLora that was as close as I hope I ever come to knowing it firsthand.

Outside, on the other side of a sliding glass door that looked out on a large, beautiful yard, were Liz DeLora's reasons for sticking out the tough times. A pair of identical, chubby three-year-old boys with Chip DeLora's dark coloring and good looks splashed in a shallow wading pool under the watchful eye of a nanny. If Michael and I had had children, how much longer would *we* have stuck it out, I wondered. Well, every marriage was different, and maybe Liz's was worth saving. Mine had not been.

Liz got up to open the back door and give some special instructions to the nanny. She was a little unsteady on her feet, and I wondered if she'd been drinking before I got there.

"Let's get back to Tuesday evening," I suggested when she sat back down. "You said you and Chip left the party early."

"I always left as early as I could manage it," Liz said. "Especially since I found out about . . . Anyway, we got there about six, and dinner was served around seven, I guess. Then there was a birthday cake and champagne, and presents. I don't think it was possible to leave gracefully until at least eight."

"Then you came home?"

"Yes. Oh, Chip went back to the office for a while later that night to catch up on some paperwork for a meeting with an important client Wednesday morning. I fell asleep before he got home. Champagne does that to me."

And what kind of mental tap dance did you have to do to enable you to believe he was really working late at the office? I wondered, but only to myself. Chip DeLora's current state of fidelity would have to be an article of faith for his wife if she were going to get through the day. And the nights. I didn't envy her the task. I asked a few more questions for form's sake, but I already had what I'd come for.

I wasn't all that far from the Garrett house, so I swung by before getting back on the freeway. Lila Jensen had Sundays and Thursdays off, I had learned from Annie, but unless there had been some special arrangements made on account of the household tragedy, she should be there today, and so should congressional-hopeful Raymond Garrett, if his young assistant was to be believed.

It was easy to recognize the house after all the pictures I'd seen of it lately. It was large and spreading, an updated and classier version of the classic fifties ranch-style house. There were lots and lots of windows, and I was glad I didn't have to pay the power bill.

A carefully tended lawn stretched out a full fifty feet deep from the house to the sidewalk, and borders of shrubs lined up under the front windows and along the long, curving walk from the street to the front door. A low split-rail fence along the sidewalk completed the illusion of a barrier between the Garretts and the world beyond.

The triple garage door was closed, and a silver Mercedes sedan was parked in the driveway. I figured it for Raymond's car; the drop-dead red Ferrari that Katherine used to drive around town was probably under lock and key inside the garage.

I looked—casually, I hoped—into the windows as I approached the front door. Most of the drapes were drawn, but at the left-hand end of the house the drapes were absent from a long series of tall windows. Beyond, I thought I could glimpse bare walls and floors. The dining room? My stomach did a flip. I took a deep breath and rang the doorbell.

From far away there was a deep chiming, then footsteps. Raymond Garrett, or the housekeeper? I waited for the door to open, but the footsteps stopped, then started up again, moving away from the door. I rang again, but with less optimism. Nothing. If I wanted to see Raymond Garrett, I was going to have to be a lot sneakier.

What I really wanted to see was that dining room, but I didn't have the chutzpah to walk up to the window and peer inside, when I knew I could be seen by someone looking out, and there *was* someone looking out, I was certain. So what I did instead was turn around and walk back to my car and drive away.

# CHAPTER 20

I WASN'T EVEN THINKING ABOUT PAUL GREGORY until
I saw the building that housed KASK-TV coming up on
my left as I drove back toward downtown. The station had
recently relocated from its old facility—a former ware-
house—to this spiffy new stone-faced building near the
river, rubbing elbows with the Civic Auditorium and the
county art museum. I had an hour before I was supposed to
meet with Annie's sister Susan, and when I saw the station
it occurred to me that maybe I could do something positive
for Sam. Maybe I could start the process of reunion between
father and son.

Cascade is too small a town to boast a television station
for each major network, but it does have a PBS station and
one other major network affiliate, the one Paul Gregory had
been working his way up in for the past twenty years. His
was a well-known face about town, and that was what he
hoped to parlay into votes for the local congressional seat
come November. I saw that face from a distance behind the
glass window of a studio as I waited by the front desk for
permission to go back.

The receptionist handed the message off to a production
assistant who walked across a darkened expanse of studio
floor, stepped into a circle of light shining down on the

anchor desk, and tapped Gregory on the shoulder. Paul Gregory turned his head, looked out at the reception area, and nodded. I had been granted an audience.

I walked through two sets of soundproofing doors, into the studio area and past the sets for a half-hour interview show which was also hosted by Paul Gregory, and a locally produced music show that featured bands passing through on their way to more prosperous venues. In the far corner a handful of young men and women wearing headsets swarmed over a permanent news set constructed of ply-wood covered with indoor-outdoor carpeting. Somehow it all looked classier on television.

"Hi. How can I help you?" Paul Gregory smiled as he extended a firm, dry grip that would do credit to his political aspirations. He was in his mid-forties, handsome enough to go over well on TV, with slightly graying brown hair flawlessly cut to just above his collar and blow-dried to casual perfection. In many ways, I realized for the first time, he was almost a younger version of Raymond Garrett, and that made me wonder. Was there only one basic poli-tician model, which could be equipped with slight physical and ideological variations for a small additional cost, like ordering passenger-side airbags for your car? I guess that's what comes of reading science fiction.

It was something of a relief to see on closer inspection that Paul Gregory varied in some degree from his opponent. There was a little more native intelligence in the gaze, and more physical energy in his body language. He wouldn't be on the air for a couple of hours yet, and had put aside for now the buttoned-down image usually associated with TV anchors, loosening the tie on his honey-colored dress shirt, and rolling the cuffs up twice. The smile he offered was so perfectly rehearsed to seem spontaneous that I had to stop myself from looking around to see if we were being taped for a Gregory for Congress spot.

"My name is Caley Burke, Mr. Gregory. I'm here to see you on a private matter."

I had to hand it to him—he was smooth. If I hadn't been looking for a change of expression, I wouldn't have seen the slight narrowing of his eyes. The smile held steady.

"Perhaps we should talk in my office, Ms. Burke." He let go of my hand. "I'll be back in a few, Gloria," he said to the nearest of the production people, and led me out of the studio and down a narrow carpeted hallway lined with indifferent paintings by local artists. We reached an office with his name on the door, and he waved me in peremptorily and closed the door. "Okay," he said as he moved across the room, putting his desk between us. "What do you want?"

I watched him for a moment before answering. This was a man clearly expecting an attack of some sort, and since I wasn't planning to attack him, I couldn't help but wonder who was. I reached into my jacket pocket and brought out a card. "I'm a private investigator," I said, reaching across the desk to hand him the card. "I'm working for Sam Holland, Katherine Garrett's son. He's just seen his birth certificate for the first time, and learned you're his father."

Paul Gregory snatched the card from my hand and stared at it, then at me. "Then what's the purpose of the phone calls?"

"Phone calls?" I echoed. "What phone calls are those, Mr. Gregory?" I sat down, uninvited, in a guest chair.

He collapsed into his chair, and if I could read his expression accurately, he was pretty damned disgusted with himself for revealing his big secret.

"Somebody's calling you on the phone? About Sam? Who would know?"

"I thought it was Katherine."

And then you went to her house late the other night and clobbered her with her own birthday present, perhaps? Of course I didn't say anything like that to Paul Gregory. "But the calls kept on coming after she was dead?"

"I got one yesterday." He put a hand over his eyes, supporting his elbow on a chair arm as he slumped into the leather seat, the picture of exhausted desperation. "Someone threatening to go public with the story about Katherine and me." He sighed deeply and looked at me. Then he kept on talking.

Paul Gregory had life so good for so long that he forgot that his past might catch up with him. He had a swift, transient affair with a young girl, then paid her to have an abortion and get the hell out of his life. Until recently, he had always assumed she had done just that.

Katherine Garrett had returned to Cascade after a few years, but she'd zeroed in on Raymond Garrett and built her little empire of influence and made no attempt to contact Gregory, which was just fine by him. He'd stayed in the same marriage and sent two children through college and made a name for himself in Cascade and environs. Now he was closing in on a congressional seat and a future of power and influence, and someone was determined not to let him enjoy it.

In sixteen years of living in the same town with him, he had never made the connection between Annie Holland's son and his long-ago indiscretion with Katherine, until shortly after he had announced his political candidacy. That's when a woman started calling him and threatening to expose his secret.

"The phone caller—what did she say?"

"At first she just said she knew what I'd done seventeen years ago." The anonymous caller had details of dates and places that seemed accurate, though Gregory had gone out of his way to forget the particulars of his indiscretion. "Later, in another call, she told me Katherine had gone away and had a son. It was the first I'd heard of it. After Katherine left, I didn't see her again for more than three years."

"You said you thought the person who called you was Katherine. Did it sound like her?"

His gaze wandered away as he remembered the voice. "It sounded like her, or at least like I remember her sounding.

We haven't spoken to one another much since . . ." His hands fluttered, helpless to find a gesture appropriate to his meaning.

"And the woman who called referred to Katherine as 'her'?"

"Yeah, but I was still pretty sure it was Katherine. She wouldn't want me to know it was her blackmailing me. That would be beneath her image. What she *would* want would be to spook me out of running against Raymond."

"And did she ask you for money?"

"No. That didn't seem to be the point. The point seemed to be to frighten me."

"Did she tell you who the boy was? Did she say it was Sam?"

Gregory sighed. "She hinted. She said the boy lived here in town, that he'd lived here all his life. Once she told me he lived with a relative of Katherine's. It didn't take me long to figure it out after that. I'd always assumed the baby Annie came back with was hers. Everyone who knew her thought the same thing. She never said any different."

"Did you ever try to meet Sam? Or see him?"

"Ms. Burke, is it?" He referred to the card I'd given him. "Ms. Burke, I may not always have been the best husband on earth, but I've been married to the same woman for twenty-three years. I have two grown children that I love very much. I have a life I've worked hard for, and a certain reputation in this town."

"And a political career to protect."

"Yes, goddammit, I do. And don't sit there and judge me for it!" His expression echoed the anger in his voice, with undertones of impending panic.

He's running scared, I thought to myself, watching the sweat break out on his forehead, and yes, I was judging him, now that I thought about it. Sam deserved a father, and while I might not be overflowing with respect for Gregory, he was almost certainly better than no father at all. "Would you agree to meet Sam if I set it up? No one would have to know but the three of us. I think you and he should get acquainted."

"Ms. Burke, I already have a family. I never knew this boy, never even thought about him until a few months ago. Katherine and I had a very sudden and very brief affair, and soon after, she told me she was pregnant." He ran his hands through the perfect hair, mussing it a bit. "You can't possibly know the position that put me in."

"You're right. I couldn't." And wouldn't want to, I added silently.

"I couldn't imagine a greater disaster than to leave my wife for a girl I didn't really care for, so I cashed in some securities I'd been holding since before my marriage— money my wife didn't know about—and gave her enough money to take care of her problem."

"Well, her problem is now a sixteen-year-old boy who might like to be acquainted with his father. And you might just end up liking him. I do. A lot."

Gregory shook his head. "You're beating the proverbial dead horse, Ms. Burke. There was no real love between Katherine and me. Sure, I wanted her, but she wasn't interested at first. I was almost relieved when she turned me down. Then she came back around and said she'd changed her mind. I was weak. I couldn't resist her, but I never loved her. Conceiving a child was the farthest thing from my mind."

"That's usually the case," I commented. "But it's always a possibility. I suppose you used some form of birth control."

"I don't think that's any of your business," he said through clenched teeth.

It wasn't, of course, but asking intrusive questions was a good way to throw a person off guard. When the target was someone like Paul Gregory, I sort of enjoyed it.

"My guess is you just assumed Katherine was taking care of it. Apparently, you guessed wrong. Now you have a son you didn't know about, but he's your son all the same."

"Ms. Burke, I don't enjoy you coming in here and trying to make me feel guilty for something I worked out with myself and my own conscience years ago. As for my relationship to Sam Holland, we have no real ties to one another except an accident of birth."

"And you're not interested in forming any ties now, is that what you're trying to say?"

"That's what I *am* saying. I'm sure Sam is a fine young man, but he's also, frankly, a complication I don't need right now."

"I see. By the way, where were you around midnight on Tuesday night?"

He shot me a look of barely concealed hostility. "Is that when Katherine died?"

"Approximately."

"My wife and I were on an overnight trip to Reno. We like to take off sometimes on the spur of the moment and come back the next afternoon. Does that satisfy your curiosity?" He was wearing his hostility openly now; I had finally succeeded in pissing him off.

"I'm not actually curious, Mr. Gregory. Not if you didn't kill Katherine Garrett. And I'm not interested in spreading your deep, dark secret."

"Someone else is, though," he reminded me, tight-lipped, "and I don't think they'll stop at trying to ruin my career on account of it."

"Well, it isn't me, and it isn't Sam." I got up from the chair, eager to be out of there and never to see Paul Gregory's face again if I could help it.

"I'm not going to tell Sam about this meeting, so I can't guarantee he won't try to contact you on his own someday. You won't have to worry about seeing *me* again in your lifetime, however." I walked to the door and opened it. "Oh, and by the way," I said over my shoulder on my way out, "I'm not going to vote for you, either."

# CHAPTER 21

MY JOB LEADS ME TO PERVERSE PLEASURES AT TIMES. Right now, as I drove away from the television station toward Susan Brock's house on the bluffs overlooking the Sacramento River, I was feeling a sense of satisfaction; I had found yet another person with reason to hate Katherine Garrett enough to murder her, and even if his alibi held up, it was just more evidence that there were a lot of people besides Annie who might have been willing to do the job.

Chip DeLora had been used by Katherine, and his wife had been emotionally shattered. People have been killed for less. Paul Gregory believed she was blackmailing him in order to cut short a political career that was obviously important to him, and that sort of thing leads to murder so often that if ever I had the urge to make threats of that kind, the statistics on dead blackmailers would change my mind real quick.

But honesty forced me to admit that Gregory was a poor choice for Katherine's murderer. I searched my memory of our meeting for any sign that would make me believe he might have had the *cojones* to take his fate into his own hands and end Katherine's life for the threat he had believed her to be. I couldn't find it. This was a man trying to hide from an indiscretion and hoping his tormentor would just go away.

It was just as well, I realized. How awful it would be for Sam if, on top of everything else he'd been through, he had to face the fact that his father had murdered his mother. I hoped he would be spared that, and I was pretty sure my hopes were on track with reality for once.

Paul Gregory had a lot at stake in his reputation as a wholesome family man. Public office was a demanding profession—ordinary flawed humans need not apply—but I'd need more evidence than the fact he was the victim of crank calls to make me think Gregory might have killed Katherine, then pinned his crime on Annie. Stranger things may happen all the time, but it just didn't ring true somehow.

My next stop was a few minutes away, and I had time to spare. It occurred to me that I'd neglected to eat today, so I solved my nutritional dilemma by taking a detour to a convenience store, where I popped a cheese enchilada into and out of the microwave, and washed it down with a bottle of juice.

Susan Holland Brock was a slender, dark-haired woman who bore a superficial resemblance to her late sister, Katherine Garrett, especially in her curly dark hair and the fine-boned quality of her face. She was dressed casually but expensively in shades of camel and green. She smiled graciously as she held out her hand at the front door, but a tightness around her mouth betrayed the strain of the last two days.

"Caley Burke?"

"Yes."

"Come on in," she said, stepping aside to admit me to her tastefully decorated living room. "I was just looking at this picture album." She held up an imitation leather album with "Susan" engraved in gold script on the cover. "Annie got together all the negatives of our childhood snapshots and had prints made for all of us a few years ago at Christmas."

"That sounds like something Annie would do."

"Do you know her well?" she asked as she led me across a large expanse of deep pile carpet toward a sofa and chairs clustered around the fireplace.

"I've known her for a long time, like a lot of people in town, but never well."

"Cafe customer?"

"Uh-huh. Annie's always been the bright spot in my weekday mornings."

Susan smiled. "Annie has that effect on people. Most people, anyway. You mentioned on the phone that you were investigating her case." She motioned me to a generously stuffed sofa covered in a creamy white fabric and punctuated with deep green and wine pillows. I set my portfolio down on a massive oak coffee table artistically strewn with pictorial books and copies of *Architectural Digest,* and sat down. Susan sat across from me in a matching white chair.

"Yes. I know this is a bad time for the whole family, but I'm looking into the circumstances of Katherine's death. I don't believe Annie killed her."

Susan nodded in approval. "I'm glad you feel that way. I don't believe it, either. I went to visit her today, after you were there. She told me what happened that night after the party, and *that's* what I believe. Annie isn't a killer and I don't know anything that would turn her into one." Susan Brock's voice didn't betray a lot of emotion, but her determination to stand behind her sister showed plainly in her eyes.

"Do you have any idea who else might have wanted to harm Katherine?"

"Almost anybody." She absorbed the look of surprise I'd been too slow to hide. "Katherine wasn't what you call a people person, Ms. Burke."

"Caley. And I've gotten that impression from others, too. . . ."

"But you were surprised to hear me say it. That's all right; I understand perfectly. I'm known to be outspoken and I had very few illusions about my sister."

"And do you know anyone who might have killed her?"

She considered this for a moment. "Not Raymond. He's nothing without her and nobody knows it better than him. Katherine *created* Raymond."

"Created him?"

Susan leaned forward, putting her elbows on her knees and giving me a conspiritorial smile. "All Raymond Garrett had when she met him was good financial sense and a half-way decent face. Katherine had him groomed for public life for the past ten or eleven years—image consultants, voice lessons—the whole nine yards."

"I had no idea. Why was it Raymond who had to be successful? Why not Katherine?"

Susan sat back and shrugged. "No intrigue. Katherine believed real power is usually hidden. She loved being the real power behind Raymond's public career."

"Who else do you think might have had something to gain from getting Katherine out of the way?"

"Raymond's girlfriend might have *thought* she had something to gain."

"There's a girlfriend?"

"Raymond's administrative assistant, Sherry Freeman."

I nodded, remembering the protective young woman guarding the portals of Garrett's privacy.

"This has been going on for almost two years now," Susan continued, "and I think she's getting a little impatient. She may even have figured out that Raymond was never going to leave Katherine. If so, it's about time. Raymond wasn't going anywhere. Katherine wouldn't be caught dead in anything as tacky as a divorce."

It occurred to me that Katherine *had* been caught dead, and I was certain she would have liked *that* choice far less.

It was perfectly understandable to me. As Amelia Rose had noted, the human capacity for self-delusion is monumental, and in my experience no one is more willing to delude herself than a woman in love with a married man. "You said Annie made 'most people' feel good. Was Katherine the exception?"

Susan nodded. "As far as Katherine was concerned, everything Annie did was wrong. The way she dressed, the way she talked, the way she was raising Sam . . ."

"They had a fight at Katherine's birthday party, didn't they?"

"A whopper." She held up a hand as if to stop me from jumping to an unwarranted conclusion. "You have to understand about Annie—the term 'mild-mannered' refers to someone much more likely to blow a gasket than my big sister. I've heard her raise her voice half a dozen times in my whole life. Come to think of it, it was usually at Katherine, back when we were kids. Katherine had a way of driving everyone around her crazy if she didn't get her way."

"So she usually got it."

"It got to be a habit to give in and preserve the peace. And not just for Annie, I might add. We all did it."

"When did you stop doing it?"

"Me personally? When I left home. I wasn't as much a part of the family dynamic after that. I could look at it from outside and choose not to participate. I could choose to stay away from Katherine."

"Except on holidays and her birthday," I put in. Nobody seemed to have the courage to turn down a summons to one of Katherine's special parties, even the ostensibly independent Susan.

"Yes. Except then."

I indicated the album on her lap. "Would it be all right if I looked at that?"

"Please." She handed it to me. "I'll get us something cold to drink."

The temperature in Susan's house was comfortable, but driving around in the Cascade summer kept me perpetually thirsty. "I'd like that," I replied. "Thanks." I opened the album and began turning pages.

The earliest pictures were of Annie as a young girl with a small Susan and Joey clinging to her skirts. The parents were in some of the pictures, too, but seemed more like background figures, watching their children grow and change in a distant sort of way. Later, Katherine showed up, first as an infant in arms, later taking center stage and dominating each picture with a burning vitality. The rest of the family seemed to fade all around her as she grew brighter.

As she entered adolescence, Katherine's sexual presence was considerable. Her blue eyes flamed from the pictures, the dark brows and delicate features framed by dark, curly hair. She could make anyone else who dared appear in the same shot look practically invisible. The way she used her body to occupy space and to relate to the males in the pictures showed a very early awareness of the power she possessed. She was frequently seen next to Joey, older than her by six years, and frequently laying a possessive hand on his arm or leg as if to establish some special claim to him.

It was impossible to tell what Joey thought of all this. He looked slightly uncomfortable, but that was also true of the pictures of Joey by himself. He didn't look like a person who felt at home in the world in general. By this time there were no parents in the pictures.

Susan came back into the room with two glasses of iced mineral water and handed me one as she sat down. She glanced at the open album on my lap. "Mom and Dad died just before Katherine turned eleven. She seemed to take it better than the rest of us, but some people suffer inside where others can't see." She shrugged. "At least that's what I've always told myself. All I could see with my own eyes was that it didn't really seem to affect her one way or another."

Part of me really wanted to hear all the gruesome details about Katherine's childhood, but I had a feeling it would take all day just to scrape the surface. The basics were fairly obvious: For whatever reason, Katherine Garrett, née Holland, had turned out to be nobody's friend, and nobody's idea of a loving sister. My immediate interest in Katherine lay in the more recent past, like about seventeen years ago.

"When Annie was staying up on the north coast, before Sam was born, that is, you were the one who gave Katherine her phone number in Trinidad, weren't you?"

"Well, Katherine was in trouble and she needed someone. I wasn't the someone she needed."

I decided to ignore the arch tone of that last part and pushed on. "What kind of trouble?"

Susan hesitated, seeming to mull it over. "I don't suppose there's any harm in telling you. I'm sure it will come out soon, anyway. She was pregnant."

"She told you that?"

"She didn't have to. I knew she was seeing a married man—I'd seen them together more than once—and she was clearly desperate to get out of town. She was already showing. She had such a tiny figure, it was obvious. She was probably three months along by then, at least."

"So you sent her to Annie?"

"There was nothing I could do for her." There it was again—a coolness in Susan's voice that said volumes remained unspoken here.

"Did she continue the pregnancy?"

Susan sipped her tea. A slight smile was beginning to form on her mouth. "You haven't heard this story yet from Annie, have you?"

I wasn't about to let Susan's version of the family history get by me for the sake of being honest. "What story?" I inquired as innocently as you please.

"I guess all this was supposed to stay under wraps, but I don't know how they planned to make it work forever. I don't know why it worked as long as it did." She leaned forward slightly. "Katherine had the baby and Annie raised him. Sam is actually Katherine's son."

I allowed my eyes to widen in an expression meant to convey surprise. "I see. That explains a lot."

"It explains their whole relationship from that day on," Susan agreed. "And it was a rotten one. Everyone would have been better off if Katherine had released him for adoption. Even Sam."

"Did Katherine know you knew about this? Does Annie?"

"Hey, it meant so much to them to have their little secret, I just let them think I was as ignorant as everyone else. But no way did I ever believe that Annie was the one who'd gotten pregnant and left town. I knew Annie better than that. She'd have married Robby Fry and they'd have a houseful of kids and pets by now, and Katherine wouldn't have had an excuse to make Annie's life miserable for the next sixteen years."

"So you probably also know who the father was," I prompted.

Her expression became heavily guarded. "His name is Paul Gregory. You may know him from local television."

"Of course. Isn't he also running for Congress? Against Raymond Garrett?"

"Yes," she replied, looking evenly and deliberately into my eyes. "I believe he is."

It was time to change the subject before I betrayed my interest in Susan's reaction to the subject of Paul Gregory. "Your brother Joey was in the house when Katherine and Annie had their argument."

"Yes, Joey and I were watching television in the family room, and Annie and Katherine were in the dining room." Susan seemed to lighten up a bit now that the conversation had taken a different direction. "Neither of us paid any attention to what they were saying until it started to get loud."

"They were shouting?"

"Katherine never shouted in an argument. She made other people shout. And scream, and tear their hair. It was Annie who was shouting."

"You heard her threaten to kill Katherine?"

"I heard the words 'I'll kill you.' I couldn't swear to the context."

"So you went into the dining room to see what was happening?"

"Yes. They stopped talking as soon as we came in, and Annie was terribly embarrassed as you might imagine, and even Katherine seemed a little shaken. I remember Joey making her a drink and comforting her after Annie ran out."

"Were Joey and Katherine very close?"

What I saw on Susan Brock's face for just an instant might almost be called a smirk. Then it was gone, replaced by studied neutrality. "Yes," she said, "very close."

# CHAPTER 22

· · · · · · · · · · · · · · ·

JOEY HOLLAND HADN'T RETURNED MY PHONE MESSAGE, either, and after reviewing his childhood in photographs, I was ready to get a good look at the man in person. As long as I was driving around town dropping in on people, I looked up his address in my notes and headed in that direction until I came to a quiet neighborhood of ever-so-slightly run-down houses and not quite new cars.

I found Joey's house and parked out front, hoping I'd get a better—or at least a more useful—reception than I had at Raymond's. A dusty brown sedan occupied the middle of the driveway, sporting several intersecting rows of cat footprints and a long-haired black and white cat who opened his eyes slightly as I pulled up, then seemed to decide I was of no interest in his scheme of things.

Joey Holland's house was a little better-kept than most of his neighbors, but it had seen better days. A few roof shingles had gone south, and the exterior paint was a year or two past its prime. Attached to an iron lamppost at the corner of the driveway and sidewalk was a black mailbox and a hanging sign that read JOSEPH AND REBECCA HOLLAND. I opened the car door to the summer afternoon with a sigh of regret and walked up to the front door.

I could hear the chime of the doorbell, but this time there were no footsteps mysteriously advancing and retreating. There was also no answer. I knocked and got the same result.

As I stepped away from the front porch, I heard a scraping sound coming from behind the house. Where the driveway ended at the house line I noticed a narrow cement walk that extended back to a tall fence with a gate. I followed it, and the cat jumped down from his perch on the fender and followed me in turn as far as the gate. There was no latch on this side, and the hole that might once have held a latch string was empty.

"Hello. Anybody home?" I called over the gate.

A moment later there was a fumbling with the latch, and the gate was pushed toward me. I stepped back and let it swing open across the narrow walk. The cat stepped through and darted past the man who stood there.

It was easy to recognize Joey Holland from the photographs I'd seen just a little while ago. He was six years or so older than Katherine—perhaps forty—but his face retained a rounded softness that was totally childlike. His dark blue eyes were a bit overlarge in an unlined face under straight light brown hair, and his smile belonged on a shy little boy. "Can I help you?" The voice was also young— slightly high-pitched and very soft.

"I'm Caley Burke, a private investigator working for your sister Annie. I called yesterday, but . . ."

"Burke. Yes, I got your message, but I'm afraid I haven't gotten around to answering it yet. Come on back." He turned and walked through the gateway into a well-kept backyard, terraced with railroad ties and brightened with carefully cultivated perennials that looked healthy and bloomed like crazy. It looked like Joey worked hard on his garden to maintain such perfection. That, or some mad gardener had been here and planted all this stuff a couple of hours ago.

"Pardon the dirt," he said, brushing his hands, clad in cotton garden gloves, against his khaki chinos. "It's a full-time job just keeping up with the weeds and the bugs. And to tell you the truth, it also keeps my mind off all these things. . . ." He sighed deeply. "My sister Katherine was cremated today."

"Yes, I know."

Joey stood, hands down at his sides, looking off into the distance. A silence began, growing stronger the longer I let it live.

"You've done a beautiful job with the garden," I commented sincerely. I had finally learned to keep house plants alive, and the little balcony outside my French doors was crowded with spider plants and cactus and wandering Jews, but anything that flowered, or in my case didn't, was a total mystery to me.

Joey regarded me expectantly, a certain tension evident in his posture. He was being perfectly polite, but it was easy to see he'd rather be alone right now. Well, I never said I liked this part of the job, but people frequently say the most useful things when they're a little off-balance. If I needed a reminder of that, I had only to remember my conversation with Liz DeLora.

"I hate to bother you, Mr. Holland, but I'm trying to clear your sister of murder charges, and I'm hoping you can help."

He didn't comment on that, but seemed to come out of his distracted state a little. "Let's find some shade. I'll get us some iced tea."

He led me to a picnic table under one of those back-yard pavilion things of the sort that people rent for weddings. This one was a little small for a wedding, but it tamed the relentless afternoon sun and let through a breeze that was almost cooling for Cascade in July. "I'll be right back," he promised.

I sat in the shade and looked out over Joey Holland's painstakingly cultivated garden. A high fence of dark wood surrounded a deep green lawn and a system of decks. A colorfully striped swing set and sandbox dominated one section of the yard.

Joey and his wife of ten years had recently separated, Susan had told me, and she and the two kids had gone to live with her parents in Oregon. It must be hard on him to stay here alone with all these reminders of his family, I thought, and at the same time I couldn't help wondering if Rebecca Holland had timed their separation to avoid an obligatory appearance at Katherine's birthday party.

Joey came back with two brightly colored plastic glasses full of ice cubes and tea and handed me one as he took a seat on the opposite bench. "I forgot to ask if you take lemon or sugar," he said.

"This is just fine," I told him. I sipped at the tea, fearing the worst and finding my fears vindicated. It was instant. I was thirsty, but maybe not that thirsty. I took a drink for the sake of form and set the glass down on the table.

"Mr. Holland, I appreciate that this is a difficult time for you and your family. I'd rather not be disturbing you right now, but I can't emphasize enough how important it is for Annie that I find some evidence—any kind of evidence— that might clear her. I know the police don't agree with me, but I don't think Annie killed Katherine. I'm doing some investigation into the night Katherine was killed, trying to find any information that might help me prove that."

"You mean you want to find someone else? Another murderer?"

"Well, I think there *has* to be someone else, don't you?"

"Yes. I suppose there must be."

"You don't sound too convinced," I ventured.

"That's not it at all," he assured me. "It's just that I heard the argument between them—you know, when Annie said she'd kill Katherine? I guess you know that much already."

"Yes, Annie told me about it."

"Well, it scared the shit out of me, if you want to know. I've known Annie all my life, and I never heard her so angry. She was mad enough to kill Katherine right then."

"I've been mad enough to kill a time or two myself," I said. "Haven't you?"

Joey nodded thoughtfully.

"But being angry at someone—even angry enough to *think* you want to kill them doesn't mean you're going to do it. Pardon me for bringing up something so unpleasant, but killing someone the way Katherine was killed takes a lot more than a burst of momentary anger."

"I suppose you're right. I've never given it that much thought—what makes people kill. But if it wasn't Annie, who could it have been?"

"I don't know. I'm going to be following up on some leads, though. I've already talked to Annie, and I'm going to be getting some more details from her. Have you been by to visit her yet?"

The question made him squirm, and I was without sympathy. "I haven't really been able to get over there yet. I've been pretty busy. Susan's been to see her," he added, as if that let him off the hook.

It didn't. "Did you know she was arraigned this morning on a charge of first-degree murder?"

His eyes widened. "First degree?"

"That's right. What were you expecting?"

Joey shook his head. "I don't know . . . I guess I thought it would be a lesser charge."

"The prosecution is claiming premeditation. Katherine was killed several hours after she and Annie argued— plenty of time for Annie to have gone away and planned the murder. Only I don't think she did, and that's why I'm on the case."

"I see." He waited for me to go on.

"I think Annie needs to know that the people who love her are on her side," I said, hoping to elicit some family feeling from Joey Holland. "I'm sure it would mean a lot to her to see you right now. But that's really none of my business." Not that I'd let that stop me, I noted silently.

"Now I'd like to get back to the argument. You and Susan were in the family room when Annie and Katherine started arguing. How much of their conversation did you hear?"

Joey looked exasperated. "You know, I've already answered that question and about a hundred others for the police."

"Yes, I know. But the police aren't going to give me access to those interviews. My investigation isn't an official one, so I have to cover all the same ground, with less to go on."

Joey sighed. "Okay. Here's what happened." He took a thirsty gulp of his drink, and I smelled the unmistakable scent of cheap bourbon. It seemed this was a hard day all around.

"Susan and I were watching television. Raymond had disappeared right after Katherine opened her presents—I think he was in his office. Everyone else had gone except for Lila, who was in her room, I guess. Annie and Katherine were in the dining room having this conversation, and after a few minutes we could hear it getting a little loud in there."

"Is that when you went to the dining room to see what was going on?"

"No, not right away. I figured it was personal, and Susan seemed to feel the same way. Every now and then one of us would look over in that direction, but we thought we'd wait it out and let them settle it between them."

"Could you understand anything of what was being said?"

"Not at first. Then we could hear some of what Annie was saying. Susan didn't seem to want to hear it, though. She got up and turned up the volume on the TV to drown them out."

"What made you decide to go into the dining room, finally?"

"Annie was losing it." He shook his head, remembering. "She was shouting at Katherine, something about 'I'd kill you before I'd let you do that.' "

"Do what?"

He shrugged. "I don't have a clue. As soon as we came in, they shut up. Katherine left the room and Annie just stood there trying to pull herself back together. Susan acted kind of disgusted with both of them. She went back in the other room until after Annie left."

"Did you ask Annie what the fight was about?"

"No. Not that I wasn't curious, but there wasn't time to ask her anything. She looked at me, and she looked at the door Katherine had gone through, and she started crying and ran out of the house."

This was pretty much the story I'd had from Susan, minus the part about acting disgusted. Neither of them had heard anything except Annie's shouted death threat, and Raymond seemed to have heard nothing at all, or ignored what he did hear. Same with Lila Jensen.

I felt the need to tiptoe through this next question, but however delicately, it had to be asked. I'd been finding that when I scratched Katherine Garrett's family and "friends," strange information sometimes came to the surface. "I don't mean to give offense, Mr. Holland, but I've met some people since Katherine's death that didn't like her much—you might even say hated her."

Joey nodded slowly. "Yes, I guess that's true. Katherine was a strong woman—ambitious. A lot of people don't like strong women."

I like strong women and I was pretty sure her inner strength had little to do with Katherine's popularity rating. I tried coming from another direction.

"I understand you and Katherine were close."

He blinked. "No, not particularly." He must have seen my eyes widen. "I mean I loved my sister, of course, but we didn't really have that much in common, even when we were kids. She was six years younger than I was, had different friends . . . ."

"I understand. Not all siblings are close, of course." Not all siblings are close, but it didn't fit with what Susan had said about Joey and Katherine earlier that day.

"Well, then, would you say you got along with Katherine?"

"I suppose, whatever that means. We seldom argued, but no one really argued with Katherine."

"So I've heard. But that wasn't the same thing as getting along, was it?"

Joey chuckled, but without a feeling of real humor. "No, it was actually more like learning to give up before the fight."

"So you all learned to let Katherine win no matter what?"

"We learned to stay out of the way when Katherine made up her mind she wanted something."

"Or some*one*?"

Joey wiped the sweat from his forehead with one of his gloves. "Yeah," he said, his mouth forming a bitter line that couldn't exactly be called a smile. "Especially some*one*."

# CHAPTER 23

"A LOT HAS HAPPENED SINCE THE LAST TIME WE HAD tea together," Miss Rose commented as she poured my cup.

A fragrance like flowers drifted up to me. I smiled with unexpected pleasure.

"Jasmine today," said Miss Rose. "My favorite flavor for a contemplative afternoon. Oolong is my choice for mornings, and I don't care for Earl Grey at all, do you?"

"I don't know. I'm not sure I've ever tried it."

"Tastes like perfume. Some swear by it, but I don't even keep it for company." She proffered one of the delicious shortbread biscuits.

"Thank you. I take it you've heard about what happened to Katherine Garrett?"

"From several people. In excruciating detail. In some ways, this town is as small as it ever was. I just sit here and the news comes right to my door, just like always."

"And poor Annie!" She sighed with feeling as she picked up a sugar cube with little silver tongs and placed it carefully in her empty cup before pouring tea over it. "I can't imagine what it must be like being locked up like that. And for killing your own sister, too."

"Do you think she could have killed Katherine?"

Miss Rose shook her head firmly. "The Annie I knew couldn't kill *bugs*. I remember when Annie was working for me, I had to have my nephew in to get rid of roaches in the kitchen. These old houses all have them, you know. But Annie was too softhearted to do away with them. Of course I suppose that doesn't mean you couldn't kill a person. It's a completely different impulse, I'm sure. Still, my money's on Raymond."

"Susan told me Raymond knew he was nothing without Katherine."

"Well, people get tired of being nothing. Katherine had great plans for Raymond—this congressional race in the fall, a few years in the governor's mansion, then—who knows? But she never let Raymond forget how much he needed her to get there. I can easily imagine him chafing under her low estimation of his potential. That, and I understand they very seldom slept together."

I thought back to Toby's photographs—the bed with one rumpled side, and Raymond's statement that he hadn't been worried when he woke in the night and she wasn't there. Her things were in the night table drawer, though.

"They shared a room," I said.

"And a bed. But from what I've heard, you could have built a stone wall down the middle and not made much difference in their sex life."

I choked on my tea and had to cough into my napkin for several seconds.

Miss Rose laughed merrily. "You mustn't make the mistake of thinking your generation invented sex. As a matter of fact, if my generation hadn't been indulging with some regularity, we'd never have gotten around to yours, now would we? Or perhaps you think because I never married I've remained pure as the driven snow the past eighty-seven years."

I was still coughing, but managed to shake my head.

"All right, then. Try some lemon for that cough." She pushed a dish of lemon wedges over to my side of the tray.

"I could tell you stories"—she sighed—"but some things are better left private, I suppose."

I set down my cup and regained my composure, though I couldn't keep from smiling. "Thanks for setting me straight."

"No bother. So I've got Raymond Garrett in the 'who killed Katherine' pool. Who have you got?"

"Nobody yet. I'm trying to keep an open mind."

"Or maybe there are just too many likely suspects, eh?" She gave me a little smile as she raised her bone-china cup to her lips.

"That about covers it."

I sipped at my tea. It was even more wonderful than what she'd served the last time, and as Miss Rose asserted, perfect for contemplation, or so it seemed to me. I was feeling more contemplative as I sipped, and more relaxed, too. I settled back a bit in the high-back Victorian chair. "I guess if I had to bet, I'd put a nickel on Chip DeLora. Or his wife. They both had reason to hate her. But then, so did a lot of people."

Miss Rose nodded. "Chip, yes. Raymond's young business partner. Gossip has it he's the brains of the outfit. And I understand he's quite handsome, too."

"Quite. A fact that wasn't lost on Katherine."

"Not surprising," she remarked. "It was always someone."

"That reminds me. There's another development I thought you might like to know about, but this one has to be kept under your hat."

Miss Rose patted her silver hair. "There's a lot under this hat, Caley Burke."

I knew the feeling, and I knew Amelia Rose could be trusted with this information. "I've seen a copy of Sam Holland's birth certificate. It lists his mother as Katherine Garrett and his father as Paul Gregory."

Miss Rose didn't bat an eyelash as she considered this information. "That's not possible," she said flatly.

"Yes. It seems Katherine got pregnant and told Gregory. He gave her money for an abortion, but she didn't want one. She went to Trinidad, where Annie was staying, and Annie stayed with her through the pregnancy. Then Annie talked Katherine into letting her keep Sam."

"That all sounds plausible," said Miss Rose. "I have no trouble believing Katherine could be the mother. What I'm saying is that Paul Gregory couldn't be the father."

"She was seeing him. Susan Holland told me she saw Katherine and Paul out together shortly before Katherine left town seventeen years ago."

"Oh, I'm not saying she didn't sleep with him. I'm saying he couldn't be Sam's father."

"I don't get it."

"What color are Sam's eyes?"

"Dark brown. Almost black."

"And Katherine's?"

I gave this some thought. "I have no idea."

"I'll tell you, then. They were blue. And so are Paul Gregory's. I see him every night on the news, and I've noticed. He's very attractive, you know."

"Only on the outside. So Katherine and Gregory couldn't have had a brown-eyed child together? Is that from all your years of observation?"

"No, it's from Gregor Mendel."

The name was familiar, from tenth-grade biology. "Peas?"

"Genetics. Peas, people, what have you. It takes a dominant gene to produce brown eyes, and people with blue eyes, which comes from two recessive genes, don't have any dominant genes for eye color to contribute to the job."

I shook my head in admiration as I filed this fact away for future reference. "Why did she put Gregory's name on the certificate, I wonder?"

"Perhaps she believed he *was* the baby's father. Or perhaps he seemed the most likely candidate to give her money. Or perhaps she was trying to protect someone else."

"Do you know of anyone else she might have been seeing at the time?"

Miss Rose gave this some thought. "Boys were always chasing Katherine, I suppose. I don't know of any boy in particular." She smiled, reminding me somehow of a fox with shining white hair. "Of course, Katherine wasn't looking for a boy."

"You mean she was looking for a man?"

All I got for that was another sly smile.

So if not Paul Gregory, who? I'd thought the case of Sam's parenthood closed, if not entirely happily. Now it was just as up in the air as ever, and I was growing more confused by the minute.

As I drove away from the big house by the river, I looked over in the passenger seat where a white gift box rested; a gift from Amelia Rose. "I think you'll enjoy your tea at home more if you drink it from the proper kind of cup," she said, handing me the box as I was ready to leave.

I'd opened it to reveal a bone-china cup and saucer—pale and delicate and translucent, hand-painted with a design of perfect pink roses.

"This was a gift from my father on my sixteenth birthday," Miss Rose told me, pleased with my evident admiration of her gift. "He brought it back from a trip to England."

"Then I couldn't possibly accept it," I said with genuine regret, handing back the box. "It's too important to you."

"Oh, my dear," said Miss Rose, "my father gave me a bone-china cup and saucer every birthday for twenty-two years. I'd hate to see them go to someone who wouldn't value them, so every now and again I give one away to someone who will." She pressed the box into my hands. "You must take it, or you'll make me unhappy."

I was pretty uncertain of my voice right then, so I gave Miss Rose a hug which she returned warmly. Now I was looking forward to going home and making a pot of tea after Sam and I got back from the mall.

Poor Sam. I hated to think of him in those terms, knowing how much he'd hate thinking anyone pitied him, but it hurt me to think of what he was going through. First he couldn't find out who his father was, then someone came and took his mother away, then out of the blue he got two new parents, one he didn't know and one he didn't like, and that one had been brutally murdered.

Now he was finding himself haunted by the image of his natural mother being bludgeoned to death by a faceless killer, and somewhere in there, I was sure, were feelings of guilt for his lifelong dislike of her. I felt very tired when I thought about having to break the news that she had created yet one more mystery before she was through: the true identity of his father.

Why had Katherine wanted Paul Gregory to think he was the father of her child? Was it because she believed it herself? Had she been seeing someone else at the same time and picked Gregory as the most likely father, or at least the most likely to pay for her silence? Did she order Annie to keep Gregory's identity a secret because she knew he wasn't responsible for her pregnancy? And who was this mysterious other man? Who was the dark-eyed man who didn't know he had a son?

Susan had said Katherine was at least three months pregnant when she came to her for help. What month did that make it? I realized that I'd been so intent on certain parts of Sam's birth certificate that I hadn't even registered other parts. I didn't have a clue as to when his birthday was. I'd have to see if I could get a look at it without alerting him that there was yet another mystery surrounding his birth—the poor kid had been through more than enough and there'd be time to tell him later when he'd had a chance to recover.

"Let's get out of here and get some dinner and go shopping," I said as I walked into the apartment.

Sam looked up from his book and smiled. "I thought you were never going to ask," he said.

•  •  •

We walked up and down the inside of the mall, which wasn't terribly large as malls go. This one had been a block of one of the main streets in the center of town. Those streets now ran around all sides of the enclosure in a system of one-way streets that managed to confuse most visitors to downtown. Instead of trendy new shops, the storefronts were the originals, some dating back more than fifty years. The asphalt had been replaced by polished stone, and lots of trees and shrubs and the skylights to keep them growing completed the decor.

Once we saw a sheriff's deputy prowling near the arcade. We ducked into a card shop and waited for her to go past, then continued in the opposite direction, laughing nervously and feeling a little like fugitives. We chose a cafe and settled into a booth to have dinner.

I'd sneaked a look at the birth certificate while Sam was in the bathroom, before we'd left the apartment. According to record, Samuel John Holland was born in mid-October weighing eight pounds and thirteen ounces, which seemed to settle any question of his being premature.

I did the math quickly. Sam would have been conceived in January. Katherine had come to Susan visibly pregnant, perhaps in her fourth month. That would make it around April or May. When had she sprung the news on Gregory, and how soon after they'd started sleeping together? When I knew that, I'd know whether she'd set Gregory up for a sucker, but even without knowing, I had a definite feeling she had. It just fit Katherine's style.

"How much of a person do you think is like their parents?" Sam asked me while we ate our dinner.

"Do you mean how much is born into a person as opposed to how much is learned later?"

He nodded.

"I wish I knew. I don't think I'm anything like my parents, but sometimes I'm surprised by how much I look

and sound like my mother. They gave me my looks, but I
don't think anything like them." This was not only what I
knew Sam would be relieved to hear, but pretty much what
I was relieved to think. My parents are strangers to me in
many ways, though I love them. They love me, too, but
I'm an alien child, unlike any they ever planned to comfort
them in their old age. "I'm actually a lot like one of my
father's sisters—the black sheep of the family. The thought
pleases me."

"I wonder who I'm like," he said.

I wondered, too. Annie Holland's influence was all over
Sam in the way she'd loved him unconditionally and nur-
tured his self-esteem, but there was a kind of intensity to
him that she lacked. A fire burned in there somewhere that
was unlike Annie or Susan or Joey, and there was an inner
humanity that was totally unlike Katherine. Annie may have
been responsible for raising him to be a human being, but
the shadow-father had left his mark on Sam in his dark good
looks and that inner electricity. As we left the restaurant and
walked through the mall, I found myself looking at the men
we passed and wondering, much as Sam had wondered all
his life.

# CHAPTER 24

. . . . . . . . . . . . . . . . . . .

"HERE'S DRAKE'S," I SAID. "WANT TO LOOK IN HERE FOR a while?"

"Sure," Sam replied, and followed me inside the big glass doors.

I looked up and saw the windows to the store offices overhead. The curtains to Melissa Drake's office were open, and I could see her gesturing to someone with a lit cigarette. "Pick out some jeans and shirts and whatever else you need," I told Sam as I handed him a credit card. "I'll bill you. I have to talk to someone upstairs for a minute."

"Oh, it's you," Melissa Drake greeted me. "I'm sorry I've forgotten your name. How rude."

"It's Caley Burke, and by the end of the day I've sometimes forgotten it myself. Can I come in?"

"Sure. We were just finishing up. I'll go over those orders in the morning," she said to the woman she'd been talking to when I knocked. "Put the folders on my desk and I'll see you at eight-thirty."

"Yes, Mrs. Drake." The woman set down the folders and left the room, rolling her eyes at Melissa as she walked past me and turned to close the door.

I gave her a quick grin, then turned back to Melissa, who, I was not surprised to see, was lighting a cigarette from the glowing end of her previous one. "Do you remember the matter we were discussing a few days ago?" I asked her by way of introduction. In fact, I was pretty certain she never forgot anything having to do with her ex-husband.

"Of course." Her eyes glittered. "Is there something new I should know about?" There was no mistaking Melissa Drake's eagerness for any nobler emotion; she wanted more dirt on Richard the way some people want sex or money. I was about to disappoint her and I didn't feel at all bad about it.

"Richard doesn't seem to be the father of Annie Holland's son," I said.

"You believed him when he told you that?" she asked, wide-eyed. "Of course he wouldn't admit it—he never admitted it!"

"There are tests that could prove it conclusively one way or another," I told her, "and Richard admitted to me that he wasn't faithful to you, but I'm pretty certain he got a bad rap on this one."

Melissa took a deep drag on her cigarette. "I'll be god-damned," she said. "I wonder if you're right. Who *is* the father, do you think?"

"That's confidential, I'm afraid." And utterly unknown to boot, since my talk with Miss Rose, but that could remain my little secret. "I just thought it was something you'd like to know."

"Of course." Her voice was utterly flat, her eyes fixed on an imaginary dimension. She sat down in her desk chair. "Thank you."

Poor Melissa. I'd just removed a support she'd been leaning on. It might take her a while to find another one.

I let myself out.

The sight of a bank of public phones just around the corner from the stairway to Melissa's office made me stop and reach into my portfolio for my address book and Robby Fry's home phone number. I was either going to do a good deed or be a meddling busybody, depending on your interpretation. Whichever it turned out to be, I was determined to go through with it.

"You think she'd really like to see me?" Robby asked. "It's been an awfully long time. She has another life now."

"I think her life is always going to need friends in it, Robby," I said. "And I think she might have something to tell you that you need to hear."

We came out a side entrance of the mall with our packages—clothes for Sam and a china teapot for me—and as I looked south I could see lights burning in the offices of Garrett Financial Services. Was it Chip DeLora working late, or was Raymond Garrett spending some time at his office? Possibly neither, but there was no harm in finding out. I walked Sam back to the apartment, and after making arrangements with Julian and Carl for him to do his laundry downstairs, I left again in my car.

The light upstairs was still on when I pulled up across the street and about fifty feet down the block from GFS.

The Mercedes sedan I'd seen in Raymond Garrett's driveway was parked under one of the big oak trees, and close behind it was a sporty little red job with a personalized plate reading FREEWOMN. Sherry Freeman was not, apparently, worried about having to be inconspicuous; not in *this* vehicle.

I got out of my car and walked to the pay phone in front of White Mountain Burgers, now dark and locked tight. The phone directory attached to the tray beneath the telephone was missing a lot of pages, but fortunately not the one that contained Paul Gregory's home phone number.

I kept an eye on the upstairs office windows as I dialed. After three rings a woman's voice answered, out of breath. "Hello?"

"Mrs. Gregory?"

"Yes . . ."

No sense getting Gregory in any more trouble than he'd already managed for himself. I decided to do what I do so well—lie. "I'm calling from the station. There's been a change in his interview schedule tomorrow—I need to go over it with him."

"Okay."

"And one more thing," I hurried to add. "I'm filling in some logs and I can't remember what night it was last week that Mr. Gregory was out of town. Was that Wednesday?"

"No, it was Tuesday. We went to Reno. I'll get Paul for you. Hold on a minute."

In a lot less than a minute, Gregory was on the line. "What's up?"

"Mr. Gregory, this is Caley Burke."

"What the hell are you trying to pull?" This in a voice barely more than a whisper—Mrs. Gregory was probably not too far away.

"You're covered for the night of the murder, so I'll make you a deal. I'll tell you something you need to know if you tell me something I need to know."

"I don't need anything from you."

"Don't be too sure. Answer this question for me, and be absolutely certain of your answer." Before he could refuse, I went on. "When did you have your fling with Katherine Holland, and how soon after that did she tell you she was pregnant?"

There was a long moment of silence. "It was March. Early March."

"And it only lasted how long?"

"A week, ten days at most." There was a hint of impatience in his voice, or maybe he just didn't like being reminded of his youthful indiscretions, this being an election year.

"And she showed up again, what, six weeks later to tell you she was carrying your child?"

"Yeah, that's about right."

"You're sure about March?"

"Yes. I'm sure." He was clearly impatient now. "Why the hell are you asking me this?"

"And your eyes are blue, right—those aren't contacts or anything."

"Are you completely nuts?"

That was a subject for another time, I thought, but not an entirely irrelevant one. "Answer the question, please."

"They're blue, goddammit. Now it's your turn."

"Congratulations, Mr. Gregory—you're not a father. At least you're not Sam Holland's father; you'll have to ask your wife about the other two."

"Are you sure?" His voice contained a mixture of doubt and relief.

"Absolutely. I can't do anything about your mysterious phone caller, and even you admit to cheating on your wife, but you can feel free to deny paternity, at least."

The phone went dead. That's gratitude for you, I thought. Not so much as a thank you.


It seemed like days later when the office lights went off upstairs at Garrett Financial Services. According to Mickey it had only been a little more than an hour, but he wasn't sitting there going numb in the behind and trying desperately to stay awake for something that might or might not happen.

Now something was definitely happening, and my level of alertness jumped several degrees at once. The door to the street opened and a man and a woman stepped out, arguing loudly. I slid down in my seat and rolled down my window, slowly and quietly.

"I can't believe I've given up the last two years of my life for you, and this is what I get!" The woman's voice was shrill and verging on tears.

"Sherry, please!"

"Oh, you'd like me to be quiet, huh? Well, I've been quiet, Raymond. For two years. I've kept your dirty little secret until the time was right to tell Katherine. *Now* what's your excuse, Raymond? There *is* no Katherine!"

"Sherry, I never meant to mislead you, but . . ."

The next thing I heard was the unmistakable sound of a slap. It had a lot of force behind it, too. I could imagine the mark on Raymond's face.

"It's always 'Please wait, Sherry,' and 'Please be patient, Sherry,' and 'Just a little more time, Sherry.' " Sherry's voice, none too controlled to begin with, rose higher and higher, until I could have heard it a block away with my windows up. "You miserable son of a bitch! You never meant to leave her at all, did you? Even when she's *dead* you can't leave her!"

Raymond apparently had nothing to say to that—nothing I could hear, anyway. A car door slammed and a car roared to life and pulled away with an angry screech of burning rubber.

I peeked over the bottom of my car window. Raymond Garrett stood on the sidewalk next to his Mercedes, looking more than a bit lost. I waited until he had pulled off and turned the corner; then I started my car and drove in the direction he'd gone.

Raymond's situation seemed sadly typical of the married man who wants to play with the idea of leaving his wife. He'd found a woman willing to settle for the job of professional rival, but not forever. Almost no woman ever thinks she's going to settle forever, and Sherry was probably not an exception.

The truth is, though, and I knew this from sad experience, no matter how sincere you may think a man is about wanting a new life and a new woman in it, most men will keep two women on the line just about indefinitely, because one may be his hope (or in the worst-case scenario, his dope) but the other is his safety line.

Raymond Garrett's safety line had been cut suddenly, and Sherry Freeman had been forced to face the fact that he would never have let go on his own. Raymond had never intended to leave the shelter of Katherine's ambitions and Katherine's plans and Katherine's influence; even now that he was a free man, he wasn't willing to legitimize a back-street relationship that he probably had never intended to be anything else.

It had taken her a while to stop fooling herself about her chances of becoming Raymond's wife, but Sherry had finally figured out the facts of her clandestine romance. It seemed a safe bet that if Raymond Garrett were to catch fire right now, Sherry Freeman wouldn't throw her drink on him, unless maybe it were brandy.

Raymond took the most direct route home, and I followed him without taking any particular precautions against being seen; it seemed unlikely he'd notice in his present state. Even on the best of days people don't really notice if the car in their rearview mirror is one they've been seeing for several blocks or several miles unless it's a memorable car, and detectives seldom drive memorable cars.

Jake Baronian usually owned two or three nondescript vehicles besides his own silver Honda hatchback that looked a lot like millions of other cars on the street. When one of us had to do a long haul surveillance, we'd switch cars every night to avoid looking too familiar when the target looked out his window.

To avoid appearing in his view as much as possible, we'd park down the street or even around the corner if we could find a spot with a clear view of the place in question, and when tailing, we'd pay attention to the target's head. If he seemed to be checking his mirrors a lot, we'd hang back or even pass and turn off if we thought we could do it without losing the guy. It was easier with two people. Almost no one thinks about the possibility of a second tail once they've thrown the first.

In Raymond Garrett's case, like that of most ordinary citizens, a pair of headlights half a block back meant less than nothing. He drove across town to his own neighborhood and his own street, and I stayed behind him all the way. I'd been dying to talk to this guy, and I couldn't think of a better time than this.

# CHAPTER 25

"MR. GARRETT!" I HURRIED UP THE WALKWAY AND CAUGHT up with Raymond Garrett before he reached his front door. I was just a little out of breath when I got there. "Mr. Garrett, my name is Caley Burke, and I need to talk to you."

He stared at me blankly. It was the same handsome and distinguished-looking face that graced the Garrett for Congress posters, but the trademark look of calm confidence had been replaced by one of bewilderment. Raymond had a lot of other things on his mind right now, and from the impression I'd gathered of his intellect, there probably wasn't enough computing power in there to handle one more.

"Do I know you?" he asked. The voice was pleasant, controlled; not too deep, but well modulated. Voice lessons, Susan had said. It seemed they'd paid off.

I stood a few feet from him as he fumbled through a ring of keys for the right key to unlock his front door. "No, you don't know me. I'm a private investigator with Baronian Investigations, here in Cascade. I'm doing some investigative work on Annie's case."

Another blank look.

"Your sister-in-law?"

"Of course. It's a bit late, isn't it?" He consulted his watch to confirm this suspicion.

It was late, I realized—at least ten o'clock by now. I abandoned immediately the idea of telling Raymond I was here so late because I'd waited outside his office and followed him home. "I guess it is at that. I've been interviewing a lot of people connected to the case today, and I guess I just lost track of the time."

Raymond opened the door, hesitated a moment, then seemed to dismiss the idea of brushing me off. "Won't you come in?"

Total déjà vu. The door opened onto a place scarcely less familiar to me by now than my own apartment. There was the hall tree, the *ikebana,* the wood-block prints. The hallway to the bedrooms was on my right, I knew, the high-ceilinged family room straight ahead; to the left was the living room, now dark, and beyond that the dining room. *The* dining room. I suppressed a shudder.

My steps slowed as we passed that shadowed doorway. I had to stop myself from staring into that darkness, knowing what had taken place only a few feet away, beyond the next wall. I had to fight the feeling that Katherine Garrett was still lying in there under the dining table in a puddle of her own blackened blood.

"We can talk in the family room," Raymond said. If he was aware of my fascination with what lay beyond the doorway, he didn't show it. I followed him into yet another eerily familiar scene—oak floors and high windows and big couches. I knew the kitchen was to my left and Lila Jensen's rooms beyond that. I knew a swimming pool lay beyond the windows in the big back yard, an arrangement of redwood decks surrounding it. It was almost impossible not to crane my neck around and stare at every detail.

"Have a seat. I'll get us something to drink."

I sat down on one of the couches, pulling myself up to the edge of the seat so as not to look inappropriately relaxed on Raymond's home turf. Raymond disappeared into the kitchen and I took the opportunity to look around without being totally rude. As I compared the crime scene prints to reality, my mind shifted back and forth between the pictures and my real-time experience, taking mental snapshots to compare with the ones Toby had taken. It was making me dizzy. The photos hadn't always shown the exact relationship of each room to the others, but now I was getting a clearer picture of how this part of the house, at least, was laid out.

I peered into the darkened doorway to see how much of the living room I could see from here, and saw a flash of light as a car pulled up into the driveway. In the brief few moments before the engine cut off, I could see that the carpet had been taken up and the furniture removed from the room. I remembered the dark spots and splatters on the pale carpet. A Siamese cat regarded me calmly from the shadows.

All reminders of the violence that had taken Katherine's life would have been removed as soon as the police released the scene, I imagined. Still, I wanted more than anything I could think of to see it with my own eyes, to experience the reality of it that the photographs couldn't give me. This time next week there'd be new carpet and new furniture and new paint on the walls. I wondered if Raymond would continue to live here in the house. If it were me, I would already have moved far, far away.

Raymond came back with two bottles of cold beer. "Would you like one of these?" he asked, handing me one.

Well, what the hell. I took it. "Thanks." It was Sierra Nevada Pale Ale, I noted with appreciation, a California beer that stands up well to the best imports. I would have taken Raymond for a Bud drinker. "I think you have more company," I said, pointing in the direction of the driveway. There was the sound of a car door closing, followed by footsteps approaching the front door.

"It's probably just Lila coming back in," he remarked, sitting down and putting one leg up on the low coffee table. A moment later the front door opened and a tall, blond woman came into the entry hall.

Lila Jensen was fortyish and a bit severe-looking with her hair all pulled back on her neck, and not nearly attractive enough to have been a threat to Katherine, which was probably a good thing. I couldn't imagine being another woman in the same house with Katherine Garrett. She nodded at Raymond and me, then walked into the kitchen and through a doorway on the other side. I remembered that Lila didn't have a private entrance to her rooms, and wondered how much of a hand Katherine may have had in the design of the house. That kind of petty control seemed like her.

"I hope you don't mind me coming by at such a difficult time," I began, knowing full well that he must, "but I don't want to see Annie Holland stand trial for a murder she didn't commit."

Raymond sat down across from me and twisted the cap off his beer. "I'm only just now beginning to realize Katherine's really dead," he said. "It's taken me all this time to have it really sink in." A frown line appeared between the silver eyebrows, making him appear more petulant than bereaved.

"I know it must be difficult," I offered.

He took a drink of the beer. "But she is dead, and someone killed her. The police say it was Annie, and they're professionals." The implication, punctuated by a raised eyebrow, seemed to be that I was not.

"Does the term 'presumption of innocence' ring a bell, Mr. Garrett?"

"That's for the courts to decide when Annie goes to trial, Ms. Burke."

I could see we were getting off on the wrong foot, here. Jake would have handled this better, I reminded myself, but I couldn't exactly call him and ask him to take over. I took a deep breath and a drink of my beer, and started over. "I'm sorry. It was wrong of me to expect you to jump on the bandwagon for Annie's defense just because I come in here and declare her innocence. Will you answer a few questions for me, though?"

Raymond seemed mollified by my conciliatory gesture. "I suppose that wouldn't hurt anything."

"Tuesday," I began, "during your wife's birthday party, you left the festivities and went into your office."

"Yes," he said. "I had some work to catch up on. I'd already given Katherine her present."

"The vase. A Souvelle, I believe."

The eyebrow went up again, this time in surprise. "Yes. It's one of a kind, you know."

"I know. It's also the murder weapon."

Raymond frowned at this reminder. "So what was your actual question?"

"Just that I wondered if you heard the argument between Annie and Katherine, or anything that was said afterwards."

"No. I can't hear anything much when I'm in my office. I didn't hear about the argument until the next day."

"Mrs. Garrett didn't tell you about it later?"

"Katherine and I didn't speak again that evening," he said, lowering his eyes. Barring the possibility that Raymond had been her killer, he and Katherine had never spoken again, and I wondered how many things may have remained unstated between them.

"So you went to bed alone, and Mrs. Garrett didn't come into the bedroom?" Of course I already knew she hadn't, but I was curious about how he'd handle the question.

I wasn't disappointed as I watched Raymond compose his face for what was probably a familiar lie. He'd never looked so much like a politician. "Katherine had a problem sleeping," he said in carefully controlled tones. "She didn't want to disturb me, so she frequently slept in another room."

"I see. When did you get up and go out to the dining room?"

"I guess it was about six the next morning. I went into the kitchen and put on some coffee. Then I walked into the dining room . . ."

I knew what came next, and it would have been kinder of me to interrupt him at this point and go on to something less traumatic. I made a quick decision to forsake the humanitarian award in favor of a first-hand reaction. "Yes? Then what happened?"

"I saw blood everywhere. Smelled blood." His eyes had gone unfocused as he went back in his mind to that morning, a trip I didn't envy him. "I could just see her arms sticking out from under the table on that side. At first I thought it might be someone else, but then I recognized her rings." I could see the emotions playing back across his face as he spoke. Raymond seemed to wear everything on his face when he wasn't in politician mode. He'd make a piss-poor liar.

"Is that when you called the police?"

"Yes." The eyes refocused and looked at me. "And they spent hours here and at the police station asking me everything you've asked me and a hell of a lot more. I'd just as soon not go through it again, if you don't mind." His guard was back up again, in spades.

"How long were you and Mrs. Garrett married?"

"Thirteen years."

It was enough to make a person superstitious. "How much do you know about her early life—her life before you met her?"

"There's not much to know. Katherine was barely twenty-one when we married. She barely had a life before she met me."

I thought about bursting his self-satisfied bubble, but life was about to do that for me, I was pretty sure. With no Katherine to invent Raymond Garrett the politician and do his thinking for him, and no Sherry to comfort his abused ego, Raymond Garrett's easy life was about to take a flyer, and he'd figure it out soon enough.

I stood up. "Is it all right if I come back and see you again if I think of something else I need to ask you? I'd call first, next time." I offered an apologetic smile to smooth the way.

"Actually, I'm leaving town tomorrow morning," he said, walking me to the door. "I need to get away from this house, away from town for a while."

"I understand. I hope things will be easier for you when you get back." If the truth were told, I really didn't care what things would be like for Raymond. I'd run out of patience with Katherine Garrett's near and dear today—with the exception of my clients, of course—but it didn't cost anything to be nice.

I was seized with an urge to park around the corner and walk back to the Garrett house, open the side gate and tap on Lila Jensen's window, but she might not be in the mood to talk to me, and I wasn't in the mood to get arrested for trespassing. Instead I noted her car, a middle-aged hatchback with a fading blue paint job. Maybe I'd run into her one of these days when she wasn't on Raymond Garrett's turf. Maybe I'd make sure I did.

# CHAPTER 26

I WAS ALMOST HOME BEFORE IT OCCURRED TO ME HOW exhausted I was. I'd tried to cram too much into a day, get too much out of too many people, generate too many pages of nearly illegible notes. My head hurt and my shoulders were tense and I knew it would be a long time before I could fall asleep.

Imagine that. A week ago I'd have been thankful just to assume I'd be able to sleep at all, much less to sleep a full night without waking up in a state of panic. For the past few days I'd been too busy doing my job to think much about my formerly overwhelming problems. Maybe I should recommend investigation therapy to Maggie Peck as a cure for emotional complications brought on by investigation. I started to laugh out loud. I was *really* tired.

I opened the apartment door and tossed my portfolio onto the floor. Sam smiled as I shuffled zombielike to a chair and dropped into it.

"Let me guess. You're really tired."

I managed to nod.

"It's eleven o'clock," he said, glancing at my kitchen wall clock. "Maybe we should give up on this day."

"I have to make some sense of these notes," I said, pulling a battered little spiral notebook out of my pocket and turning the pages. "I've talked to your mom, your uncle Raymond, his business partner, the partner's wife"—I skipped over the pages I'd written after seeing Paul Gregory—"your aunt Susan, your uncle Joey, and a woman your mom used to work for. That's not counting incidental conversations and a trip to the mall."

Sam pointed to the little notebook. "And it's all in there? Everything you've been finding out?"

"Yeah. The facts are all in there. The conjecture is all in here." I tapped my head with a forefinger.

"I don't even know the facts," he pointed out.

I raised myself up and looked at him. "I've kept you pretty much in the dark about all this, haven't I?"

He shrugged. "I figured you had your reasons. I figured you'd tell me when you were ready."

"God, I'm sorry, Sam. You're not a child, and I've been treating you like one. I guess I just don't know how much I should protect you from all the shit that's flying around out there."

"Is there anything I'm not going to find out by the time Mom's case goes to court?"

I shook my head. "Not a goddamned thing. Let's talk."

"I'll make a pot of coffee," Sam offered.

I accepted.

I started at the beginning, with Robby Fry and Miss Rose and Melissa Drake. While we curled up on opposite ends of the couch and sipped our coffee, I told Sam about how Annie had come to be his mother and about the speculation that had followed him around this self-absorbed little town since the day Annie had showed up with him in her arms; how he'd been a mystery to a lot of people besides himself.

"I never knew there was so much talk," he said. "I guess I'd have felt bad if I'd known everyone was paying so much attention."

"Well, there's an old saying: 'If they're talking about

you, they're leaving someone else alone.' For all the good that does you."

"Now that we know, what's going to happen?"

I sighed. "There's something else I found out today," I said. "Paul Gregory isn't your father, Sam."

Sam set his cup down on the couch arm and closed his eyes. "When is this going to be over?"

"I wish I had an answer for you that I could believe myself." I outlined Miss Rose's (and Gregor Mendel's) theories about the inheritance of eye color. "So now we're looking for a man with dark eyes like yours."

"Who wants to apply for the job of instant father," Sam added wearily.

"Yeah."

We sat there in silence while Sam assimilated the latest blow to his search for identity. After a minute or so he opened his eyes and turned back to me. "Okay, we'll worry about that later. Now tell me what's going on with my mom and all this other shit."

Sam's courage in the face of what he'd been living through the past few days brought stinging tears to my eyes. I covered up as best I could by putting down my coffee and shuffling through my notes until I trusted my voice to speak again.

"Okay, here goes. The cops have your mom's fingerprints on the vase your aunt Katherine got for her birthday—that's the murder weapon, by the way—but she has an explanation for how they got there, and it's a perfectly good one. And there's a question about the vase—it seems to have been in two different places at the same time. When we figure out how that happened, we may know who really killed Katherine."

I still didn't want Sam to see the evidence photos, so I didn't mention I had them in my possession. Maybe I was still being overprotective, but I couldn't think of a good reason to put him through the disturbing experience of walking through the scene of a violent crime involving his closest relatives. Instead I told him what I knew about the conflicting evidence on the vase in the form of prints and blood, taking care not to be overly graphic in my descriptions.

We went over everything I had found out over the past two days and tried to find the connections. Chip and Liz DeLora; Raymond Garrett and Sherry Freeman; Lila Jensen and the stoneware vase; Annie's accidental leaving of fingerprints.

"So that means Mom left her fingerprints on the vase after Lila wiped it down, but before Aunt Katherine was hit with it," Sam said.

"Exactly. And whoever hit Katherine with it used it within a few minutes of the time your mom was there. According to her statement, Lila cleaned the vase before she went to her room around nine o'clock that night. Your mom says she was there a little after midnight, and your aunt Katherine was killed between twelve and one."

"And the murderer must have seen her handle the vase," Sam said. "Whoever it was could have killed her, too." His eyes were frightened as he considered that possibility.

"If she'd stumbled upon the killer, that might have happened," I said. "She didn't, but she provided them with a perfect set of her fingerprints."

"Except to use the vase, they would have had to pick it up."

"Don't remind me. The vase was the murder weapon, it was also five or six feet away when the murder took place, and it was only picked up once. I've got such a headache." I got up to find some pain relievers and glanced at the clock. It was two A.M. "It's two A.M.," I croaked.

"I'm tired, too," Sam said. "I think we've done all the thinking we can do tonight."

"And there's always the hope we'll find out something new tomorrow," I offered, sounding a lot more optimistic than I felt right then.

"Where are you going tomorrow?"

"To church," I replied. "For the first time in about twenty years."

# CHAPTER 27

St. Martin de Porres Catholic Church occupied a corner lot about six blocks west of my apartment. It was faced in gray-brown stone and featured a well-trimmed lawn, going a little yellow now with the heat, and beds of shrubs and flowers all the way around. A short flight of cement steps led up to wide double doors with iron handles. I dragged myself out of my car and up the steps, cursing myself for not having picked up a cup of coffee somewhere on my way. From inside, I could hear the steady sound of hammering.

It was nine-thirty—later in the morning than I'd intended to be starting my day, but my late-night brainstorming session with Sam had robbed me of sleep and hadn't produced much in the way of new insights. Sam and I agreed that Chip DeLora was awfully conveniently unaccounted for at the time of Katherine's murder, and it might be interesting to know if he'd dropped by the Garrett house while he was away from home that night, supposedly working late.

Maybe that's why Katherine slept in another room some nights, I thought—to make it easier for gentleman callers. It seemed awfully ballsy, but from what Sam and Susan had both said, Katherine wasn't terribly concerned with keeping her extramarital activities a secret.

That was a secret I wanted to get to the bottom of today, but it was the secret of Katherine's youth I was pursuing this morning, and with any luck at all there might be a piece of it waiting for me here in this place.

The church doors were ajar, and I stepped into cool semidarkness inside. The hammering stopped. A stocky gray-haired man in jeans and a black shirt got up from his knees and put down his hammer. He walked up the aisle toward me, dusting off the knees of his jeans. "Good morning!" he exclaimed cheerily. "What can I do for you?"

"I'm looking for Father May."

"That's me. Frank May." He offered a plump but callused hand. For the first time I noticed the white clerical collar above the shirt.

"I'm Caley Burke. I'm investigating the death of Katherine Garrett."

"Ah. Police?"

"No, I'm a private investigator. I'm working for her sister, Annie Holland."

"I see. Have a seat, please." He indicated a pew and I sat down at the end of it. The soft light coming in the colorful windows and taking on a golden color from all the lovingly polished wood of the old church's interior reminded me of how much I'd loved coming to church as a child. The scent of votive candles called up memories so deep, I couldn't say exactly where they came from.

Father May sat in the pew just in front of me and turned sideways, leaning one arm over the back. "So what do you need to know, Ms. Burke? Is Mrs. Garrett's death connected to St. Martin's in some way?"

"No, not really," I assured him. "But there are some things I need to know about her past—about the period of her life when she *was* connected to your church. Seventeen years ago or so. Were you here then?"

"Oh, yes indeed." Father May chuckled softly. "I've been with St. Martin's for more than twenty-eight years."

"Then it's possible you can help me. What do you remember about Katherine when she used to come here?"

"Well, let's see. Katherine Holland . . . Katherine Garrett, that is—and I was very sorry to learn of her death, by the way—attended this church with some regularity that long ago, if my recollection is correct. She moved out of town around that time, and I'm afraid she never came back—at least not back to this church. At least not when I was here to see her."

"What I'm trying to find out is if anyone remembers who Katherine may have been seeing at the time."

"You mean a boyfriend? I'm afraid I wouldn't know about that. You know how young people are—they form romantic attachments so easily and dissolve them just as quickly. Everything for them is so vital and at the same time so transient. I was never good with teenagers, I admit. Even that long ago I was too old and cranky to handle the youth groups. I left that to Father Neall."

"Is he still around?"

Father May shook his head. "Not for many years, now. He came here soon after Seminary and lasted barely two years in our little parish before he was all afire to get away to a real city. Cascade was a lot smaller then, you know."

I nodded. Cascade still couldn't be called a city, or not with a straight face, anyway. It spread out in all directions as it gained population, becoming more scattered into distant neighborhoods with each passing year. Only downtown never changed, except to become a bit more run-down and lose a little more business to the outlying shopping malls. The names on the stores and restaurants changed more often than they had in years past, but it was my belief that any of the homeless men who crowded the park benches late at night could fall asleep for twenty years and still find their way around downtown Cascade when they woke up.

"Do you remember a young man by the name of Don Harris, who came here around the same time as Katherine?"

Father May beamed. "Donald James Patrick Harris," he said. "I gave him first communion soon after I came here. In time I confirmed him, married him to a lovely young woman, and now I've baptized both his daughters. It's one of the privileges of staying with the same congregation for twenty-eight years."

"And you don't remember anyone else you might have seen Katherine with that long ago?"

"There may have been someone, but it's been so long. . . ."

"I understand. What color are Don Harris's eyes?"

"Excuse me?"

"Okay, it's a strange question, but do you know what color his eyes are? It's important."

Father May crossed his arms and wrinkled his forehead in thought. "I think blue."

"You think?"

"That's what I seem to remember, but I can't be absolutely sure."

"Do you happen to know where he works?"

"He's a realtor with the Sierra-Cascade Company. The downtown office. Why do you need to know that, Ms. Burke, if you don't mind my asking?"

"Well, it's not because he's in any kind of trouble, or suspected of anything," I offered.

"Perhaps it's because you want to get a look at the color of his eyes?" Father May cocked his head and regarded me with curiosity and just a bit of amusement.

I nodded. "Something like that. And do you know how I could get in touch with Father Neall?"

"I'm not sure where he's posted these days, but I could find out with a couple of phone calls, I'm sure. Come on back to my office, and I'll have a number for you in five minutes."

"I'd appreciate it, if you wouldn't mind."

"No bother at all. You can use my phone to call him and ask if his memory is any better than mine."

• • •

Father May made a phone call to the Sacramento Diocese and found Father Neall with his second call. Daniel Neall had left Cascade for Sacramento in the early spring of the year Sam was born. If Katherine's secret paramour had shown his face at the church, maybe Father Neall would remember it. When he had made contact, Father May handed over the phone and left the office.

After identifying myself to Father Neall, I got to the point. "Do you remember a young woman named Katherine Holland who attended St. Martin's about seventeen years ago? She was a member of the young adult service club."

There was a pause on the other end. "Katherine Holland. Yes, I do remember. What is it you want to know?"

"Whether you're aware of anyone she might have been romantically involved with around that time."

The silence was longer this time. "I recall that Katherine was dating a boy named Dan, or perhaps Don. . . ."

"Don Harris," I supplied, "but her sister told me they stopped dating soon after she joined the club. Do you remember how long it was between the time they stopped seeing one another and the time Katherine left town?"

"No. Not really. It's been a very long time."

"I'd like to give you my phone number. If you remember anything, would you call me?"

"I'd be happy to. Why is it so important to know who Katherine Holland might have been seeing that long ago?"

I thought it over and could come up with no pressing reason he shouldn't know. "Katherine left Cascade in May of that year and had a son that October. She gave him to her sister Annie to raise. His name is Sam Holland, and he's a really great kid, and he needs to know who his father is."

"Do you think Don Harris might be the father?"

"It's not likely. Another man's name is on the birth certificate—a local man—but he's definitely *not* Sam's biological father."

There was a moment of silence from the other end of the line; then Father Neall spoke. "Can't Katherine tell him herself?"

Oh, God, I had forgotten that one little bit of unhappy information. I felt like a fool saving it for last, like some sort of punch line. "I'm sorry," I said. "I should have said something right away. Katherine is dead."

"I see. How . . . how long has she . . . ?"

"It happened Tuesday night." More bad news coming up. I felt like shit, but there was no point in pretending. "She was murdered."

"Dear God. I had no idea."

"Well, it probably didn't even make the papers in Sacramento, but Katherine had gotten to be a personage around Cascade the past ten years or so, and she was pretty well known in the community." But not liked, I added silently. And not loved, either. "If Sam's father isn't Don Harris, it might be someone else you remember."

"Someone I might have seen her with around that time."

"That's right. It would mean a lot to me if you'd give it some thought." I gave Father Neall my phone number and hoped he'd be able to come up with a name.

# CHAPTER 28

IT ONLY TOOK A FEW MINUTES TO STOP BY THE REAL estate office and verify the color of Don Harris's eyes. Having done this, I departed, leaving a very confused Mr. Harris and an equally perplexed receptionist.

I wasn't sure if I was disappointed that my search for Sam's father had come up against another wall, or relieved that our mystery man was not the uptight, anal-retentive man behind the spotlessly clean and compulsively neat desk. His intense pale-blue eyes gazed out at me from a pair of horn-rimmed glasses as I approached him from the receptionist's desk. "Sorry," I'd said, beaming. "Wrong Don Harris." Then I'd turned around and walked out.

Now I was parked around the corner from Raymond Garrett's house, flipping a mental coin as Raymond started up the Mercedes and pulled out of his driveway. The flip came up "wait," but there's a chance I cheated. Raymond had been going from the house to the car with luggage for five minutes, and I had no doubt he was leaving on the vacation he'd told me about. I also didn't doubt that I wouldn't learn much by following him, so I decided to stick around for a while and see if the little blue hatchback went anywhere.

I didn't have to wait long, which was fortunate. I still

hadn't taken care of my dangerously low caffeine levels, and the boredom of sitting in one place and watching one house for signs of activity was stupefying even to an awake and alert mind, which mine was certainly not this morning. For this reason, when Lila Jensen—looking quite unlike anyone's housekeeper, in jeans and white shirt and hair down around her shoulders—came out the front door and got into her car, I uttered a heartfelt sigh of relief.

When she turned onto San Francisco Street near the park a few minutes later, and then into JavaLand, my sigh was one of gratitude. Lila and I shared a favorite spot, it seemed. Maybe I'd even seen her there before without knowing it.

JavaLand was an espresso house decorated something like your aunt Minnie's parlor, with dark antiques and soft floral fabrics and polished wooden floors. The light was subdued, but adequate for reading. There were a dozen out-of-town newspapers to choose from, and the coffees were perfect. Its charm was of a different brand than the Cascade Hotel Café, and none of the servers were a day over twenty-two, but it was a great place for an afternoon pick-me-up or an evening spent talking with friends. I avoided it at breakfast on weekdays because of the highly addictive pastries, but could frequently be found here on a weekend afternoon.

I drove by JavaLand and hung a U-turn at the next opportunity, then parked and watched Mickey's second hand journey around the clock face five times. No sense getting off on the wrong foot with Lila by letting her know I'd followed her here.

Stepping inside, I ordered a latte from the young man at the magic caffeine machine and waited patiently while he went through the steps of grinding the beans, filling the little aluminum cup with coffee, and hooking it up to the flow of boiling water that would transform it into a couple of ounces of espresso. Anything worth having is worth waiting for, my mother used to tell me, and she was never proven more right than during the interval between ordering a caffe latte and taking the first bracing sip.

It was a rhythmical ritual of copper and brass and steam, not unlike a religious observance, at least to a hard-core latte junkie like me. I acknowledged the familiarity of each action as he held the milk pitcher up and into the boiling stream from the steam nozzle, causing a fragrant white cloud to form above it. When he was through compounding the coffee and milk into a golden mixture swirling in its tall glass, the High Priest of Espresso handed over the result and acknowledged my adoration with a smile. I paid and put a dollar in the collection plate marked "Tips." First church, now JavaLand, and it wasn't even Sunday yet.

I turned around and spotted Lila Jensen sitting alone behind this morning's *Chronicle* with an identical latte by her elbow. I walked over to her table and she looked up expectantly.

"Ms. Jensen, you don't know me," I began in a tone of voice that attempted to beg her indulgence while establishing some sort of instant acquaintance.

"You were at the house last night talking to Mr. Garrett," she supplied. "Sit down, if you like."

So far it was going better than I'd dared to hope. Maybe there was a secret sisterhood of caffeine fiends, after all. I pulled up an antique wooden chair and sat down, keeping my latte close to hand.

I introduced myself and offered the usual explanatory phrases, ending with "I don't believe Annie Holland killed Katherine Garrett, and I'm trying to find some evidence that might clear her of the charges." I had certainly said all those things a lot of times since Thursday.

Lila set down her newspaper. "What makes you think I can help with that?" she asked, taking a long spoon to the foam on the top of her glass.

"I'm not sure you can," I said. "It's just that I figured since you worked for Katherine Garrett, you had to be pretty well acquainted with her, and with the comings and goings around the house."

Lila chuckled. "Especially the comings and goings." She

took in my look. "Katherine Garrett changed boyfriends only a little less often than her underwear, and she had about as much care and concern for them, too. She made her husband look like even more of a fool than he actually is, and she managed to destroy the marriages and/or reputations of anyone who ever believed they were her friends." She paused for breath, and a wry smile crossed her lips. "I don't think I need to have any more respect for her now that she's dead than I did when she was alive, do you?"

I shook my head, still a little surprised at her candor, if not her information. "I've been talking to people all over town who knew Katherine, and I don't think I've met anyone who liked or respected her yet, and that includes her closest relatives. I never even met her, and I'm not too crazy about her, either."

"I've lived in that house for two and a half years and I've seen shit you wouldn't believe, and heard more."

"Anything that might be relevant to my case?"

"I'm not sure. What would be relevant?"

"Who came visiting Tuesday night after the party?"

"Well, Mrs. Garrett's brother Joey was there after everyone else went home. He wanted Mr. Garrett to go bowling with him, but Mr. Garrett said he was too busy."

"Raymond Garrett goes bowling?"

I must have shown how incongruous that seemed to me, because she hastened to explain. "It's just the sort of down-home recreational thing Katherine was always trying to get Raymond to do. That's where a lot of his constituency was, she was always telling him—the blue-collar crowd—and he should go out and mix it up with them."

"So Raymond took a pass on bowling and Joey went home," I prompted. "Who came by later who might still have been there around midnight?"

"You mean besides whoever killed her?"

"I don't know that there's a difference."

She stared at me hard. "I do."

"Okay, help me out here. There's something you didn't tell the police, isn't there?"

"Maybe. If I tell you, is it going to get to the police anyway?"

"Only if it directly impacts on their investigation. I can't keep any important secrets if I want them to cooperate with me some other time. The other case would be if you said something that I could use to get Annie Holland off the hook."

She looked down thoughtfully for a few moments, then met my eye again. "Okay. I like Annie, and that seems fair to me. Let me put it this way: Someone came to see Katherine, but she was still alive when he left. I didn't want to get him in trouble, so I didn't mention it when the police were questioning me."

I nodded as I took the first sip of my latte. "Let me make it easier for you. Was it Chip DeLora?"

Lila's look reflected a sort of amazed respect. "You already know a lot about her, don't you?"

"I could write a book, but I don't think I'll bother."

"We could collaborate on one of those tell-all biographies, but who'd care outside this town?" Her voice dropped a level. "Mr. DeLora came to the house about eleven. He was only there for a few minutes. I think they had words, but I couldn't hear any details. After I heard him drive off I came out into the kitchen to get a drink of water. Mrs. Garrett was pouring herself a shot of vodka. I went back to my room and put on my headphones."

"He could have come back."

Lila sighed. "He did. He knocked on my window a few minutes later. He was with me until almost two."

I don't like showing that someone has surprised me. In fact, I do all kinds of displacement tap dances to keep someone from knowing they've just knocked me off my pins; I've got a whole repertory of them, and they work pretty well. This time I was caught flat-footed with my mouth wide open. Chip, Chip, what a busy boy you are,

I thought as I tried to get some of my composure back. "And neither of you heard anything that went on in the dining room?"

She shrugged. "We were pretty absorbed."

Well, so much for Chip as a suspect, if Lila was to be believed. Part of me hoped she wasn't, I realized, but this all made a kind of sad, sorry sense. "So had this been going on awhile? You and Chip?"

"I know it probably seems pretty sleazy to you, but it's not like that, really. I've never fooled myself that he's in love with me, and I'm not in love with him, either. It all started because I felt so damned sorry for him. He really needs someone in his life who understands him."

Well, don't we all. "And you didn't mind that he was seeing Katherine at the same time?" It wasn't any of my business, but I was seized by an undeniable curiosity about the whole thing.

"Katherine had a hold on him." Lila's fist clenched reflexively as if to illustrate it. "It's hard to understand until you've seen her at work, but he was having a tough time breaking it off with her. He came to the house to tell her it was over between them. She tried to get him into bed—that was her way of getting around any obstacle with a man—but he got disgusted with her and left. Then he came back to my place to tell me it was *really* over between them. I let him in the window."

Then he went home to his wife and didn't tell *her* anything. I suppressed a sigh and a headshake of disgust, taking the opportunity to sip at my latte.

"Of course," I put in thoughtfully, "you could also be protecting yourself. What if Chip *didn't* tell you he was through with Katherine and you decided to off her yourself? That could be a possibility."

"It could," Lila acknowledged, "except I didn't hate Katherine enough to kill her. She never considered me competition, so she pretty much treated me like furniture. I didn't like her, but hate takes a lot of energy and I've never been able to put forth that kind of effort for Katherine Garrett."

She set her glass down on the table. "Anyway, you can ask Chip, if you want. We were together in my room during the time Katherine was being killed. Every time I think about it, it makes me cold inside. I can't stomach the thought of making love with Chip again, knowing what was going on two rooms away." She shuddered visibly.

I'd visited that scene more times than I cared to think about through Toby's photographs, and barring Lila having actually done the deed, I was even more familiar with what went on in the Garretts' dining room that night than she was. I could sympathize, after a fashion, with her reaction. "So you and Chip have a mutual alibi if you ever need it," I admitted.

"He'll probably lie about it at first," Lila warned, "but if you pin him to the wall, he'll admit he was there."

I wasn't sure I wanted to pin Chip DeLora to any walls—his wife was bound to do that some day—I just wanted someone to look good for Katherine Garrett's murder and keep looking good no matter how many of his or her lovers I talked to. The powers that operate the universe didn't seem to give a good goddamn. "Are you absolutely sure you didn't hear anyone else come in, any voices or noises?"

She shook her head. "Nothing. You can see why I couldn't say anything to the police, can't you? Chip would have been a suspect, and I know he didn't kill her. Will you have to tell them what I told you?"

The sigh I'd been holding onto sneaked out. "Probably not," I said. "I think Liz DeLora's been through enough for now, and nothing you've said would lead them to think Annie didn't kill Katherine, anyway." I didn't mention that it might make pretty good ammunition for Mike Gold when Annie's case came to trial. No one had asked me to keep information from Annie's attorney.

A shadow crossed Lila's face at the mention of Chip's long-suffering wife. I was sort of sorry I'd brought her into it—it wasn't my job to make Lila's life miserable because she was a fool about some man, but on the other hand it didn't pay to pretend she didn't exist, either.

It was a good time to change the subject. "So are you going to keep working for Raymond Garrett?"

Lila shook her head. "I gave notice Wednesday afternoon. I can smell the blood no matter how much the cleaning service goes over that floor. I can see her lying there with her head all . . ." She swallowed hard and looked up. "Mr. Garrett asked me to stay a few days until he could put his affairs on hold and get away from town for a couple of weeks. I'm putting my things in storage today, and after that I'm never setting foot in that place again."

I thought about my desire to visit the murder scene firsthand, the feeling that something might come clear to me if I could experience that room with my own senses. "Could you let me into the house?"

"Uh-uh. I have a bonus check to collect from Mr. Garrett after he comes back. If he knew I'd let you in there while he was gone, I could kiss it goodbye."

"Well, I wouldn't tell him, and if you didn't . . ."

"I'm sorry, but I'm just not comfortable with the whole idea. Mr. Garrett's very territorial."

About his house, perhaps, but not about his wife. I shrugged to cover up my disappointment. "It was worth a try. Is there anything else you'd like to tell me?" I asked her. "Any more of Katherine Garrett's little secrets that might help me out?"

"Yes. She's the mother of Annie's boy, Sam."

"I knew that already, but how did *you* find out?"

"Mrs. Garrett liked to make war in the kitchen when there were guests in the living room. I can't tell you how many times she dragged Annie in there and gave her shit over Sam. I felt bad about overhearing it. I overheard so much stuff I didn't want to know, I took to wearing earphones when I was in my room."

I couldn't blame her. I'd heard things this week I wished I

could forget, and Lila's confession about Chip DeLora was one of them. Oh, well, I'm not the best person for people to model their lives after; if I were, we'd be ass-deep in millions of work-obsessed hermits pining away in tiny little walk-up apartments.

I finished my latte and thanked Lila for her help, but I didn't mean it—not completely. I had to admit I'd been pretty happy with Chip DeLora as a suspect, and now I was going to have to beat the bushes for another one.

# CHAPTER 29

I STEPPED OUT INTO THE ALREADY TOO-WARM MORNING sun and checked my watch. It was a few minutes past eleven, and I wanted to catch Susan at home. I should have gone by before I staked out Raymond's, but then I would have missed out on my rather enlightening chat with Lila. A bicycle whizzed past, then braked and turned back around. The rider smiled and took off his helmet, and I recognized Joey Holland.

I smiled and tried to look pleased to see him, but the truth was it was lousy timing. "Mr. Holland. Nice to see you again."

"I was just out getting a few miles in before it gets too hot," he said, wiping his brow with his forearm. "I'm a pretty serious rider, but I can't deal with that afternoon heat. Seeing a familiar face was a good excuse to stop for a minute."

He was wearing a tank top and spandex bike shorts and even those little leather gloves with the ventilated backs, so I guessed he did take his biking seriously. The bike looked pretty serious, too, with a heavy-duty frame and gears on top of gears, but like Joey's house and car, it had seen better days. "How's the investigation going?" he asked.

"I wish I could say really well, but Annie's still in jail." Too late, I heard the pointed tone I'd meant to leave out of that statement.

Joey smiled sheepishly. "I went to see her first thing this morning—that's why I was late getting out for my ride. She seems to be doing okay." His voice went up a notch at the end as if to ask my approval of his opinion.

"I haven't seen her since yesterday, so I couldn't say," I replied, trying to keep my attitude from slipping by this time. "But I still don't think it's a really good experience for her, and I'd still like to see her out of there as soon as possible."

"If there's anything I can do to help . . ." He gestured widely as if to say the sky was the limit.

Well, as long as I was reaching for the sky, anyway . . . "Okay. Tell me how to get into Katherine's house without breaking any laws."

He regarded me quizzically. "Why do you want to get inside the house?"

"I'd just like to walk through and see if anything occurs to me. It sounds silly, even to me, and I know it probably won't make any difference, but it's something I've been thinking about a lot lately."

Joey reached into his nylon belt pack and withdrew a ring of keys. "I've got keys to the front and back doors," he said, jingling them. "Katherine used to ask me to watch the place when no one was there. When did you want to see it?"

I took back all the petty things I'd been thinking about Joey Holland since our visit the day before. "Raymond left on vacation this morning and Lila's moving out today. What do you say we meet there tonight?"

Joey took a key off the ring. "I'm going out of town myself this afternoon—up to Oregon to visit my kids. This key fits the front door." He handed over the key. "Try not to disturb anything," he added as he zipped up his pack and put on his helmet. "Raymond would be really unhappy if he knew I'd let you in there. I'll go by before I head out and disarm the security system, so don't let any burglars in, and re-arm it on your way out. There's a box inside the front door and one on the outside."

I stood there staring at the key to Katherine Garrett's house, and barely recovered in time to yell thank you to Joey as he pulled out onto the street and pedaled away. He acknowledged me with a wave of his hand as he leaned to the right and turned down toward Riverview Park.

"I told you everything I know about Katherine's inconvenient pregnancy," Susan said, turning off the television and sitting down across from me with her glass of iced tea. She was dressed in a blue chambray shirt and jeans, and the feet she propped up on her coffee table were bare. "She played around with a married man—it happens all the time, or didn't you know? She was an idiot if she thought he was going to marry her."

"But you weren't, were you?"

Susan blinked. "Excuse me? What does that mean, exactly?"

I shrugged. "I guess it means that you were more realistic about Paul. You knew he wasn't going to marry you."

Susan flushed deeply and looked away. "How did you find out about Paul and me? Did he tell you?"

"No," I said. "You did."

She looked back at me, her face drawn, her usual flip self-assurance put aside for the moment. "I'm not very good at hiding my feelings, am I?"

"Not especially, but that's not necessarily a bad thing. Maybe trying to hide your feelings about Katherine and Paul is what's made them take on such huge proportions in your life." Listen to me, giving someone advice about their mental health! Look out, Maggie Peck—here comes Dr. Burke.

"I guess it's gotten a little out of hand lately," she said in a choked whisper as tears sprang into her eyes. She wiped at them with her hands. "I'm sorry, I never meant to get out of control like this. He hurt me so badly, and I never got over it, even after I married someone else. I never stopped loving him."

I could understand her feelings, but I wasn't going to let up on Susan just yet. "Did you think you could hurt him back by threatening to expose his affair with Katherine? If you did, why didn't you do it seventeen years ago?"

Her voice was so soft, I had to lean forward to hear her words: "Because his wife is my best friend."

This was a genuine surprise, but this time I kept my face impassive. I'd been insensitized to sordidness over my morning coffee.

"And you managed to keep her from finding out for all these years?"

"I never wanted to hurt her, to have her know any of this. Then he started campaigning with this bullshit family-man image, and I just . . ." She trailed off, her gaze imploring me to comprehend her motivation.

"Why didn't you threaten Katherine with exposure instead?"

"Because I couldn't imagine she'd care. I hated her for taking Paul away from me, for having his child and then pretending it never happened. Nothing I could threaten Katherine with could hurt her because she knew me too well to think I'd have the guts to go through with it."

"So you picked Paul as the weak link and went after him."

"You have to believe I was never going to go public with any of this," Susan said, wiping furiously at her eyes with the tail of her shirt. "I just wanted to scare the shit out of him."

I sat back, unable to control a slight chuckle as I remembered Paul Gregory sweating in his air-conditioned office. "Well, it worked. He thought it was Katherine, and when you called again after . . . well, you had him on the run, all right, but for the wrong reason."

"I don't understand."

"Paul isn't Sam's father. You saw Paul and Katherine together—when, in March?"

Susan nodded. "That would be about right."

"Then you saw Katherine a couple of months later, pregnant. What you didn't know was that the affair hadn't been going on that long. She was pregnant when they started sleeping together; she needed for him to think he was the father, probably so she could hit him up for hush money."

Susan seemed to absorb this slowly; I had only thought of Paul Gregory as Sam's father for a few hours before I'd been disabused of the notion; she'd held the belief close to her heart for seventeen years and experienced a lot of pain on that account, so much so that she'd never troubled herself about the arithmetic. Finally, she came out of her haze and looked at me with a slightly stunned expression. "Then who is?"

"I haven't got a clue, but I'm working on it. Can *you* think of anyone else it might have been?"

I watched her face undergo a strange transformation from curiosity to horror. "Oh, my God!"

"What? What is it? Who else was Katherine involved with back then?"

"One day I came to the house after work," Susan began, shaken. "Annie's house. I didn't live there anymore, but I still had a key. Annie always told us never to knock. She liked to feel like we still lived there—Joey and me—she missed us after we moved out on our own, and I tried to visit as often as I could."

She stared at the far wall and went silent for a minute or so. I waited for her to go on, afraid to interrupt and afraid to hear the rest of it.

"I heard voices coming from another room, and I went toward them. As I got closer, I could tell it was Katherine and Joey. I didn't think anything about walking in, of course." Her eyes went wide at the memory. "I saw . . ."

Another silence—longer this time. Finally I couldn't stand it any longer. "What did you see?"

"Katherine. And Joey. They were lying on the bed together, half-dressed. When they saw me, Joey jumped up and grabbed his clothes, and he was so—I don't know— devastated, I guess. He tried to explain, but nothing came out that made any sense. Katherine just lay there with this little smile on her face as if she'd won a prize. She seemed to be daring me to say anything to anyone about it."

"*Did* you ever tell anyone?"

Susan shook her head. "I walked out. Joey followed me when he got his clothes and shoes on—I was still sitting in my car in the driveway when he got outside—I couldn't get it together enough to start the car and get out of there. He got in the car and sat there in the passenger seat for a long time before he said anything."

"What did he say?"

"That Katherine had been trying to seduce him since she was thirteen and he was nineteen, and he'd been struggling to resist her ever since. That nothing had happened in there—nothing had ever happened. He thanked me for walking in on them, because if I hadn't, she'd have finally won her little game." She looked up, stricken. "Suppose she *did* win, finally?"

"When did this happen?"

"It was just before Christmas, the year before Sam was born."

"Well, it doesn't matter for the purposes of our discussion. I just remembered Joey's eyes are blue."

Susan stared at me, wide-eyed.

"They are, aren't they?" I asked.

"Yes, of course. But Paul's eyes are blue, too."

"Well, yes, that's the other reason he can't be Sam's father. Dominant versus recessive genes."

She shook her head in amazement. "Why didn't I ever notice that?"

"Because you were seeing what you wanted to see. Whoever Sam's father is, his eyes are dark." I pictured Sam in my mind, his handsome young face that was on the way to maturing into a man's face that resembled someone unknown. "And I think his face is a bit narrow," I went on, "and there's a fire about him somehow. It's in Sam's eyes—a peculiar kind of intensity—not like Katherine's or like anything I've seen on his mother's side of the family. People resemble their families, you know—sometimes in quite subtle ways, but it's usually there if you're looking."

I felt a bit like Amelia Rose tracing resemblances through families, but I felt she was right. Looking at Annie and Susan and Joey, and even pictures of Katherine, I could see all the things she told me about in their faces. And other things, too. Their closely held secrets seemed in my mind to become a part of their features, lending a different cast to their faces. Their awful, awful secrets.

"Did you ever talk about . . . what happened . . . with Katherine?"

"Never." Susan shook her head emphatically. "I couldn't forget the look on her face when I walked in on them. She wasn't ashamed the way Joey was—she knew she'd scored some sort of victory over him by knowing he'd go that far with her. If I hadn't interrupted them . . ."

I didn't prompt her. I could imagine the rest without any help.

"So I knew it was only me that had stopped them, and they knew it, too. Joey was always terribly apologetic around me, as though he had to justify himself to me constantly."

"And Katherine?"

"She was amused. As much at my reaction as anything else, I think. After that, she'd always go out of her way to get close to Joey when I was around—to touch him in some familiar way when I was looking at them, to say things only Joey and I would understand the real meaning of."

Her eyes clouded over again. "Poor Joey. You can imagine how that made him feel; yet at the same time he could have tried a lot harder to stay away from her. He could have moved out of town instead of settling down only a few miles away. It was a cat and mouse sort of thing, only the mouse didn't really seem to be trying to escape."

Why didn't anything I heard about Katherine Garrett surprise me that much anymore? How could this one woman have caused me to develop such a jaundiced view of human nature, especially hers? Katherine sexually tortured her older brother, held his own weakness over his head for most of his life, and did her damnedest to destroy him while flaunting his destruction in their sister's face because the idea amused her. And all I could think was that it fit. It just fit.

# CHAPTER 30

I WAS EXHAUSTED AGAIN WHEN I GOT HOME, AND IT WAS only mid-afternoon this time. I'd gone by to see Annie and take her some reading material, but her emotional state was scarcely improved despite Joey's attempt to pretend otherwise, and I made a quick decision not to tell her most of what I knew. I couldn't see it doing her any good at this point. I confined my remarks to assuring her I was doing my best to make everything come out all right. I'd been pretty sure it was all she really wanted to hear anyway.

"How's Sam?" she asked. "Is he feeling all right?"

"He could be better. He *will* be better when we get you out of here."

"Paula says they miss me at the cafe. They had to put on two waitresses to take my place."

I smiled. "That doesn't surprise me. You're one of a kind."

Annie smiled back, a little heartened. "That's what Sam always says. Oh, and you'll never guess who came to see me!" Her face lit up for real, now. "Robby Fry. After all these years!"

"No kidding? That's great!" As a matter of fact, it was nothing short of terrific.

• • •

I opened the apartment door and tossed my portfolio on the floor, collapsing two seconds later in a chair.

"Another one of those days?" Sam asked.

"Yeah." I proceeded to fill him in on the general drift of the day without going into any details, like the key I'd gotten from Joey. After sitting a few minutes, I realized I wasn't as tired as I was fed up. I needed a change of scene, and Sam must need one even more. "Are you as sick of this place as I am?" I asked him. "What do you say we blow this joint and go see a movie?"

Going to the Rio reminded me of my office upstairs, and Jake and Terrie slaving along without me. Of course I hadn't received a phone call begging me to come back a few days early and handle things as only I could; I couldn't really say whether I'd been expecting one. I wanted Jake to feel like he couldn't get along without me, but even if he did he wouldn't go back on the deal. Jake was nothing if not dependable, and that had been a source of great comfort to me for the past three years.

I stood on the sidewalk and looked up at the office windows on either side of the big neon theater sign. I thought I saw movement in Jake's, but it might just have been a reflection from the street.

"We going in?" Sam asked.

"Sure," I replied. "I was just getting ready to do that."

There were three movies we wanted to see, and we couldn't make up our minds, so we made a marathon of it, like I do on weekend afternoons sometimes. I never have to pay for my tickets, anyway, and Angela, the pretty dark-haired woman in the ticket booth, waved Sam in, too. We loaded up on popcorn and large drinks and Milk Duds, and began our six-hour orgy of movie viewing. It was after nine when we staggered out, laughing, into the street. "Amazing!" Sam said. "I've never seen three movies in a row before!"

"You should do it more often," I told him. "It's good

for you." My stomach rumbled loudly. "Popcorn and Milk Duds for supper is less good," I admitted. "How about a sandwich at The Ice Cream Man?" I pointed down the block to the garishly decorated ice cream parlor along one side of the mall, which was frequented by a lot of movie patrons around the time shows let out. "We can get a booth in the back where everyone can't see us. I'll face the mall, and if I see a cop I'll throw myself in front of you."

"I'm so tired of having to worry about that, I've got an urge to flag down the first cop I see and turn myself in," Sam said with a sigh as we crossed the street.

"It's up to you, of course, but you'd be turning me in, too. I'm the one who's been hiding you out, you juvenile delinquent."

He smiled at that. "Maybe it won't be too much longer, huh?"

"I hope not, Sam. I really hope for your sake it won't be too much longer."

When I could hear deep, even breathing from the couch across the room, and when I was absolutely sure Sam was asleep, I stared at the ceiling for another ten minutes before getting quietly out of bed and carrying some clothes into the bathroom, where I dressed in the dark. A couple of minutes later I was locking the apartment door behind me and tiptoeing down the stairs to the street. Fifteen minutes after that I was strolling down the quiet residential street toward Katherine Garrett's house, trying to look—for the sake of any prying eyes behind the darkened windows— like I might actually belong there.

I had parked my car a block away, coasting in with the lights out and the motor off to minimize my impact on Katherine and Raymond's neighborhood. I wore soft shoes and dark clothes and felt utterly conspicuous every time I passed under a street light, which was pretty often. The chances were good, I told myself, that all these people were

sleeping soundly this time of night, safe and cozy and pro-
tected by their handy household security systems. I hoped
Joey had remembered to disarm the one in Katherine's
house, or that key he had given me this morning wasn't
going to do me much good.

I touched my pocket for maybe the hundredth time today,
feeling for the shape of the key against my leg. For maybe
the hundredth time I wasn't surprised to find it there, but
this time I reached in, took it out, and held it in my hand
as I turned up the winding walk toward the Garretts' front
door, and clutched it nervously. The security box near the
door was dark and dead as Joey had promised, and the
porch light had been turned off. There went my last excuse
for not going in. I put the key in the lock, turned the knob,
and walked into the entryway.

I'd been here only last night, seeing the house for the first
time in person, but that was a house of the living, bathed
in light. This was something entirely different. This was a
tomb. I remembered what Lila had said about smelling the
blood and hoped my imagination wasn't as good as hers.

There was light from the family room windows that
looked out onto the floodlit back yard, and there was moonlight coming in the front windows that made a shadow-play
of tropical plant leaves from the window boxes onto the
bare living room floor. It was a surreal, high-contrast version of the scenes I'd seen so many times already.

I could make the entire grand tour in the dark, using
what little light came in the windows of the bedrooms,
following the path of Toby's crime scene photographs, but
I already knew Katherine Garrett's house by heart. What I
didn't know was what it felt like to be there in that dining
room when it was happening—when Katherine was losing
her life to someone she knew. The closest I was going to get
to that was walking through the two rooms to my left and
standing there where her killer had stood, trying to puzzle
out what must have been in his mind.

Or her mind, I corrected myself. If the police thought

Annie capable of wielding the heavy vase efficiently enough to club the life out of Katherine, then the real killer might just as easily be a woman.

I turned left at the wide doorway and stepped across the threshold.

Lila had apparently turned off the air conditioning when she left, an environmentally commendable action, but one that left me stifled, already starting to sweat by the time I was halfway across the living room. My steps echoed slightly, even in Reeboks, against the hard surface of the floor and off the bare walls. The dining room doorway loomed ahead of me and in my mind I began to put the missing furniture back in place—the tables and chairs and sofas and ottomans, and the narrow stand that had held the heavy stoneware vase.

At the thought of the vase I started, as though I could see it in front of me, descending toward my face. I fought off the urge to put my hands up in front of my face, and stopped short of the dining room, breathing hard. I tried to calm the beating of my heart while I took note of the place where Annie had picked up her purse Tuesday night. There was no cat to jump out, Peony doubtless being at the vet while Raymond was out of town, but in the state I had put myself in I didn't need one. I swallowed, took a deep breath, and looked around.

She had been this close, I thought, standing just outside the doorway to the dining room—Annie had been *this* close. Close enough to hear Katherine if she'd cried out, to smell the blood—though most people don't recognize the smell of large amounts of blood until someone identifies it for them—to see her if there'd been any light, which there had not been. Just like tonight. It was easy to imagine the shadows forming a high sideboard, a dining room table, a pair of legs.

A breeze hit my face from the direction of the kitchen. My heart hammered. Without looking, I turned and ran back through the living room, gasping for breath. I jerked on the front door, but the knob slipped from my hand. Cursing, I grabbed it again and flung it open, hearing it bounce off the hallway wall and bang shut again behind me. I ran and didn't turn around until I reached my car, sobbing for breath. The street was empty.

The phone rang. I opened one eye to pitch blackness and reached for it, pressing it up against my ear. "Yeah?" I hate hearing the phone in the middle of the night—it's always either bad news or some heavy breather. This sounded like the latter at first, and I started to hang up, disgusted.

"I made a terrible mistake," a man's voice said, choked with tears.

I put the phone back up to my ear. "Who is this? What do you mean?"

"I never meant to. Dear God, I'm so sorry."

I sat up in bed. "Please. Tell me who you are!"

The phone went dead. I held it in my lap as it buzzed insistently. "Who called?" Sam asked from the couch.

"I don't know," I answered. "But I wish I did."

The whole next day was slow torture. I knew I had to go back to Katherine's and finish what I'd started, but I couldn't go back until late at night, and this time I couldn't let my imagination get the better of me. I felt bad keeping things from Sam, but I couldn't bring myself to tell him that last night's phone call had been some sort of confession from an unknown man.

I also couldn't tell him about leaving late at night and going to Katherine's house. I didn't want him to know I'd been there, only feet from where his natural mother had bled her life out into her fine plush carpeting. It was too creepy, and the only thing creepier was that I planned to go back tonight.

I left the apartment after breakfast, promising Sam I'd be back for lunch and conversation. After checking in with Mike Gold and filling him in on my recent interviews, I stopped by to see Annie. She tried to be cheerful for me, and I did the same. I said the usual comforting things I wasn't sure I believed anymore, and hoped I was a better actress than she was.

Since I was already in the neighborhood, I went by Tech Services. Toby was covering another tech's shift in return for a four-day weekend to be named later, and she was bending over a drawing board with a pencil and a straight-edge, re-creating a crime scene she had painstakingly photographed and measured the night before.

"That would be a lot easier with a computer and a CAD program," I told her as I looked over her shoulder.

"Tell it to those tightasses at the C.P.D.," she muttered, then, "Hi, Caley. You're here a little early for lunch, aren't you?"

"Yeah, well I'm sure you could eat a little something if forced at gunpoint. I just wanted to thank you again."

"Why, whatever for?" Toby batted her thick eyelashes in a parody of innocence.

"Oh, nothing, really," I replied with equal coyness, "but nothing has been a lot of help to me, and I wanted you to know how grateful I am. Of course it hasn't led me to figure out who did it, but I'm grateful anyway."

"Good. I like to keep you grateful. Who knows, I may need your services someday. Keep yourself handy, huh?"

"Sure thing, boss."

After leaving Toby drawing shrubs and trees into her crime scene, I crossed the parking lot to my car. Behind me, I heard a second-story window slide open, and a familiar voice called, "You still staying out of my business, Burke?"

"Fuck you, Farmer," I replied under my breath, but lacked the gonads to repeat it in a voice that might carry all the way to his office. I liked and respected a lot of people on the C.P.D.—why couldn't one of *them* have drawn this case?

I killed the rest of the morning going over my notes in the park to the tune of the river rushing by my favorite spot. The deep shade of old oaks kept the worst of the heat away, and this close to the water it was almost nice for July. I arranged and rearranged little pieces of paper, made lists connecting one person to another, one event to another. The last note said: "Late night phone call. Who?"

Who, indeed? I couldn't recognize the voice, distorted as it was by emotion, but I remembered it as slightly deep and resonant, and totally unfamiliar, and it bugged the hell out of me that I couldn't match it up to anyone connected to the case.

And what was he confessing to? "I made a terrible mistake," he had said. And something about not meaning to. Not meaning to cave in Katherine's skull? Not meaning to pin the murder on an innocent person? "What didn't you mean to do?" I asked aloud. No one answered.

# CHAPTER 31

NIGHT CAME EVENTUALLY, THOUGH IT TOOK ITS SWEET time about it. My thoughts were never far from Katherine's house no matter what I was doing, and even closer to Katherine herself. I had spent most of the day trying to get into her skin, feel her emotions, which couldn't really be so alien to mine, after all. We all feel the same things, I think; it's just that we feel them for different reasons. I wanted to know Katherine's reasons. The more successful I felt at this mental exercise, the closer I felt to Katherine Garrett. I still didn't like her, but I understood some things.

Katherine was probably born to be the kind of person she was. Desire of one kind or another had seemed to be her entire motivation from early childhood. Katherine wanted things with an intensity most people don't have to give to the task. She *wanted*. And what she wanted, she made sure she got. If it was something she wasn't supposed to have, it was only more irresistible.

Susan had stopped Katherine from consummating her seduction of Joey so many years before, and for all anyone knew she'd been successful on some other day, but I didn't think so. Not that I thought she'd ever given up her cat and mouse game; Joey was merely postponed, I was sure, until such time as she could make him pay for the weakness of wanting her.

She wanted her husband to be a powerful man, and she made him one. She wanted her family to acknowledge her natural superiority, and without saying it in so many words, they did just that for most of her life. Katherine may not have had everything she wanted, but until the moment she realized she was going to die, she had no doubt she would have it someday.

From time to time that evening I saw Sam looking at me with an unspoken question in his eyes. I was afraid to ask him to voice it.

After a dinner of takeout tacos and a late-running poker game, we called it a night around midnight with Sam seventy-eight cents to the good. As I had the night before, I waited for Sam to fall asleep before I made my move. Imagine my surprise when I stepped out of bed and the light came on.

Sam sat up on the couch with his hand on the lamp switch. "You got out of here without me last night, but tonight I want to go with you."

"You don't know where I'm going."

"Wherever it is, it's about this case and it's important. You can't deny that."

"I won't try. It's also more than a little grim, and I don't want you there."

"What can it hurt for me to go with you?"

"You," I said. "I think it could hurt you, and I'm not taking you. I'm sorry, Sam." I carried my clothes into the bathroom and closed the door.

When I came out again, Sam was gone. I hurried down the stairs, but could see no sign of him on the street. My car was parked in front of Studio J and the doors were locked, so I knew he wasn't hiding inside to hitch a ride. I spent a few minutes driving around the nearby blocks to see if I could catch sight of him, but he was nowhere to be found. I'd left my apartment door unlocked, so when he cooled down and came back he could get in. It was the best I could do; he was a big boy now.

The front door of the Garrett house was still unlocked after my hasty departure of Saturday night. After my usual—probably meaningless—attempt at an inconspicuous approach, I turned the knob and let myself in, closing the door quietly behind me.

The expensive possessions lined up along the walls of the entranceway hall took on a new meaning for me tonight as I saw them through Katherine's eyes—lovely things that validated her as the lovely person she somehow knew she could never be without them. Visible proof of the wealth that insulated her—as her conquests had—with implied power over her secret inner powerlessness.

I reached out and touched a hand-carved antique half-table and the vase of slightly wilted fresh flowers that sat on it. It was a wide-mouthed vase not unlike the one that had taken Katherine's life, at least in size and shape. A more delicate porcelain in deep blue and white, it probably wouldn't withstand the kind of blows that had shattered Katherine's skull, but it would do a fair amount of damage before it broke.

On impulse, I picked up the vase and the flowers and carried them through the family room into the kitchen. I wasn't ready for a repeat of last night's freakout, thank you—I'd just take a few minutes to psych myself up for the dining room. I was starting to sweat again from the stifling heat of the house.

I hoped Raymond wouldn't miss the flower arrangement when he came back from vacation, since I'd promised Joey I wouldn't disturb anything. Maybe if I were careful, I could put it all back as good as new before I left.

I pulled the flower stems from the vase gently, and set the flowers down on the countertop next to the kitchen sink. I reached into the tepid water and removed the arrangement of tiny metal spikes that held the stems in place, then poured the water into the sink and hefted the empty vase. Not heavy enough by half, but good enough for my purposes.

I walked through the doorway between the kitchen and the dining room, then beyond to the threshold of the living room, turning my back to the front door and holding the vase in both hands the way Annie had held Katherine's stoneware peasant vase to keep it from falling. Now it had its perfect set of fingerprints. I knelt down and set it on the floor, walking all around it and thinking.

The trick now was to stop thinking like Katherine and start thinking like someone who wanted to kill Katherine. I've never hated anyone that fiercely, so I tried to work up the proper emotion as I circled the vase. Someone had come to see Katherine, or waited for her, or been here all along, hating her and wanting her to die. Or maybe he didn't come with the intention of killing her, but had been driven into a murderous frenzy by something she said or did. *That* wasn't too hard to imagine.

*The person in the shadows hates Katherine's guts. It's someone she's played her little power games with and finally pushed over the edge, someone who knows he'll be destroyed if he doesn't destroy her first. He doesn't just want to kill Katherine, he wants to annihilate her, erase all trace of her; that's why he's going to smash in her face.*

*And now a murder weapon has come to hand or was brought along for the job, and the killer raises his hand to act on the hate that's been burning in him for so long. He raises his hand.*

"Caley!"

My knees gave out entirely and I lurched against the doorway, grabbing on with both hands to right myself for defense.

"It's Sam, Caley! I'm sorry—I didn't mean to scare you!"

"Sam, I really hate it when you do that," I said, pressing against my chest with one hand as though I could slow my heart that way.

"I took a cab," he said. "It wasn't too hard to figure out where you'd be."

"I guess I gave enough hints, didn't I? God, I didn't even hear the door open," I said, shaking my head.

"You seemed pretty wrapped up," Sam admitted. "What were you doing?"

Remembering what I was doing made me remember why I didn't want Sam to come along in the first place. "Sam, I still don't think you should be here. It can't be a good thing for you."

Sam looked around at the familiar surroundings of Katherine's home, the darkness, the strange barrenness of the rooms. "Well, none of this has been especially good that I can see, but it's all a part of what happened, isn't it? And I'm one of the people it happened to, aren't I? I think I have a right to be here." He crossed his arms in front of him as though daring me to deny him that right. I couldn't, of course.

"Okay, it's your call. Stick around." I put an arm around his shoulders. "Just don't sneak up on me anymore, okay?"

He crossed his heart with a forefinger. "Promise. Anything I can do?"

"You can listen to me talk to myself—it's bound to be endlessly entertaining." I turned back to face the dining room. "The vase there is standing in for the vase the police say is the murder weapon," I told him. "The question seems to be now that Annie has left her prints on it and set it back down, how do I pick it up without leaving my own prints or disturbing hers?"

Sam walked around me into the dining room and knelt down by the vase. "If I pick it up, I fuck it up," he said. "I can slide something under it and pick it up that way, but then I can't hold it to use it."

I squatted down beside him and looked down into the mouth of the vase. Unlike the real thing, which was dark and featureless in the photos, the inside of this vase almost glowed with soft white light as the translucent porcelain gathered in the moonlight from the street-side windows. A cool breeze brushed the back of my neck, but this time I ignored it. There was probably a window open somewhere in the family room.

"Maybe there *is* a way at that," I said, gazing into the interior of the vase. Reaching inside, I made my hands into fists and applied outward pressure with my wrists. I lifted the vase as I stood, and Sam stood with me. "Behold the weapon," I said. "I've got more than enough control over it to smack someone a few times. My hands and wrists aren't particularly strong, but this vase isn't particularly heavy. Whoever picked up the other vase was stronger than I am, probably."

I faked a couple of blows against the air, feeling the cool glazed porcelain against my knuckles. "But Katherine's vase wasn't smooth inside like this one," I said. "Carl said it would be rough, with chunks of ground-up fired pottery inside."

"So if it was rough inside, and really heavy," Sam said, "and if someone picked it up like that and used it, they'd probably tear up their hands."

"The knuckles, mostly," I said, feeling the places where the vase exerted the most pressure on my hands. "So how would you hide that kind of damage?"

"I guess you could wear gloves," Sam replied. "But people might wonder why you were wearing gloves in July."

Gloves. In July. "Oh, Jesus Christ!" The vase fell from my hands and smashed into a thousand pieces on the floor.

"What's wrong? Caley, what's wrong?"

"Joey has the key to the back door. We're getting the hell out of here, now!"

# CHAPTER 32

· · · · · · · · · · · · · · · ·

I GRABBED SAM'S ARM AND HEADED FULL TILT FOR THE front door, but a black shape filled the doorway, arm upraised.

"Don't move!" Joey shouted, but Sam was already rushing him. The arm came down and that's when I saw the moonlight glinting off the blade of a knife. Sam cried out and crumpled onto the marble hallway floor. Joey raised the knife again.

"Over here!" I shouted, and ran back the way we had come, back toward the dining room. I had to get him far away from Sam. I heard his feet pounding after me, felt the knife brush past me as I gained the dining room, skidded on the broken vase and went down on my hands and knees in the shards of porcelain.

Joey's arm snaked out and encircled my neck, drawing me up against his right side. The knife flickered by in the light from the dining room window, a kitchen knife with a long, gleaming blade—probably from Katherine's kitchen. "I said not to move," Joey said slowly and deliberately, raising me to my feet.

Fragments of the vase were stuck in my knees through my jeans and in the palms of my hands, and the pain was raw and terrible. I wanted to cry like a baby and I wanted to kill Joey Holland. I felt the blood slicking my fingers and I twisted my head so that I could see Sam lying against the front door, utterly still. *Move!* I willed the still form silently. *Move!* In this light I couldn't tell if he was breathing.

"God damn you!" I told Joey, biting back tears, and I meant it as much as I've ever meant anything.

He had the knife in the hand he was holding me with, and I figured there wasn't much he could do with it while he was controlling me. I hoped there wasn't. I tried to roll out from his grip, but he squeezed his arm against my throat until I saw red through the darkness. Then he took the knife in his left hand and put the edge of it against my throat and eased up on my neck a little. "Why won't you listen to me?" he pleaded, and the edge in his voice was one of hysteria.

Sam moaned and pulled himself up on one arm. My knees went weak with relief. His other arm hung useless at his side, a dark, wet stain spreading over his T-shirt and running in rivulets down to his hand and onto the floor. He snarled at Joey and raised himself up onto his feet.

"You just stay right where you are," Joey warned him. "Come at me again and I'll cut your heart out."

Sam was alive. So was I. Now to keep us that way. I couldn't see Joey's face from this position, but I could imagine it. Katherine was dead and his troubles had just begun. In the end it hadn't been his sister that had driven him over the edge, but himself. "How did we do, Joey?" I asked him. "Did we figure out exactly how you did it?"

His arm tightened on my neck and the tip of the knife pressed against my throat. "I didn't do it with the vase," he said. "Not at first. First I did it with the bowling ball. Later I did it with the vase."

"I know."

Sam took a step forward. "Let her go, Uncle Joey."

"I'm not letting anyone go, and if you don't keep your distance, I'll cut her throat."

The edge of the knife stung my neck. "I'm okay, Sam," I said, but I don't think I convinced him. I didn't feel okay.

"I understand why you killed her," I told Joey. "I'm surprised you took so long to get around to it."

"She was killing *me*," he whimpered.

"Why did you have to pin it on Annie?"

"I thought she'd get off lighter. I thought they'd take it easy on her," he whined. "I've got little kids to worry about!" He punctuated this speech with touches of the knife. I tried not to wince, but Katherine's knives had a terrific edge on them.

Sam took another step into the living room. Joey's grip on me tightened convulsively.

"Sam, I want you to turn around and go out the front door," I said as calmly as I could manage.

"Caley . . ."

"He can't kill both of us unless you stay here and let him! Now get the fuck out of here!"

"Shut up!" Joey shouted. "Stay right where you are!"

I turned my head as far as I dared against the knife blade, felt it bite into my skin. I gave Sam a look meant to singe his eyebrows. "Go!"

Sam walked slowly backward toward the front door, then stopped.

Joey moved forward, trying to drag me across the floor to Sam. I pulled against him, pressing the soles of my shoes against the floor. "Don't let him kill us both, Sam. You've got to get out of here *now*!"

"You shut up!" Joey screamed.

Sam flung the door open and ran out.

Joey trembled with indecision. I braced to run in case he dropped me, but he renewed his grip and started dragging me back into the dining room. "You couldn't just mind your own fucking business, could you?" he spat at me. He wasn't the first person to voice that sentiment, and I hoped with all my heart he wouldn't be the last. Lookie here, Maggie Peck, I thought. Here I am doing it again. And why? Because I went after the truth and I found it. I went to do a job and I did it, however this turns out. I did my job. Annie's finally off the hook.

But I wasn't—not by a long shot. "She must have worked pretty hard to make you mad enough to kill her like that," I said in what I hoped was a sympathetic tone. "She must have said things that really hurt. I know how she could be. I know how she treated people, and how she tortured you especially. She *made* you kill her, didn't she? I guess it's harder to kill in cold blood, though. It's harder to kill someone who hasn't been devoting her life to destroying you."

We were standing almost on the spot where Katherine must have died. The fact didn't seem to be lost on Joey, who began to sob uncontrollably. "She made me! She made me! She *wanted* me to!"

Almost, I felt sorry for him. "I want you to think about this, Joey. They're not going to gas you for killing Katherine, but if you kill me you're going down for murder one and I can guarantee you they'll want your life for it."

"I'll give them my life," he said, grown suddenly calm again. "They can have it. It's not worth shit to me anymore. But I won't wait for them to come and get me."

That calm attitude, that resignation to the consequences of cutting my throat and watching me die, was bad news. Joey wasn't just waving a knife around—he was planning a dramatic exit for himself once I was out of the way. It had to be now. I wouldn't be any more dead if it didn't work. I pressed myself back against Joey's leg. He pulled my upper body closer against his side, straightening the leg and pulling himself upright, balanced against any attempt I might make to pull free. Good. That was just where I wanted him.

There was a rattling sound from the kitchen. Joey turned his head. Before he could take a step, I lifted my leg and drove the flat of my foot backwards into the side of his knee. His scream was cut short by a wet smack as Sam hit him a roundhouse blow with an iron skillet. Joey flew backward and slammed into the dining room wall. The knife flashed by my face and clattered onto the floor. I spun around to face Joey, but he was down for the count.

Sam dropped the skillet with a clang onto the bare floor and pushed it away with his foot. "Are you all right?" he asked, taking my arm gently.

"Uh, yeah." I took a quick inventory of body parts. "I am. How about you?"

Sam had wrapped his T-shirt around his arm and it was almost soaked through with blood. "I'm okay," he said, looking me over. "Your hands look awful. He cut your neck, too, but not very bad."

It could always be worse, a wise man once said. I fought the urge to laugh at my own joke. "Is there a phone around here? We should call an ambulance, I think. How do you feel about stitches?"

"I hate 'em."

"Me, too." I looked down at my hands, and a wave of nausea twisted my stomach. "You'd better dial."

"You'd better sit down," said Sam, putting his good arm around me and leading me into the family room.

I collapsed onto one of Raymond's couches and closed my eyes, arms out and palms up. "I guess we could turn on the lights now; the cops will be all over this place in a few minutes, anyway." Sam flipped a switch and the lamp next to me came on, bringing a welcome brightness. He brought me a phone and sat down next to me on the couch.

"Who should we call first?" he asked.

"First the ambulance, then the police," I answered. "I can't wait to tell Johnny Farmer that I haven't really been minding my own business."

# CHAPTER 33

"ENJOY YOUR WEEK OFF?" JAKE BARONIAN POKED HIS head in my door and gave me a welcoming smile.

I smiled back. "It was fine. Just fine. Sorry I ended up taking an extra two days, but I'm back now."

"And you kept your appointment with Maggie, and you got lots of rest and good, healthy food, and took your vitamins?"

"Sure thing."

"You look better," he said, crossing the rug and perching himself on the edge of my desk, "except for one thing." He leaned over and pointed to my throat. "You do that shaving?"

I put a gauze-covered hand up to touch the gauze wrapped around my neck, covering a row of little butterfly bandages. "I look like a mummy," I admitted, "but I'm ready to go back to work."

"Uh-huh. How's your typing?"

"Oh, a bit painful. But not impossible."

"And you're walking okay?"

"A little stiff. The knees don't bend really well, but the stitches will be out in a week or so."

Jake nodded, eyes twinkling. "You did this to get back at me for making you take the week off, didn't you?"

"Well, I do seem to be safer at work than just about anyplace else."

"I guess you're right," he admitted. "And you're sleeping okay?"

"Well, Sunday night was a little rough. . . ."

"I'll bet." He tossed down the Monday edition of the *Cascade Beacon,* which sported a headline reading: "Local Investigator Apprehends Murder Suspect."

"Yeah, I read it." I tapped the subhead. " 'Cascade Detective Nabs Knife-Wielding Culprit in Bloody Fight for Life.' That's pretty dramatic, isn't it? 'By Michael Carlson,' as you might have guessed." I handed the paper back.

"It was on my doorstep Monday morning when I stepped outside looking forward to seeing my favorite investigator," Jake said, "and feeling guilty about kicking her out of her office, and hoping she hadn't been too awfully bored while she was away."

I shook my head. "Not bored, no. Forgive me?"

"Always." He got up and walked to the door. "Lunch at the Grill? We can go over some new cases, and you can see if any of them are dangerous enough to keep you interested."

I held up my hands. "Better give me something I can do with both hands behind my back."

"Promise. If you'll promise *me* something."

"Shoot."

"Next time I give you some time off from work, don't go out and get your throat cut."

"Honest, Jake, this one won't even leave a scar."

Jake went out and closed the door behind him.

I sat back and closed my eyes, wishing I'd been able to cop a few more hours sleep. I'd been up late talking to David on the phone and saying some things I'd left unsaid for too long, and listening to some things I'd been waiting too long to hear. He was coming up Friday to spend the weekend, and it was going to be a long, difficult two days until he got here.

This would be Sam and Annie's first day back at work, too, and I felt bad that I hadn't been able to drag myself out of bed early enough for breakfast at the cafe. I decided I'd have to settle for a cup of Terrie's coffee. I picked up my "Hire the Left-Handed—It's Fun to Watch Them Write" mug and carried it into the front office.

"You want me to hold the mug for you?" Terrie offered, pointing to my gauze mittens. "You seem to be manually challenged."

"I can handle it, Santini—just pour it in there."

She poured the coffee, then watched me quietly while I took the first sip. "How are you feeling, really?" she asked.

I laughed. "You mean am I still crazy?"

"Are you crazy, are you scared—whatever. You've been through a hell of a lot. How do you feel?"

"I feel pretty good, Terrie. Jake wanted me to get some sleep, and as soon as I had something useful to do, I slept like a baby. Maggie Peck wanted me to look for some answers and I think I've found some that work for me. Sam wanted his mother back, and he got his wish, too."

"What was your wish?"

"Let's see—to feel like I was doing the right thing. To be sure I was doing more good than harm, no matter what went down. To feel real again."

"Oh, you're real, all right," Terrie assured me.

I smiled. "That's the same conclusion I came to. Still want to be a detective?"

"You gonna teach me everything you know?"

"Eventually," I told her. "Stick around."

My intercom buzzed. "There's a man on his way back to see you," Terrie said. "He says his name is Daniel Neall."

The man who walked into my office dressed in blue jeans and a soft cotton shirt was in his late thirties. He was on the tall side of medium height with straight dark hair and burning dark eyes in a narrow, good-looking face.

I felt like Amelia Rose's star pupil identifying one familiar feature after another as he stood quietly by the door, looking serious and uncomfortable. "I'm Daniel Neall," he said, coming forward to shake my hand. "I called you the other night, but I don't think I made much sense. I think we need to talk."

I gave him my happiest smile as I got up stiffly and grabbed my jacket from the back of the chair. "Would you like to have a cup of coffee with me, Father Neall? There's a great place just across the street, and there's someone there I'd like you to meet."

He took the jacket, helping me ease a bandaged hand into each sleeve, then gave me a smile of surprisingly familiar sweetness and courage. "I can't tell you how much I'm looking forward to it."